What the critics are saying…

4 *Stars* "*Love Me Tomorrow*…Passion rides high in this book and readers will love *Sally Painter's* creative and intriguing characters and interesting plot." ~ *Kay Smith Just Erotic Romance Reviews*

4.0 "*Love Me Tomorrow*…Passion rides high in this book and readers will love *Sally Painter's* creative and intriguing characters and interesting plot." ~ *Angel Romance Junkies*

4 *Stars, Heat level: H* "This descriptive tale captivated me from the beginning. I admired Mecah's ability to continue to woo Shalene, in spite of her resistance… Pick up this enjoyable tale." ~ *Kay Smith Just Erotic Romance Reviews,*

fated mates

Delilah Devlin
Sally Painter
Charlotte Boyett-Compo

ELLORA'S CAVE
ROMANTICA PUBLISHING

An Ellora's Cave Romantica Publication

www.ellorascave.com

Fated Mates

ISBN # 1419953036
ALL RIGHTS RESERVED.
Warlord's Destiny Copyright © 2005 Delilah Devlin
Love Me Tomorrow Copyright © 2005 Sally Painter
Secrets of the Wind
Copyright © 2005 Charlotte Boyett-Compo
Edited by: Briana St. James, Sue-Ellen Gower and Mary Moran
Cover art by: Syneca

Electronic book Publication: June, 2005
Trade paperback Publication: December, 2005

Warning:

The following material contains graphic sexual content meant for mature readers. *Fated Mates* has been rated *E-rotic* by a minimum of three independent reviewers.

Ellora's Cave Publishing offers three levels of Romantica™ reading entertainment: S (S-ensuous), E (E-rotic), and X (X-treme).

S-*ensuous* love scenes are explicit and leave nothing to the imagination.

E-*rotic* love scenes are explicit, leave nothing to the imagination, and are high in volume per the overall word count. In addition, some E-rated titles might contain fantasy material that some readers find objectionable, such as bondage, submission, same sex encounters, forced seductions, etc. E-rated titles are the most graphic titles we carry; it is common, for instance, for an author to use words such as "fucking", "cock", "pussy", etc., within their work of literature.

X-*treme* titles differ from E-rated titles only in plot premise and storyline execution. Unlike E-rated titles, stories designated with the letter X tend to contain controversial subject matter not for the faint of heart.

Contents

Warlord's Destiny

Chapter One

So, that's what Kronaki warriors look like!

Every story ever whispered about the fearsome warriors came rushing back to set Mora's body trembling. How they fought like ravaging beasts, cutting bloody swaths through Graktilian mercenaries during the war. How they lived in rough stone fortresses made of blocks carved from their frozen mountains. How they fostered their children to rival clans so they would be raised without gentleness.

How they fucked with such fury their women's screams echoed throughout their valleys.

Mora felt a tremor rumble beneath the polished, marble floor of the great hall, so explosive was the swell of conversation that arose at the warriors' arrival.

They were seven, dressed in furs and leather, armed with bows slung across their shoulders and scabbards at their sides.

She couldn't drag her gaze from the man at the head of their formation, striding toward her — her husband in name, if not yet by deed. Although she had never seen him before this day, she knew it must be him, for he looked the fiercest, the strongest — only one such as he would be chosen to rule from amongst their ranks.

He was from a race of barbarians, seemingly as proud of their reputation for brutal warfare as their orgiastic sexuality. The latter Mora could well believe for the man stalking her now looked every inch a sensual marauder.

A shiver of awe bit the base of her spine and trembled upward until the fine hairs on the back of her neck stood erect.

Taller by a head than any Mellusian, his broad shoulders nearly blocked out the sight of the two heralds dogging his steps as they attempted to halt him. He seemed not the slightest bit interested in following protocol by waiting for his name to be addressed to the assemblage. As if anyone attending the ceremony hadn't already guessed who he was!

He'd also eschewed the fine wedding tunic Mora's mother had personally designed—an embroidered silk affair that would have stretched absurdly across his bulging chest and arms.

No, he wore a vest of gray animal pelts that parted at the front, no doubt to tempt a woman's gaze to ogle his obscenely muscled chest and follow the dark arrow of hair down his hewn abdomen. The black sueded leather that encased his legs strained over thickly corded thighs and the alarming swell of his manhood.

Mora's heart tripped and then fluttered like the wings of an *aradil*.

Her mouth dry, she forced her gaze upward to look at his face but found no comfort there.

Lord Tetrik of Kronak—his name was as harsh as the angles of his square jaw and the sharp blade of his nose. His hair was dark like a moonless sky and worn like the old warriors in the paintings in History Hall—hanging past his shoulders with small braids on either side of his inflexible face. But his eyes frightened her most of all—chips of blue ice froze her in place as his gaze found hers across the noisy hall.

He would have to know she was his bride. She wore her wealth and importance in the weighty jewels studding her hair and gown and encircling her neck. She saw fury in that first glance. Had he already guessed he'd been cheated of the true prize? That her rich adornment was a ruse?

Her mother moaned behind her. "His ambassador said he was too busy to attend such an insignificant event. You should have worn the pink gown!" her mother hissed.

"It was covered in dirt, mother," Mora whispered, keeping her gaze pinned on the man walking straight toward her. "It's too late now, anyway. The ceremony is over."

"He may still repudiate you. Oh, what were you thinking, digging in the garden on your wedding day?"

"I wanted a tuber rose to take with me to my new home."

"As if a rose will grow in their rocky soil," her mother said, her voice becoming thin and breathy the closer the warrior drew.

Mora hoped her mother didn't choose this moment to faint. She suspected the Kronaki leader would scorn a woman frightened by the mere sight of him.

"That green makes your cheeks sallow," her mother lamented, working herself into a high state of agitation. "You look as though you're attending your own funeral."

Mora couldn't resist delivering a little dig. "Am I not? What do you think he'll do once he finds himself wed to the wrong sister?"

"You should have worn the pink! It would have shown you to advantage." She sounded on the verge of tears.

Her mother's diatribe wore on Mora's nerves. "Mother, it doesn't matter if I wear the pink or the green, I'm no beauty. He will know. And by the look of that scowl he wears, he already does."

"May the Goddess save us!"

"Hush, Hespha!" Her father finally intervened. "You frighten our daughter."

Only that wasn't quite true. Her mother's words had the opposite effect, reminding Mora that by rights, her older sister should have been the one sacrificed to honor The Promise. But her sister had been deemed too delicate and hidden away when the day came to repay the decade-old debt owed the Kronaki. "She'd never survive the rigors of life on that harsh planet," her father had said.

Her mother had been only too eager to agree to the substitution. Her delicate, slender little flower wouldn't be surrendered to the barbarian. Instead, Mora stood in her place.

She was anything but delicate—a fact that had pained and embarrassed her parents to no end all her life.

A flush of anger heated Mora's cheeks. Try as she might, she couldn't suppress the primitive emotion. Her parents thought so little of her they were willing to marry her to a beast. A black-haired beast that grew more enormous and intimidating as he approached the dais upon which *most* of the members of the Mellusian royal family stood.

Mora straightened her shoulders. Jewels and a fine gown would not deceive the man. She was dull quartz against the bright, blonde diamonds glittering inside the hall.

He stopped in front of the dais. The room fell silent while all in the assemblage strained to hear what he might say. His cold gaze raked her from head to toe. Even standing on the raised platform, she had to tilt her head to meet his glance.

Panic had her body tightening. Mora raised her chin another notch, unwilling to let him see her fear.

He lifted one dark brow, and his gaze swept her face, lingering over her lips. "What is your name?"

He knew! "Mora. I am Mora," she said, surprised the words escaped her tight throat. Would he reject her? Strangely, she wasn't certain she'd feel relief if he deemed her unfit. Humiliation at his hands would be the harder emotion to swallow.

His gaze cut to her father, and he nodded once. "It is done," he said, his deep voice terse. Then he turned and offered her his hand.

As Mora realized his curt statement meant he would accept her as his bride, emotion pricked her eyes. He would have her. Although she wasn't the beauty he'd been promised, he accepted her as wife. She blinked and drew in a deep breath. She'd not shame herself by giving way to tears. Although she might be the least favored daughter, she was wed now—and to the fiercest warrior of the covenant worlds. She placed her hand inside his and stepped down beside him.

Immediately, she felt swamped by his tall, broad body, a sensation foreign to her, living all her life among the slender elegance of her people. She lifted her startled gaze.

"You're short." A frown drew his dark brows together in a daunting scowl.

Mora drew back. "I am tall for a Mellusian woman."

He snorted and glanced down her body again. "We leave now," he said, letting go of her hand.

"But we've prepared a banquet," her mother's voice quavered behind her.

"We're leaving now," he said again as though grinding his teeth, his ice-cold gaze never leaving Mora.

She sensed a question in his statement and nodded her assent. Best not to annoy him so soon in their marriage. That would doubtless come later.

He raised his arm, and she placed her hand atop his forearm. His skin was warm, the hairs dusting his arm crisp— the muscle beneath felt hard as stone.

"But her trousseau!" her mother cried. "Her things must be packed."

"I will see to her clothing." To Mora, he asked, "Is there anything else you would bring with you?"

She thought of the small bundle containing her personal treasures and the bundled roots of her tuber rose. "There's a package on my bed."

He turned then to her mother. "Fetch it. Bring it to the mage's chamber."

Her mother was so startled, she didn't question his authority to command her. She swept up the train of her gown and rushed from the hall.

Lord Tetrik strode out of the room, past the glittering assemblage without so much as a sideways glance.

Mora found herself enclosed at the center of the formation of tall warriors and lengthened her stride to keep apace. So tall were they, she was denied her last glimpse of her home, only catching a glimmer of gold leaf from the panels in the ceiling. Too soon, she was descending the steps to the mage's chamber in the dark, ancient dungeon beneath the golden keep.

As they stepped inside, the shadowy cavern seemed, for once, cramped. Her escorts fanned out around the perimeter of the room, their legs braced as if for battle.

Gwimmel, the castle's mage, turned from the cooking pot suspended above a crude wood hearth. His gaze darted to Mora's, and he raised his bushy, white brows. "That was rather quick. I had thought there would be celebrations above."

"Lord Tetrik desired to depart immediately," she murmured to her one true friend, aware of her husband's scrutiny. "And since the ceremony took place before his arrival …"

"Ahhh…" Gwimmel nodded. He straightened as far as his hunched back would permit. "Lord Tetrik, it will only take a moment to reopen the passage."

Mora glanced to her husband, whose scowl grew darker by the moment. *If Gwimmel doesn't hurry, he'll change his mind! Disaster has not yet been averted.*

Suddenly, her mother rushed into the room, halting to catch her breath as she spied the warriors. She stepped timidly into their midst and thrust the bundle into Mora's arms and hugged her. "Despite how it may seem," she whispered into her ear, "I wish you well, daughter." She squeezed her and stood back. Then she smoothed a hand over her perfectly coiffed hair before turning to her new son-in-law. "We have your promise you will return her if she so desires?"

"I keep my bargains," he said, the words spoken so slowly his true meaning could not be misinterpreted. He had kept his bargain—the Mellusians had not! "She may return after spring comes to the mountains if she so desires—and if she does not carry my child."

Although her mother strove for a regal nod, her hands pressed her stomach, betraying her unease. "Well, I wish you good journey." Her liquid gaze met Mora's one last time before she turned and departed the chamber.

Mora let out the breath she'd been holding and tried not to shiver at the chill encasing her heart at her husband's words. *If she does not carry my child...* With a husband so virile, how would she not?

"Mage!" Lord Tetrik spat the word, impatience apparent in his tone.

"Oh, yes, yes. Just a moment." Gwimmel bent and lifted a stone from a basket of magical stones beside the hearth.

He opened his palm and a rough-cut yellow diamond caught the flickering light from the hearth, bending and fracturing it until rays spread in a fiery prism—yellows, reds and oranges bursting like a tiny sun. Then he closed his eyes and murmured an incantation that sounded more like the gurgling of a river than any spoken tongue. The slivers of fiery light curved into a shimmering circle, becoming liquid, the radiance dimming at the center.

"Come, it is time," her husband said, gripping her elbow. He led her to the circle and ducked inside, pulling her along.

Chapter Two

Once past the glimmering barrier, Mora gasped as air was sucked from her lungs. She panicked for a moment, until she saw her husband's face. He exaggerated closing his mouth and nodded toward the glowing passage.

Since he didn't appear afraid, she swallowed her fear and hurried down the passage, helped along by his large hand pressing the small of her back. Another circle of light blazed at the end of the corridor. He pushed her through it, and Mora stumbled onto the other side, nearly falling to her knees.

She dragged in cool, dank air and then slowly looked around her. Light from the passage behind her illuminated the inside of a cave.

One by one the rest of the seven warriors stepped inside, their solid expressions betraying no hint of concern for the fact they'd just passed from one dimension to another. The last of the warriors brought with him a flaming torch. Within moments, the glow of the passage narrowed and then blinked out.

Now there was no turning back.

Mora crossed her arms in front of her, already shivering from the cold.

Her husband cursed beneath his breath and took the bundle from her arms, passing it to one of his warriors. Then he shrugged out of his fur vest and handed it to her.

"Thank you," she murmured, trying to ignore the expanse of naked, dark-furred chest before her. "I didn't think about the cold when I dressed this morning." She didn't add that she hadn't thought they'd leave Mellusia until the end of the week's celebrations. It was spring on her home world.

Lord Tetrik frowned. "No, but I knew better. I should have brought a cape. Put it on."

His stare was intent, almost unnerving, as she pulled the vest over her arms. She sighed as it enveloped her in warmth, the garment falling past her hips. The soft fur still held his body's warmth, and she couldn't help sniffing to draw his scent into her nostrils—woodsmoke and herbs, and his own musk.

At the soft grunt beside her, she raised her startled glance. A frown furrowed her husband's brow, and a muscle in his jaw flexed. So forbidding was that look, she shivered with fear, wondering what she might have done to displease him already—well, besides not being the right sister.

He gripped her elbow and nodded to the man carrying the torch. The warrior led the way as they walked deeper into the cave, until they reached a set of stairs carved into the gray stone of the cave wall.

Without a handrail to clutch, Mora was grateful her husband climbed the narrow stairs behind her. She stumbled once when her feet tangled in her long gown, but he caught her before she pitched over the edge, his arm slipping beneath the vest to curve around her waist for a moment as she steadied herself.

He quickly pulled away, but not before Mora felt as though her side burned where his thick arm held her. She gathered up the hem of her skirt and continued upward, ignoring the pounding of her heart.

Finally, the staircase led to a crude wooden door, and they passed through it.

Mora blinked at the brightness, and her eyes teared immediately from the biting, cold wind that whipped at her hair. They stood in the middle of a path on the side of a mountain. Pockets of frozen snow clung to grass and weeds on either side of the trail.

But her breath caught at the sight of the valley that fell steeply away from the unpaved track. Below, dark treetops dusted with snow dotted the mountainside. A blue river cut through the center of the valley, the water flowing so swiftly it frothed white over jagged rocks. On either side of the river stood the stone buildings of a town, as gray as the mountains surrounding them.

Again, his hand gripped her elbow.

Mora kept walking, feeling more and more disoriented and detached as impressions of her new home bombarded her.

They climbed the path, but just as they rounded the curve of the mountain they reached a fortress. A monstrous, crenellated curtain wall surrounded it, its stone-block exterior broken only by a gateway that looked like a dark, gaping mouth, the grilled portcullis resembling blackened spiked teeth.

The portcullis rose, pulled up by grinding gears, and they entered the bailey of the fortress. Cobblestone paved the grounds, and wooden buildings hugged the stone outer wall. The pungent smell of manure from a stable mixed with a smith's smelter and the sweeter aroma of the coniferous forest carried on the wind.

Primitive though the place was, Mora could see order in the chaos of activities while castle folk hurried about their chores. As Mora and the warriors passed, the people gave them small bows and curtsies. She felt their stares follow her all the way to the steps of the keep at the center of the courtyard. Her lips twisted into a grimace—what a sight she must make, shivering in her rich silk and jewels while they wore warm, woolen trousers and skirts with fur jackets, vests and boots.

At the moment, she envied their comfort as she closed the edges of Lord Tetrik's vest in front to guard against the chill wind that penetrated her skirts below.

Again, her husband guided her forward with a hand at her elbow, up the broad steps to the thick wooden door. She cast a quick glance upward. Her new home jutted four stories into the sky with narrow windows that no doubt provided advantage for warriors seeking cover from arrows and missiles, but only meager light for the occupants.

She sighed her acceptance of her new circumstance and entered through the massive wooden door. Warmth fell over her like a blanket, scented by woodsmoke and sage. The source was easy enough to find—fires blazed at either end of the long hall in tall hearths.

The wood plank floor was scarred by many years of use but was buffed to a golden glow. Rows of wooden tables gleamed and smelled of a fragrant polish. A dais near the fire at the far end of the hall supported a massive carved table with chairs padded in velvet.

So the warriors liked their comforts—hearth and home. Mora began to have some hope there might be some commonality between this rough people and herself.

She glanced back at her husband, who had watched, scowling, as she took inventory of his home. She wondered if she would ever lose this trembling that filled her whenever his gaze fell upon her. If her heart would learn a calmer rhythm.

Gathering her hopes around her, she offered him a smile.

Tetrik's whole body tightened like stretched leather at the sight of her tremulous smile. *Mora!* He'd known the instant he spied her across the gold and marble hall she was not the princess he'd been promised. The Mellusians had thought to cheat him of his prize. But after his rage at their betrayal subsided, he'd felt nothing but relief.

They hadn't wanted to give the barbarian their treasure. But they couldn't have known how he'd dreaded the thought of bedding the scrawny, fey creature that should have been his wife.

As he'd approached Mora, the "unfortunate" sister, he'd been pleasantly surprised when she didn't cower in fear, although he knew she was aware of his reputation.

Instead, she'd raised her round chin and held her ground as he towered over her. Her soft, gray gaze hadn't faltered even while he'd succeeded in intimidating everyone else gathered for the wedding.

It was then he'd felt his first stirring of lust for the woman. He'd raked her body with his gaze, not missing the telltale gasp that thrust her generous bosom against the fabric of her gown. But she hadn't hesitated to place her small hand in his when he'd assisted her from the dais, nor had she demurred when he refused to remain for the celebrations.

He'd intended an insult to punish the royal house for their subterfuge, but he'd also been motivated to bring his wife posthaste to his keep to get on with the business of consummating their union.

His eagerness surprised him.

He'd chided himself silently for his uncharacteristic haste and suffered his men's amused glances. The woman was no great beauty—not by Mellusian standards, certainly not by any Kronaki scale. Her hair, a pleasant blend of brown and blonde, hung to just above the curve of her waist. Her skin was golden with brown freckles that dotted the bridge of her rather square nose. Her gray eyes were also unremarkable, but their wide set enforced the unwavering honesty he read in them.

But her form *begged* remark. Womanly, lush. And her aroma was scented with flowers and earth.

No, Mora would suit him far better for a wife. Her broad hips and sturdy frame would bear his weight, glove his sex, carry his child—and The Promise would be fulfilled.

For the sake of his world, he'd take Mora as his wife and hold to the vows his ambassador had made in his name. That his body proved eager to consummate the vows was just a pleasurable and unexpected bonus.

Something of his thoughts must have shown on his face for her eyes widened.

He shuttered his expression lest she bolt. Coming from such a *civilized* planet, he doubted she had any inkling how close he was to tossing up her thin skirts and ravishing her here and now.

When she turned from him and walked toward the hearth, he let his gaze caress her backside as it twitched beneath her gown.

At that moment, Garion, his Captain-at-Arms, pushed through the entrance. "My lord, the gates are closed for the evening." His glance swept the hall before returning to Tetrik. His brows rose. "But what of the celebration?"

"'Tis my question as well," Tetrik growled. The slow burn of anger built in his gut.

"Do you think your staff is letting you know they aren't pleased with your foreign bride?" Garion asked, his voice pitched low.

"If that is their intention, they will regret this small rebellion."

"They haven't even seen her yet." Garion's lips slid into a sly smile. "Do you think they will be as pleased with this sister as their overlord is?"

Tetrik gritted his teeth. "She is my wife; they will accept her."

Garion's smile broadened. "They've likely all fled the keep to avoid hearing her loud weeping when you bed her. Mellusian cock surely can't compare."

Tetrik slapped Garion's shoulder and shoved him. The man took a step backward but remained on his feet, much to Tetrik's annoyance.

"See to the kitchen staff," Tetrik bit out. "We will eat within the hour. I will take any absence as a personal insult."

Garion lifted his chin toward the new mistress of the keep. "Does she know about our custom of first bedding?"

"Not yet. I had thought I might spare her the spectacle."

Garion shrugged. "It is your choice, my lord. But if you do that, she may never gain our people's respect. That would not bode well for The Promise."

"I will think on it." A knot centered in Tetrik's gut at the thought of his new wife's horror when he explained the custom. Perhaps her sensibilities would have been better served had they remained on Mellusia for the first week of their marriage. The bedding might convince her to lock her door against him until springtime. He drew a deep breath. There was no going back now.

"Perhaps you should pour drink down her throat first. Or Serit could give her a potion to induce desire," Garion murmured. "I will see to the preparations for the celebration, my lord." Then he quickly turned on his heel, heading toward the kitchen.

Tetrik drew a deep breath and stared at his wife's lush figure, revealed in silhouette against the fire. He noted with satisfaction the length of her sturdy legs. "She'll need no potion," he muttered, and then followed his wife to the hearth where she stood warming her hands.

Seduction was a game Tetrik seldom played, sex being a plentiful commodity for the master of the keep. He wasn't certain how a woman who'd lived a sheltered existence would react to the open carnality of his people. The feast would only give her a small taste of what was to come.

She didn't turn from the fire at the sound of his footsteps, but continued to hold her palms up, warming them.

He wondered how her soft, warm palms would feel surrounding his cock and nearly groaned. He cleared his throat to gain her attention. "Come, I'll show you your quarters so you may dress for the celebration."

"Will I have my own quarters then?"

That left him wondering if she hoped to avoid their marriage bed, and he fought to keep a frown from his face. *Proceed slowly.* "Is that your wish?"

She glanced his way and blinked. "Whatever is the custom here…"

"You will share mine," he said, his voice sounding harsh to his own ears. *Devil, take this wooing!* "Come." He offered her his arm, as he'd seen Mellusian courtiers do, remembering how foolish he'd felt at Garion's soft snort of laughter when he'd done it the first time.

She slid her hand atop his arm, and the caress, though not intended to be sensual, had his loins filling with heat. Her palm was as warm as he'd imagined and smooth.

He gritted his teeth as he tried not to let his mind wander to the coming night when he'd coach her to cup his balls and encircle his sex with that soft hand. *Blast and damn!*

Her hand trembled on his arm, and he knew his expression must have betrayed his frustration. He led her from the hall to the stone staircase, acutely aware of the crudeness of his home after the dazzling wealth of hers. No carpets to protect her feet from the cold, no colorful banners or paintings to dress the plain stone walls.

They climbed in silence to the landing on the third floor, and he led her to his room. When he opened the door, he stood aside, again conscious of the comforts she would lack here as well. Besides the bed, a brazier and a large cupboard to hold her wardrobe, there were no other furnishings, save for a large copper-framed mirror he'd had added before her arrival, having asked the cook for advice concerning furniture a wife might approve.

Would she think him poor? Kronaki spent their days either training for battle or fighting battles. While he'd accumulated some wealth through the mercenary trade, he had few possessions to show for his gold.

"You may of course make changes," he said, watching as she entered his room.

Her gaze went straight to the bed. "It's a very large bed."

"It holds four comfortably," he said, and then wished he'd bitten his tongue off at her shocked expression. "Not that it ever has." He felt his cheeks color at that slight lie.

"I've heard things…" she said, her skin blushing a lovely rose.

The hesitant note in her voice, sounding at once shy and curious, had him cursing the fact he had to wait for the ceremony before taking her. He cleared his throat and spread his legs to ease the ache building in his loins. "What things have you heard?"

She turned so that her back was to him. "That you need to couple often and with many partners to give you strength for battle."

His lips curved at hearing that old warrior's excuse for frequent sex. "One partner can fill a man with vigor, should she have a like appetite for coupling."

She cast a quick glance over her shoulder, and then looked down to her tightly clasped hands. "What will happen between us tonight? Is it true that everyone will watch us…come together?"

He felt swift relief she had some warning of what would come. "A few will watch," he said, making the decision on the spot as a caution to limit the ribaldry. "I was promised a virgin to assure no child would exist before mine is planted in your belly. My people will expect proof at your breaching."

In profile, her face blanched white, but she nodded. "I will follow custom. I wouldn't want to bring more shame upon your house," she said, her voice so soft he had to step closer to hear her words.

"More shame?" he asked, standing so close now the rose scent in her hair tugged at his cock.

"I'm not exactly the woman you expected. You were deceived."

Stillness settled over Tetrik. *She thinks I'm unsatisfied with this bargain.* "You are a virgin from the Mellusian royal house. The Promise was kept. There is no shame."

"But you were promised...someone finer, prettier."

Intending to soothe her, he said, "It matters not which sister I have—only that she is virgin. It is not as though there will be a heart bond between us. You suffice."

"No...heart bond?"

"No love. I'm a warrior. There is no place in my life for soft emotions. I will protect you. I will give you children to love and rear. Your life will be full."

She turned to face him, her eyes wide. "Warriors don't love?"

"It is not our destiny. So you see, it matters not that you aren't your sister. In fact, I was relieved. Although I have never seen her, I was told she had slender hips. Yours are sturdy. You'll do better."

"Don't you mean *if* I breed before springtime?"

Something in her tone and the way she slowly enunciated her words told him to proceed cautiously. He nodded. "If you are not breeding, I will give you the choice to return to your home world or remain on mine." But he felt a growing certainty she would breed, because he had never felt such an attraction to a woman before. He'd keep her abed until springtime.

Her eyes narrowed to slits and her cheeks bloomed with heat. "If I'm not *breeding* by spring—I'm leaving here!"

Chapter Three

Mora could scarce believe she'd just shouted at the warlord. By the look of his gaping jaw, neither could he!

Lord Tetrik quickly recovered, closing his mouth with a snap. He drew back and narrowed his blue eyes, staring at her, as if for the first time. "I think you are overwrought. Perhaps you are nervous about this evening's festivities?"

Mora drew in a deep breath to curb her lamentable temper, reminding herself she was alone with a half-naked man. A man whose chest and arms rippled with the evidence of his warrior's training. "My lord," she said, speaking slowly as she gathered her unraveling patience, "I understand that the first time I accept a man into my body there will be an audience to witness my humiliation."

His brows drew together in a fearsome scowl. "The bedding is not intended as humiliation. And I would have you call me Tetrik—you are my wife."

Mora spun away, not wanting him to read her anxiety. "Then no one will be commenting on my body?" she asked, putting to words her deepest fear. "No one will offer suggestions as to how you shall fulfill your duty?" She glanced over her shoulder and caught his deepening frown.

"'Tis not meant to humiliate. There will be drinking this evening...and perhaps my men will become a little...enthusiastic," he said, his tone becoming impatient. "But it is their duty to ensure our coupling is successful. Be at ease, they will not penetrate you."

That was meant to calm her? "Not penetrate?" She cleared her throat as a precaution not to scream. "Do you mean to say they will actually touch me?" she squeaked.

He nodded. "As part of the inspection…and in preparation …" He shrugged his unconcern. "'Tis only meant to accustom you to a man's regard and to stimulate you."

Mora restrained herself from crossing her eyes at the lummox. "Let me get this aright. It was important that I be virgin — untouched — and yet, you will allow your men to *molest* me first?" she asked, her voice rising toward the end.

He drew a deep breath, his hands fisting alarmingly at his sides. "They will not molest you…much. It is our custom that the groom is brought a *ripened* bride. It is to your benefit they do this."

"Molesting me is meant as a favor…to me?" Mora felt a bubble of hysteria choking her throat.

"Of course. Kronaki men are not like your Mellusian men. We are…more. "

More? Of course, he was more — the rapidly expanding bulge at the front of his breeches told her that much. But he was also far too arrogant. So, despite her growing trepidation, Mora rolled her eyes. "How many times have I heard men brag about their superior manly parts?"

He raked his hand through his hair, frustration evident in his jerky action. "You will take my word on it. You need preparation."

She took his decisive nod to mean that this should end this particular line of conversation. But Mora was far from reassured and growing angrier by the moment. This cockle-brained man expected her to trust him — on just his say-so! "Since I've never seen a man's private parts, just how will I know I am being *blessed* with superior cock?"

He blinked, and his expression grew suspicious. "Are you saying you should be given the opportunity to make comparisons?"

That look, all narrow-eyed and angry, filled Mora with a reckless excitement. She fisted her hands on her hips and lifted her chin. "If I'm going to be judged and fondled by your men, I think it only fair you must also submit."

His glance flickered down her body, and a slow smile stretched his mouth. "I knew you would better suit me," he growled.

Mora dropped her fists and straightened, wondering what the devil she'd said that pleased him.

He stepped close so suddenly, she didn't have a chance to retreat. His hands closed on her waist and pulled her against him. With his legs braced wide, his sex pressed into her belly.

Mora had the fleeting thought that he was undeniably... *more*. More man, more danger than she'd ever faced in her sheltered existence.

Then his face lowered, and Mora's fears coalesced into one screaming thought—*I want him!*

Now, Mora had been kissed before—by a stable boy when she was just a girl. She'd thought the act distasteful—a sloppy exchange of spit that had her wiping her mouth with the back of her hand afterward.

But this was...different. His lips *claimed* hers with a searing heat that felt like a brand. His mouth caressed, molding, slanting over hers—drawing a gasp from her, which opened her lips.

He groaned against her mouth, and his tongue thrust inside hers, lapping at her teeth, gliding along her tongue.

Her heart leapt and pounded against her chest. She felt dizzy and warm, and her breasts tightened, her nipples drawing to points so sensitive the silk of her gown abraded the tips. Without thinking, she smoothed her hands over his furred chest, her fingers gripping the fine hairs, trying to draw him closer still.

When he drew back, her eyelids fluttered open.

Her husband grinned down on her.

That smug expression of triumph wiped away the sensual fog his mind-drugging kiss had produced. Mora straightened and stepped back, trying to gather her scattered thoughts. *Think!*

He stared at her, an assessing look that seemed to strip the clothes from her body. Truthfully, if he said that he would take her this minute, she wouldn't utter a protest. He was the most devastating man she'd ever encountered.

Beside his powerful body, hers felt small and feminine. His hard, sculpted face and the small scars that striped his arms and chest had her heart tripping and a curl of heat settling low inside her belly.

Damn him! He could flip up her skirt and take her now, and she thought she'd probably love it.

Worse, she thought she might love *him* already. He'd accepted her—thought her suitable. That she'd suffice! How pathetic was she to be *grateful* he hadn't tossed her back to her parents?

But in that instant, she also realized she wanted more than just acceptance. She wanted him to need her just as much as she knew she would grow to need him. She wanted his respect—his love. In Mellusia, where she'd been found wanting so often, she'd have settled for a tepid emotion...an arrangement.

Staring at her husband, she decided she'd have it all—or she'd leave come spring. But how to accomplish that?

If she acted the shy virgin, his people would ridicule her. She'd heard enough about their sexual appetites and carnal behavior to know she couldn't demur from the festivities this evening.

That would surprise him, no doubt. But what more could she do to rivet his attention on her—only her. She'd not have him sneaking from her bed later if he didn't find his full pleasure!

Although her stomach burbled with anxiety, she kept her posture erect and lifted her chin. "Perhaps you will not suit me."

He blinked, and a small frown creased his forehead. "Do you think I will hurt you?"

"I think you may not satisfy me," she said, keeping her words clipped, while fighting fear that had her heart beating a rapid tattoo.

"Because I don't have a fine keep?" he asked, his tone low and deadly.

Mora blinked in surprise. "There's nothing wrong with your keep that a woman's touch can't fix. It's well-built and sturdy."

Both his brows rose. "Then you think I will not satisfy you in the marriage bed?"

She lifted one eyebrow, striving for a haughty look. "You have yet to prove yourself."

His expression turned watchful, his gaze measuring. "We've a celebration to attend before I can reassure you, wife."

Her mind made up that she would do the wooing here, she looked down at her clothing and frowned. "I will look a little out of place in this gown."

"There is clothing in the cupboard for you. Shall I help you out of that frock?"

Mora's breath caught at the light of devilment in his eyes. Could she tempt him? Or would the sight of her overblown figure repulse him? She decided to find out while they had no audience. She turned, presenting her back, and shrugged out of the vest, letting it fall to the floor. "I will need help with the fastenings," she whispered.

His fingers opened each fastening, grazing her bared skin as the gown parted down her back. Mora shivered, and when the last lace was undone, she let the garment slither to the floor.

Wearing only a thin shift now, she pulled it over her head.

Tetrik's breath hissed between his teeth.

Mora didn't know if that was a good sign or not until his hands smoothed down her back and over the globes of her bottom, stroking, squeezing.

His breath came faster, for there was reverence in his touch.

A trembling started in her belly.

"Your skin is white as milk and softer than I had even imagined," he rumbled in her ear. "Turn around."

Mora closed her eyes and turned slowly. He stood so close, her breasts scraped against his chest, her nipples tangled in his chest hair. When she raised her gaze to his, she shivered at the feral look on his face.

His nostrils flared as he dragged in her scent. His scowl deepened while his glance roamed over her breasts. He stepped back, and his gaze dipped lower.

"Do I...suffice?" she asked, clamping her jaws to prevent her teeth from chattering.

"My men will attempt to inflame you, but fight against taking your release with them," he said, his voice harsh. "You will save that privilege for your husband."

Mora still didn't have her answer, and irritation overtook her natural modesty. "But will *they* find me lacking?" she asked, taking a different tack.

She wouldn't have thought it possible, but his scowl deepened. "They will find you...suitable."

Mora felt like stomping her foot. *What is that supposed to mean? That they won't lose their appetites for their dinner?* She needed to know what he thought, but wasn't about to ask him outright whether her figure pleased him. But she had another worry, too. "How will I know how to fight my...release, if I've never experienced it before?"

"You've never pleasured yourself? No man has touched you?"

She liked the way his body tightened as he awaited her answer. "I'm a virgin," she said simply, thinking that was answer enough.

"Being virgin only means no man has entered your body. So, none has ever touched you?"

She glanced away. "I was kissed once, by a stable boy."

"And that is all?" he asked, his tone deepening.

She nodded, embarrassed that he knew now how unappealing she was to the opposite sex.

One of his hands lifted and cupped a breast. "Would you like to know what you must guard yourself against tonight? Will that relieve your unease?"

She cast him a glance from beneath her lashes—a look she had seen her sister do often. Mora hoped her attempt at being coy didn't look ridiculous. "Don't you think I should know? I might become…*inflamed*…seeing as how I've never…done that."

"Good point," he murmured. His fingers tugged her nipple.

Mora gasped, and her eyelids fluttered closed.

"No," he said, his voice tight. "Look at me. I would have you know who touches you."

She glanced up. "Are you starting the lesson?" she asked, breathless beneath his intense gaze.

"I find myself unwilling to let them have the first taste of your *virgin* body."

"They will taste me?" she asked, finding the thought not nearly as offensive as it might have been moments ago. The room was growing warmer, and her woman's furrow moistened. She clamped her thighs shut to prevent liquid from trickling down her thighs.

He knelt in front of her, his hands settling on the notches of her hips.

Mora's skin flushed with embarrassment now that his face was level with her melon-sized breasts. Udders, her sister had called them.

Only Tetrik didn't seem the least bit repulsed as he tweaked her nipples, tugging them with his fingers, then letting them go. One digit fingered the tips he'd stimulated to full arousal.

She shifted on her feet, uncomfortable beneath his stare. "My breasts are overlarge."

"They'll feed a litter of warriors," he growled.

For some unknown reason, her body appreciated the comment. Her womb tightened, and her channel clenched. "Are you comparing me to a sow?" she asked, keeping her tone appalled, as she should be.

He snorted and leaned toward her, his lips closing around one turgid peak.

Mora gasped, but her hips undulated. The sensation of his tongue curling around the sensitive tip was almost too pleasurable to bear. Her trembling hands clutched his hair, holding him tightly to her breast.

Tetrik laved the dimpling nipple and then suctioned on it, drawing more of the mound into his mouth, twisting his head back and forth to pull and tug at her breast.

Heat streaked from breast to womb, tightening her sex. Her fingers dragged on his thick hair, clasping handfuls as she tried to rub his face harder against her breast. "The other! Suck the other!" she cried, then bit her lip to prevent another unseemly request.

Laughter gusted from his throat, but he complied, pulling away to use the flat of his tongue to soothe her nipple. Then he licked his way across her chest, leaving a wet trail in his wake, until he suckled the neglected breast.

Her head fell back, and her knees buckled from the pleasure, but his strong hands held her secure as he brought her body closer.

Fire licked her skin and sex—everywhere he touched set a blaze of wanton need.

Mora wanted to wrap herself around him—anything to ease the burning ache building inside her. She rubbed her inner thigh against his side and rolled her hips, seeking something she hadn't the experience to name. "Please," she moaned.

Tetrik released her breast and moved lower, nuzzling her belly, his hands now trailing up the insides of her quivering thighs, pushing them apart. When his fingers met at the juncture of her thighs, he glanced up, his expression alight with wicked promise.

Gasping, Mora braced her weight against his shoulders, afraid she'd melt to the floor in a puddle.

Slowly, he spread her outer labia and curved his back to lower himself. His breath blew over her heated flesh. Then his tongue lapped at the moisture soaking her curls.

Embarrassment heated her cheeks and chest, knowing what he tasted, what he could see of her open, clasping pussy. But his low, appreciative growls and the stroke of his hot tongue eased her past that first stab of mortification.

Her hips rolled of their own accord, and Mora learned the sounds her slick folds could make—wet, sucking murmurs that Tetrik enjoyed immensely, if his escalating groans were any calibration of his pleasure.

Mora jerked when his fingers found the center of her ache, a knot at the top of her cleft that hardened as he swirled the rough pad of his thumb across it.

"Give me your moans, wife. Let the wildness take you," he said, his voice tight and roughened. Then he planted a kiss on her inner thigh and resumed the lush tongue strokes, continuing to rasp his thumb over the burgeoning knot.

Mora felt the first deep shudder ripple throughout her channel and cried out, her hips pumping forward and back. "Tetrik...what is happening?"

"Come for me, wife. I have you—just let yourself go." His mouth closed around the hardened kernel and suctioned while his fingers took the place of his tongue and stroked over her sex, fingering her portal, massaging her lips.

Another ripple convulsed along her channel, and then she was thrust headlong into an explosion of ecstasy, nearly painful in its beauty and power. Prickling multicolored lights burst behind her closed eyelids. She bit her lips to hold back the scream tearing from her throat, and then she pitched over the edge.

When she returned to her senses, she found herself sprawled atop the large bed. Her husband lay on his side, his hand stroking her breast. His face was taut. His gaze hard.

She closed her legs and glanced away, self-conscious now that the fervor didn't rule her body. Had she acted the wanton? Conversely, she wondered if her passion approached that of Kronaki women.

His palm cupped her cheek, and he brought her gaze back to his. "Now you know what you must fight," he said, his expression frightening, yet thrilling, in its intensity. "I will own your cries. Your body will weep for me, alone."

Chapter Four

Tetrik pretended to enjoy the feast while watching his wife from the corner of his eye. Fearing his men would guess his heightened awareness, he tried not to look her way too often. For if his lust for her were discovered, they would only be encouraged to torture and tease him to unbearable heights during the bedding.

Already, the evening was proving torturous without their *aid*. His cock and balls ached for the sweet release he'd gifted his wife. His erection had yet to wane when he had only to see his wife's lips purse around the rim of her cup to reignite his desire.

He'd been relieved his threats were heeded and that his staff had prepared foodstuffs in advance, despite their earlier show of rebellion. But the spiced mutton tasted like sawdust after the headier flavor of Mora's arousal. Just the memory of her quivering awakening lessened his appetite for any meat sweeter than he'd supped between her thighs.

However, he was not so far gone with lust that he missed the condescending glances Mora received from the women in attendance. Bristling, he wished he could leap to her defense, but his interference with the women's actions would not serve his new wife. She would have to find her own way to earn their respect.

His men were another matter. They stared openly while she picked at her food. The flush of color staining her cheeks told him she was aware of their interest, and likely damning them for their coarse behavior.

Matters weren't helped by the outfit he'd selected for her to wear. It was a traditional Kronaki gown made of soft sueded leather. He had thought she would be better accepted in something less ostentatious than the glittering gown in which she had arrived. The garment he'd chosen looked like the ones worn by many of the women in attendance, but the leather bands that crisscrossed her chest accentuated her full breasts.

Already, his men had taken note, and he glared daggers to warn them from ogling her and embarrassing her with their avid regard.

His hand tightened around his goblet, no doubt leaving impressions in the hard metal. With the scent of her arousal still upon his lips, he took a sip of wine and kept his gaze from his wife's other attributes.

He caught Garion's glance as he eyed Mora's legs and cursed under his breath. He should have chosen something longer, less form fitting. As it was, the leather skirt hugged her generous bottom and exposed those mouthwatering legs. Any man looking at them could well imagine the pleasure they would give, clasping his middle as he rode between her thighs.

Cursing beneath his breath, Tetrik shifted on his chair.

Garion cleared his throat and leaned to the side, whispering, "I would never have guessed how well your wife would look in ram-skin. That shade of beige warms her cheeks."

Tetrik glared at his Captain-at-Arms.

"And her figure could make a man's mouth crave a mother's milk."

Tetrik slammed his goblet on the table, not caring that wine sloshed over the rim. "You're enjoying this, aren't you?"

"More than I had hoped," Garion said, a smug grin curving his mouth. "But she is still Mellusian. Perhaps the surprising package only clothes a tepid passion."

Tetrik snorted, recalling his wife's muffled screams and the way she'd fainted dead away when she'd orgasmed beneath his mouth.

Garion's eyebrows rose. "So, you've already tasted her passion? But what of the bedding?"

"She is still a virgin."

A loud guffaw of laughter erupted from the other man. "No wonder you look ready for battle. Sweet, was she?"

"Ambrosia," he groaned. At Garion's renewed laughter, Tetrik grimaced, vowing to beat his captain to a pulp during the next day's training.

"My lord," Mora said, laying her hand upon his arm to draw his attention.

He leaned toward her. "I told you to call me Tetrik," he growled. "You did before," he said, reminding her of the circumstance under which she'd lost her reserve.

She blushed, and her fingers tightened on his arm. "I was just wondering, *Tetrik*, whether it is permissible in your society to flaunt your sensuality so openly," she said, nodding toward Agarth, the cook, who sat upon the mage's lap, feeding him strips of meat with her fingers.

"We have no inhibitions, wife. If we desire the pleasure of a woman on our lap, *or more*, we take that pleasure wherever we please."

At that moment, Serit slipped his hand beneath Agarth's skirt. The woman smiled and widened her legs, allowing a glimpse of her naked quim and his busy hand.

"Oh!"

That one gasped word drew Tetrik's attention from the randy couple.

Mora's chest rose as she drew a deep breath. Her hand shook as she raised her goblet and took a dainty sip, her tongue darting out to wipe away a droplet. But her wide-eyed gaze never left Agarth and Serit.

Tetrik knew he stared at Mora but couldn't tear away his glance. Her cheeks reddened, and her chest rose and fell rapidly. Most interesting was the scent of her arousal that rose to tease his nostrils.

Finally, Mora's gaze slid his way. "Is it permissible for a married man to take a woman, not his wife, upon his lap?"

Tetrik chose his words carefully, so as not to offend her tender sensibilities. "If the wife has no objection, then yes," he murmured. "But he shouldn't offer her an open insult. Why do you ask?"

Her blush deepened. "I just wondered…that's all."

He leaned close to whisper in her ear. "Do you wish to sit on my lap?" he drawled.

Her eyes widened, and her face flushed scarlet. "Of course not."

"Would you like to sit on someone else's lap?" he teased to gain a brighter blush, but her blinking stare told him she considered it. "Well, ballocks!"

"No. No, I wouldn't," she said too quickly.

Tetrik lifted her off her chair and onto his lap, settling her on his erection—a pointed reminder of whose cock she should be considering. "Think on this, love."

Her bottom squirmed. "Everyone's staring," she complained, although she sounded breathless.

"They're just wondering what took me so long," he ground out.

"Are we starting the bedding?" Garion asked loudly.

"The bedding? Here?" Mora bleated, blood leaching from her face.

"Here's as good a place as any," Tetrik said, wondering why he goaded her.

A new, ruddier flush stained the tops of her breasts. "I'll not be the dessert at this feast!"

"No, my lady," Garion said, sweeping his arms wide. "You're the whole main course!"

Her gasp and the tears that instantly filled her eyes told him Garion's jest had struck her.

Tetrik cast a glare at Garion for upsetting her, and then he bracketed Mora's face with his hands. "He did not mean to wound."

She sniffed and blinked to clear away her tears. "I'm just overly sensitive. Pay me no heed."

But he could tell the comment still stung her. "Tell me, now. What bothers you?"

"Will you not leave it?" she hissed, struggling now in earnest to get off his lap.

He snaked an arm around her waist to anchor her. "Not until you tell me what is wrong," Tetrik said, not liking her distress.

She leaned close. "I know I am fat," she whispered, her voice ragged with emotion, "but I don't need the fact trumpeted!"

"My lady, you think you're fat?" Garion asked, his tone lower now. "Your curves have made your husband the envy of every man here!"

"Garion!" Again, Tetrik glared at the other man until he backed away. To Mora, he said, "Your figure is not unattractive. Think you that my cock would be hard as stone if that were true?"

Mora grew still. "Your cock wouldn't be just as...attentive... if another woman sat upon your lap?" she asked, suspicion flavoring her tone.

Tetrik combed his fingers through her hair and drew her head closer. "I've been this way ever since I had your tits in my mouth."

Her eyes widened, and then a giggle broke free. "I can't believe you just said that."

"Why? I like your tits," he said, smiling with relief that he'd managed to shock her out of her tears.

Her grin turned teasing. "I liked what you did to them too," she whispered. "But I had no idea you were so pained, husband." Her hips wriggled, grinding her bottom against his cock.

"Witch!" he muttered, and then he took her lips in a blistering kiss.

She moaned, and her tongue crept inside his mouth, tickling, gliding. Then she drew back and licked her lips. "Mmm. You taste different. I want what you're eating."

"And you shall have it." *Ah! I'll paint your lips with the flavor of your desire.*

"We'll have none of that," Garion said, his voice filled with merriment. "Save it for the bedding."

When Mora stiffened again in his arms, Tetrik scowled at Garion. "About the bedding, Garion…"

"You're ready to begin?"

"I'll want only a minimum of participants."

"So long as I am one of them," Garion said, letting his gaze roam over Mora's breasts, "I'll keep the grumbling from the rest of the men at bay."

"You and Serit, then—but a warning. You will not embarrass my wife."

"Wait a second," Mora said, tugging on his hair. "Which of them will prepare you?"

"Wife, there is no need for me to be prepared," he said, giving her a devilish smile. "I've done it before."

She crossed her arms across her chest. "But I was serious about wanting this to be equally embarrassing for you."

Garion laughed. "Perhaps Serit—he seems to like it both ways."

"I'll not give my cock to Serit!" Tetrik turned to his wife, whose expression had grown confused. "Wife, you may choose two women to prepare me."

A frown creased her forehead. Would her wish to discomfit him outweigh that hint of jealousy? She gave him a narrow-eyed glance, then let her gaze sweep over the hall. "The woman on that man's lap," she said, pointing to Agarth. "And her." This time she pointed at the stable master's daughter.

Tetrik concealed a smile. She'd chosen women with ample proportions to match her own. He nodded to Garion, who'd grinned throughout the whole exchange, his shoulders shaking from suppressed laughter. "Just get on with it," Tetrik said testily, his body tightening painfully now the bedding was imminent.

After Garion departed, Tetrik brought Mora's face around with a finger beneath her chin.

Her expression was tight, and her cheeks a bit pale, betraying her growing anxiety.

"You will not be afraid," he commanded.

"You're making an exception for me, aren't you? Limiting the participants."

He disliked the worry that creased her forehead. "I find I don't like the idea of sharing you with so many."

"But is this wise? Will your people think I'm a coward?"

"By the time Garion is done, they will know I wanted you to myself. But tradition will be served—adequate witnesses will bear the news."

Her glance fell to her fingers, which plucked the fur of his vest. "Would you think me a coward if I said I was afraid of what will happen this night?"

"No, wife. It's natural for you to fear my superior cock," he said, attempting to lighten her mood. At the smile that quirked her lips, he added softly, "Do you want to know what will happen during the bedding?"

"Will they touch me like you did before?" Her cheeks flushed a lovely rose as she met his glance.

He nodded.

"Will it be acceptable if I pretend you are the only one touching me?"

He'd have thought it impossible, but his cock grew harder. "Watch me when they touch you. I will be the only one there."

"Will you enjoy the other women's attentions?"

"Only if what they do inspires you," he said, drawling the words.

She shivered, and her nipples beaded beneath the supple leather of her garment. "When will they give me to you?"

"When you are ready." His hand cupped a breast, and he slid his thumb across the aroused peak.

She drew in a ragged breath. "How will I know I am ready?"

"Don't worry. They will know." He pinched her nipple hard. "But remember, you must not let them bring you release."

Her chin lifted, even as she pressed her breast against his hand. "Can I demand the same of you?"

Tetrik lifted his hips fractionally off his chair, grinding his aching cock against her bottom. "I may not be able to halt my release. I've been aching so long."

"Then, when you are close…" she said, her lips an inch above his, "May I help them?"

"If you help, I may embarrass myself, for it will be over all too soon," he said, groaning when she wriggled, her bottom caressing his straining shaft. "Would you have me spend myself upon the floor like a beardless boy?"

She blinked, considering his words. "How long will it take you to grow firm again?"

"Moments," he ground out. Just the thought of her curious gaze watching his sex fill again with ardor had him close to exploding.

"When I am ready, will they stay long?"

"Long enough to help us join."

Her eyes widened. "I don't think I want to know what that means."

"Some things are better left for the bedding to discover." He rasped his thumb across her lower lip. "Are you still afraid?"

She nodded. "But I think I am also eager now for it to begin."

Tetrik gave her a reassuring squeeze. "I knew I had the right sister."

Chapter Five

Despite the fire blazing in the brazier in the corner of the room, Mora shivered as the witnesses gathered inside the bedchamber. They'd been introduced, one by one, as they entered, but now stood staring at one another. *How awkward this is! Do they wait for me to give a signal that I'm ready to be ravished?* Mora glanced at her husband, who stood with his feet braced, his jaw tight—looking for all the world as if he prepared for a battle. She wasn't reassured.

She dragged in a deep breath and cast a glance at the tall warrior, Garion. "Would you unbuckle the bands at the back of my clothing?"

A small smile quirked up the corners of his lips.

Was that approval for her courage? Or amusement? Does he think me too eager?

"I'd be honored to undress you, my lady," he said, his deep voice sounding like a caress. With his long blonde hair and the facial hair that surrounded his mouth and chin, Mora could well imagine how intimidating he would look holding a sword...or bending over her breast.

Oh Goddess! And Tetrik expects me to withhold release from this man?

His fingers plucked open the buckle, and her clothing loosened.

Mora clutched the fabric to her breasts, not yet ready to bare herself to the room.

"Mora," Tetrik said, drawing her attention.

His chiseled expression renewed the curling desire his play at the feast had fostered.

"The sooner you let go of that garb, the sooner I will have you," her husband said.

How easily he takes away my will!

Holding his stare, she released her clothing, letting it slither to the floor. She fought the blush already heating her cheeks as all eyes turned to examine her. Then she caught a glimpse of herself in the copper-rimmed mirror. Standing next to the two tall warriors, she didn't seem nearly as robust of figure as she knew herself to be. The sight reassured her.

"My lord," Garion drawled, "I think Serit and I will have to linger over this feast."

A hand settled on her backside and delivered a delicious squeeze. Mora jerked, then gasped as her body reacted with a release of liquid that gushed to wet her thighs. She found she had little liking for the fact she had no control over her body's response. She tossed back her hair and feigned a bravado her quivering belly belied. Striving for a haughty tone, she said, "I think it highly unfair I'm the only one naked in this room."

Soft laughter broke the tension, and the two women flanking Tetrik pulled at his clothing until he too was nude.

Mora's first glimpse of her husband's body rocked her on her heels. As Garion's hands caressed her breasts and belly, and the mage, Serit, smoothed his over her back and bottom, Mora feasted on the sight of her husband's muscled frame.

She'd already learned the texture and tensile strength of his chest and arms, but below, his body took her breath away. His waist narrowed, an arrow of dark hair leading her gaze to the dark triangle that framed his manhood. She skipped over his straining erection for the moment, since she needed to remember how to breathe, and followed the thick thighs and calves downward. A dusting of hair clothed thick muscles that bulged and rippled as he shifted on his feet.

Oh Goddess! The power those thighs would deliver! Her gaze returned to his sex, and she swallowed to wet a mouth suddenly gone dry. She understood now what he'd meant when he said he was more. The man could fill a flagon with that cock!

Agarth's long fingers wrapped partway around his straining sex, and she nuzzled him with her nose and mouth. The other woman, whose name escaped Mora at the moment, knelt at his feet and cupped his sac with both hands, then opened her mouth to suckle his balls.

Fresh cream trickled down the inside of Mora's thighs as she watched the women tongue his flesh, suctioning the end of his cock and massaging his balls. She couldn't tear her gaze away from the sight, but strangely, she felt no jealousy for the pleasure they delivered him.

Then her torment began.

Garion grabbed her hand and tugged her toward the bed. "Our pleasure will not be over before it even begins."

She let him lead her, her legs trembling like jelly, and cast Tetrik a wild-eyed glance.

His face remained carved in stone, his eyes glittering with some dark emotion that sent shivers down her spine.

"Lie down, lady," Serit said, in his odd singsong voice. Still fully clothed, he climbed onto the bed and beckoned, his arms opening to accept her as she slid across the furs. Serit contrasted Garion's blond barbarian looks with his dark skin and leanly muscled build. He helped her recline, his strong arm beneath her shoulders, lowering her to the bed.

Garion climbed onto the end of the mattress and grasped her ankles, pulling wide her legs. Mora's breath hitched and a wicked smile spread over his lips at the small sound. "Already, you drip honey. But how sweet do you taste?" Before she knew what he intended, he moved between her feet and leaned over her sex.

A gasp escaped her lips, as his tongue lapped at the moisture drenching her curls.

Garion turned his head and grinned at Tetrik. "You were right. Ambrosia." At Tetrik's ominous growl, he only laughed, and then parted her cleft with his fingers. "I've a terrible thirst."

Mora couldn't stop her hips from jerking as he suckled her slick folds. Her bottom rose from the mattress, seeking a deeper pleasure, then trembled when his laughter vibrated against her sex.

"So eager," Serit said, his mouth beside her ear. "But I think our overlord will want the pleasure of all your cries. Can you resist us?"

Mora groaned and closed her eyes. Which was a huge mistake. Robbed of the sense of sight, her skin and sex tuned sharper to the two men's efforts.

Serit shifted beside her and tongued her nipple into an aching peak, laving and chewing the distended tip, while Garion's beard rasped her pussy as he tunneled his tongue inside her, thrusting into her clasping folds.

Her eyes shot open to meet Tetrik's heated gaze. "No penetration, you said," Mora accused, unable to contain the uncertain quaver in her voice.

The women paused in their fondling to laugh.

"They'll not fuck you, my lady, but tasting is acceptable," Agarth said, then sank her mouth over Tetrik's cock, her cheeks hollowing as she sucked.

As Garion lashed her with his wicked tongue, Mora's hips lifted again from the bed, seeking the release her husband had already conditioned her body to expect. "I can't stop!" She raised her knees, letting them fall open, encouraging Garion to spear deeper inside her.

"Mora!" Tetrik shouted, then his hips rolled forward, thrusting harder into Agarth's mouth. "Damn you!"

Mora heard his curse, but was beyond the point of caution or fear of her husband's retribution. The pleasure her two lovers visited on her, along with the visual wonder of Tetrik's seduction had her nearly mindless with desire.

The other woman joined Agarth in front of Tetrik, and her hands closed around the base of his cock. She licked up the side of his shaft and down again, matching the rhythm of Agarth's suctioning. Together, the women held him captive with their hands and mouths.

Dazed with the building pleasure and Tetrik's angry arousal, Mora was transfixed as she watched the women torment her husband.

Agarth drew back from his cock and moaned as she nibbled and laved the bulbous head of his cock, while the other woman twisted her hands around his shaft.

Inflamed, and feeling the need to compete with the women's sensual play, Mora thrust her breast against Serit's mouth. "Bite it. *Goddess*, bite it," she begged.

Serit murmured and nuzzled her breast, then took her turgid peak between his teeth and bit.

Mora slammed her hips upward, nearly dislodging Garion. But he slipped his hands beneath her buttocks and held her still as he continued to ravage her with his beard and tongue.

Sweat broke on her brow and upper lip, and she tossed her head back and forth on the mattress. *So close! Just a moment more...* A groan tore from her lips.

Suddenly, both men stopped.

Mora cried out, nearly weeping with frustration.

"Watch him, lady," Serit said, turning her face toward Tetrik.

Mora turned her dazed glance to her husband, and her breath caught.

Tetrik's hands fisted at his sides, his eyes clenched tight. Then a rumbling groan broke from his throat as he pumped hard into Agarth's mouth.

Agarth's head bobbed in opposition to his strokes — mewling, choking sounds erupting from deep inside her throat. Abruptly, she drew back.

"Ahhh!" Tetrik sighed, as a stream of creamy liquid shot from his cock, striping the women's upturned faces. As his thrusts grew shallow, his eyes opened, and he stared at Mora. "When I am renewed, I will fuck your body like I did her mouth. *Be prepared.*"

Mora shuddered at the possessive anger that stained his face and chest. She lifted one hand to caress Serit's cheek, the other fisted in Garion's hair. "Then be quick about it. I'm dying here."

Garion groaned. "Yes, my lord, be quick about it, or I'll drill a hole into this mattress with my cock."

"Bastard!" Tetrik spat.

The women giggled, then returned their attention to his slackening cock.

"Think you, we can stave him long enough to rob him of her release?" Agarth teased.

"Your next release had better be mine!" Mora warned.

Tetrik's eyes narrowed. "Keep that in mind while my men toy with you. You will resist."

"I think it's my turn to sup at the lady's cunt," Serit said, his thumb flicking her nipple.

Garion's eyebrows waggled. "Then I'll play with those glorious breasts."

The men quickly changed places.

Mora sighed as the men renewed their efforts, her body languidly undulating. She turned her fevered gaze to her husband, needing him closer. "There is room for more upon this great bed."

Tetrik helped the ladies to their feet. "I think we'll expand my wife's knowledge of the possibilities."

The women shared wicked smiles and strode toward the bed, their hips swaying enticingly. They climbed onto the bed and delivered loud, smacking kisses to the men bent over Mora's body.

Crowded now to one side of the bed, Mora complained, "Why are Tetrik and I the only ones naked?"

"We thought you'd be more comfortable," Serit murmured.

Tetrik lowered himself beside her, his glance sweeping over her nude body. "You did say you wanted comparisons."

Mora's breasts tightened at his hungry expression, and she swallowed her reserve. The more she let go of her natural modesty, the more aroused he seemed to become. "However else will I determine whether I'm receiving superior cock?" she said, feeling proud she'd managed to sound only slightly breathless.

Her bravado waned as clothing fell away amid giggles and laughter.

Tetrik reclined with his arms behind his head and grinned. "At least, I'm closer to my objective now."

As the others bounced them on the mattress while they shifted to make room for so many bodies and limbs, Mora wondered where her reticence had flown. What would her fellow Mellusians make of her wanton behavior?

When at last all had taken their chosen positions, Mora lay on her side facing Tetrik, her left thigh raised to allow Serit access to her pussy. Her arm curved around Garion's shoulder as he curled over her to suckle her uppermost breast.

Agarth lay between Tetrik and Mora, dividing the bed, her mouth surrounding his sex, her bush perilously close to his mouth. The other woman fondled his balls from behind him.

As the seduction began again in earnest, Tetrik's mouth curved into a lusty smile over Agarth's hip. "There's nothing that says we can't torment our witnesses."

Mora raised her eyebrows in question.

He smoothed a hand along Agarth's hip and thigh while Mora watched, her breath hitching as his darker hand massaged the woman's pale skin.

That's how it looks when he caresses me!

The woman parted her legs, lifting her leg to brace against the headboard to allow him to slide his fingers across her sex.

Mora watched Tetrik's play, her breasts tingling as Garion suckled, her cunt rippling beneath Serit's expert manipulations.

Tetrik halted the motion of his fingers and raised an eyebrow—an unspoken question.

With both of his men-at-arms working over her flesh, Mora's breath caught, her gaze falling to his wicked fingers as he drew circles over Agarth's pussy. The sight of another woman brought so quickly to quivering arousal excited her.

She lifted her gaze to meet his and nodded.

Tetrik's expression smoldered, a small smile signaling his approval of her daring as he stroked the woman's sopping labia.

Mora knew exactly how Agarth felt, for Serit rubbed her own wet flesh, plucking her lips, massaging the aroused nubbin at the top of her cleft until her hips rolled against his hand.

As Agarth writhed and pulsed in response to Tetrik's manipulations, so did Mora.

Soon, Agarth moaned, and her head bobbed on Tetrik's cock, her strokes growing longer as his sex lengthened.

Tetrik's gaze remained fastened on Mora even while his fingers slid between the other woman's slick folds. His nostrils flared to breathe in her arousal.

Mora's chest rose faster as more moisture seeped from Agarth's body to coat Tetrik's fingers. She arched, on the edge of exploding. Her husband's fiery stare and deepening breaths told of his own escalating passion and stripped away her last inhibitions. She wanted to see Agarth come apart—witness another woman's fulfillment beneath his skilled hands.

She leaned toward him and kissed his lips. "Do it. Fuck her with your fingers." She liked the nasty, explicit words and the taut, hungry expression they earned.

She watched as he tunneled his fingers into Agarth's body, twisting his hand to rotate and dig deeper.

Agarth groaned and her hips pumped, her belly first brushing Tetrik's chest, then her bottom pressing against Garion as he suckled Mora's breast.

Garion laughed and let go of the nipple he'd tongued to full arousal, and then aligning himself along her back, he thrust his cock between her legs, rubbing it over Mora's aching sex, where Serit turned to alternately tongue the man's cock and suckle Mora's swollen lips.

Garion's body tightened behind her and his thrusts ground harder against her sex. "Serit!" he hissed angrily, but he thrust again. This time Mora felt the shadow of Serit's beard against her cunt and knew Serit had taken Garion's cock into his mouth.

Garion's arm snaked around her belly and he pumped his hips fast against her bottom, driving his cock deeper into Serit's mouth.

Mora delighted in Garion's abandon and moaned, fighting the curling heat knotting her own belly.

Agarth's arousal wafted pungent in the air between her and her husband, and they shared a heated stare.

Then Tetrik spread the woman's thin inner lips apart and pulled to expose the kernel of her desire, framed by her glistening lips and the damp blonde hair clothing her outer labia.

That's what it looks like! Mora thought the woman's quim and reddened knot rather ugly, but the woman's moans and undulating hips excited her. She darted a glance back up to her husband.

Tetrik lifted one dark brow.

"Suck it," she commanded. "I want to watch."

The heat of all the bodies pressed close made Mora's body slick with sweat—the easier to glide her belly and legs against the woman and the two men working on her own flesh.

Moans rose in the air as everyone on the bed reached for cocks and quims and writhed against each other.

Tetrik leaned close to Agarth's fragrant sex and pursed his lips around her clitoris.

Agarth screamed around Tetrik's cock, and his eyes squeezed shut. He moaned.

"Your next release is mine!" Mora reminded him, as he kept up the grinding rhythm of his fingers as they pumped inside the other woman's channel.

Suddenly, a rippling shudder clenched around his hand, and Agarth undulated, groaning loudly. Still, Tetrik suckled her nubbin until her shudders shook the bed and all its occupants.

When Agarth stilled, panting to catch her breath, Tetrik leaned away.

Mora groaned, her eyelids dipping as she took in the sight of the moisture glistening on Tetrik's swollen lips and leaned toward him.

"Wife! Your passion pleases me," he murmured, then kissed her. "Are you ready?" he whispered.

She bit his lips and moaned. "Take me."

As if that was the signal, bodies unwound from around them and hands helped her up to straddle Tetrik's hips.

Serit parted her cleft with his fingers. Garion supported her weight above Tetrik's cock since Mora's legs quivered too much for her to control her own movements.

Agarth's hands clasped Tetrik's sex to raise his newly invigorated staff and place him at her opening. Another set of smaller hands cupped her bottom as she eased down his long cock.

Mora groaned as she was lowered onto his cock, his girth stretching her opening, cramming into her channel.

Then Serit took a nipple into his mouth as Garion positioned himself behind her, his chest against her back, his cock between her buttocks. With his arm around her waist, together, they lifted and fell while she fucked her husband, writhing inside the circle of Garion's arms.

Closing her eyes, she moaned at each rising, unwilling to let him go from her inside her body, only to sink deeper with each fall.

"Easy," Garion's strained whisper ruffled the hair tucked behind her ear. "Take him slowly, we have still to break—"

Down she slid, and the thin barrier inside her broke, allowing her to sink deeper on his cock. She cried out, not so much from pain as surprise. As if from a distance, she heard Tetrik's answering moan.

Both her breasts were suckled hard now, tongues laving the hardened peaks. Fingers massaged her sex, still straining around his erection, and rubbed her clitoris in drugging circles.

Mora's hips jerked, and her body shuddered. She reached back to clutch at Garion's hair. "More, deeper. Oh please!"

Laughter shook against her back, but Garion heeded her plea, letting her sink deeper until Tetrik's large cock butted against her womb.

Then Garion gripped her belly hard and leaned her over, changing the angle of penetration, moving faster with her to grind her pubis into the hairs surrounding Tetrik's cock and press Serit's fingers harder against her clit.

Mora mewled, a long, broken sound that earned her praise.

"That's it, lady," Serit crooned against her breast.

So much heat and sweat, their bodies glided together, Garion's cock sliding between her cheeks, grazing the other opening, friction building a fire between Tetrik's cock and her tight channel, until Mora was mindless with the need to reach the pinnacle. "Please, oh please."

"Come for me, love," Tetrik moaned.

She opened her eyes, finding his gaze boring into hers, and her body answered his command, her cunt flooding, her body shuddering, wringing cries from deep inside her throat.

Mora pumped with Garion, faster, harder, her open sex slamming against Tetrik's groin, until heat and a prickling darkness closed over her.

Her scream keened from her parched throat as she hurtled over the precipice. Mora jerked and shuddered, until finally she grew still.

"Shhhh. Shhhh." Garion held her as she sobbed.

Her gaze stayed on her husband's face. "But you—you haven't come."

His face hard as the granite of his mountain, he said, "I'll need no aid to fuck you, wife."

Garion kissed her shoulder, and then withdrew his support. The others melted from the bed to leave Mora and Tetrik alone.

Shivering, her hands braced against his chest to keep from crumpling on top of him.

He opened his arms and Mora fell gratefully against his chest, their bodies still joined.

"What do you think now of our custom, wife?" he said, his deep voice rumbled beneath her cheek.

Mora smiled sleepily against his slick chest. "Can we only wed once?"

Chapter Six

Bemused, Tetrik held his softly snoring wife. Their bodies were still joined, his cock nestled deep inside her cunt.

He nearly groaned with frustration.

But what a delight she'd proved. Already, tales of her courage and lust would be traded in the hall below. No one would question her worthiness to be his bride or carry his offspring. Mora was no tepid Mellusian—she had the heart of a Kronak.

Her passion gave him hope the provisions of The Promise were attainable now.

The sight of her lush body held inside the circle of Garion's arms, her eyes glazing as she came, pumping up and down on his cock, her large breasts quivering with each stroke, had him gritting his teeth against the need to spear upward into her molten channel. She gloved his entire length, like a lock to its key—snug, and hot, and...*clenching!*

The snoring had stopped.

He smoothed his hands down her back and curved his palms over the swell of her backside, squeezing her fleshy bottom. "So, you're awake at last?"

"I was having a lovely dream, but something kept prodding me awake," she said, sounding grumpy.

Tetrik smiled and flexed his buttocks, driving his cock upward. "Then it worked."

She snuggled closer and plucked at the hair matting his chest, stifling a yawn. "Will I ever become accustomed to this?"

He nearly forgot her question when she fingered one flat nipple. "To what?"

She pinched him. "This…intimacy!" She soothed his nipple, stroking it softly now. "To your touch."

He hugged her close. This was one of those moments most warriors avoided like bloody plague. Conversation with a woman was as treacherous as navigating a Graktilian minefield. But this was his wife. Her tender feelings mattered to him — and not just because he needed her pliant and agreeable to share more sex. Her happiness alone was important to him now that he knew her.

"You'll adjust…somewhat." *There!* He'd reassured her. Now, how long would it take her to notice he still needed to find his own release?

She raised her head and frowned at him. "That was definitive," she said, a hint of sarcasm in her tone.

"My answer didn't please you?"

She shook her head and lay down against his chest once more. "Tetrik?"

He grunted in answer, drawing on his warrior's training to restrain himself from forcing her to give his body ease.

"Was I too…abandoned?" she asked, her voice small.

How was he supposed to answer that? If he said yes, would she feel ashamed? If no, would she sulk? "Too abandoned?" he repeated, hoping she'd give him a hint how she wanted him to answer.

"Too unrestrained before…with our witnesses."

Tetrik relaxed and nuzzled her hair with his nose. "Are you asking whether I was pleased with your passion?"

She sighed. "Never mind."

Tetrik felt a grin stretch his mouth. *Ah! She wants praise.* "Can you not tell the extent of my pleasure?" he teased and gave her another "prod".

She sniffed. "It's only obvious to me that I left you wanting."

"'Twas my choice to restrain myself—but not because I found you lacking, wife. I wanted to fuck you my first time without assistance or an audience."

"But we've already…fucked."

"*You* took me, dear. That first time was meant to make your breaching less traumatic and painful—to ease you into accepting my cock. You retained control over how much of me you could take."

"I beg to differ," she grumbled. "I felt completely out of control. If Garion hadn't… assisted me…"

He didn't like the way her voice softened when she spoke his captain's name. "Let's not mention his name right now," he said, choking back anger.

She lifted her head. "Are you jealous of Garion? But this was your custom."

"Garion's attentions to you went a little far."

Mora's lips twisted in a wicked smile. "I fear I wasn't the center of his attention toward the end."

Tetrik raised his eyebrows in confusion.

"Did you not notice what Serit was doing?"

"To Garion?" Shocked at the thought of Serit…with Garion…he closed his gaping jaw.

She nodded, her gaze full of devilish humor. "Oh, Garion protested—at first…"

"Serit and Garion?" he parroted. "But Garion continually mocks Serit's proclivities."

"Well, perhaps he was a little too aroused to resist the mage's skills."

"Too aroused by you, you mean. That wife, I can well understand." Tetrik released a bark of laughter. "Just wait until I see him in the morning."

"You will not tease him! I think he might be embarrassed."

Tetrik laughed again. "He certainly will when I'm through with him." He smiled at his wife. "See the havoc your passion wreaks on my warriors?"

Her inner muscles tightened around his cock. "Then how are you able to resist me still? I'm beginning to think you're growing bored of me."

Tetrik rolled her beneath him, in a move so fast she only had time to gasp, before he was poised above her, his cock partway removed as he prepared to show her the extent of his *disinterest*. "Are we through with questions and talk of Garion?"

"I have one more question," she said, her voice deepening into a sensual drawl.

"Say it quickly! I fear my control is unraveling."

Her eyelids dropped to half-mast, and she gave him another wicked little squeeze. "Will you give me your wildness?" she asked, raking her fingernails down his back.

Tetrik groaned and took her lips. Then he flexed his thighs and hips, driving deep inside her — unrestrained — letting the "wildness" consume him. His strokes were deep, powerful, lifting her buttocks from the bed with each thrust.

But he wanted more. Wanted her closer still — to drive the thoughts of any other man from her mind. "Put your legs around me," he growled.

She did so without hesitation, hugging his waist as tight as he'd imagined, her arms encircling his back, her warmth and softness surrounding him. "Like this?"

"Perfect." Groaning, Tetrik rose on his arms to give his hips greater leverage. He tunneled into her, a sharp thrust that drove the breath from her body. "Tell me if I cause you pain," he said, although he doubted he'd have control of his body for much longer.

Shaking her head, she grasped his buttocks. "You make me greedy, husband. I would see your face when you find release — to know whether you want me as much as you did Agarth and that other woman."

"That wish is easily granted, love. But you are wrong about which woman I wanted—your greedy gaze drove me to completion. Hold on to me—tight." Tetrik thrust his cock deep and then pulled away, enjoying the clasp of her channel as he withdrew. Her body was eager as she for this joining. He stroked into her, flexing his buttocks to deliver a sharper thrust.

She grunted softly, and her face reddened as her hips rolled to meet his thrust and take him deep as he could reach.

And Goddess, her cunt! Moisture flooded her channel, coating his cock in steamy welcome. It rippled around him as he tunneled, clasping tighter each time he withdrew.

He stroked again and again, coming up on his knees to drive deeper, harder—needing to brand her body with his power and heat.

Her gasps grew thin, accompanied by thready moans as she tossed her head on the mattress. "Tetrik, Tetrik!" she chanted.

Faster and harder, he thrust into her tight quim, pummeling her womb with the head of his cock, until her channel convulsed, squeezing and releasing, milking his shaft toward orgasm.

His body tightened, his thighs turning to stone as he pounded harder, each stroke shoving her higher up the bed. He followed on his knees, crowding her, until her hips curled up higher and her legs hugged his shoulders.

Now, her sweet, tight cunt pulsed around his cock as he drove straight into her, pounding her body so hard she struggled to breathe, but still she hugged him closer.

Then Tetrik felt his release overtake him, tension making his thighs and buttocks rigid as cum jetted from his cock in one burning, endless stream. He shouted then, his relief so strong his body shuddered as he came apart.

Mora gave a strangled scream, and her arms fell away while her eyes glazed and her back arched.

Tetrik continued to pump against her pussy, loath to end this first joining. But at last spent, he collapsed on top of her, tucking his head beside her on the mattress. He didn't know how long he lingered, still joined to her, as sweat cooled on his back and his breaths slowed.

Mora's hand stroked over his hair, soothing him. "I need to lower my legs, husband," she whispered.

Groaning, he eased back a little as her legs unclasped and settled to either side of his hips on the bed. "Am I too heavy?"

"No, I like this part...too."

He sighed. Her soft body pillowed him, chest to groin, and he could imagine the joy of resting like this for many nights to come.

"Husband?"

"Yes, wife."

She yawned. "Think you we could sleep before we do this again?"

He rose to look into her face. What he saw pleased the marauder inside him. Her lips were slack and swollen, her eyelids drooping, blinking against the need to rest. Her skin was flushed a lovely rose that contrasted with the silver-gray of her eyes, and her hair was a brown, tangled cloud upon his bed. She looked well loved and happy.

"I think we will not do this again tonight," he said, smiling as he brushed back her hair. "You will be sore in the morning — and I would have you recovered for more bed sport tomorrow night."

Her eyes widened. "Will you seek another until I am recovered?"

Tetrik stilled. "I'm not sure what you've heard of Kronaki men, but we do not mate morning, noon and night. I won't seek another before we come together again."

She sighed and cast him a shy glance from beneath her lashes. "Would you tell me if I didn't provide you enough sex?"

"What is this about?" he asked softly. "Do you still believe that old warrior's tale about our needing sex to keep up our strength?"

"It isn't true?" She sounded almost disappointed.

"It is only true that we enjoy sex and make up tales to ensure our women do their best to keep our appetites appeased."

Her nose wrinkled in mild disgust. "That's very self-serving."

"I didn't say we weren't selfish."

"Arrogant is what I'd call it."

"But don't you think, after experiencing our superior skills, that we have earned a bit of arrogance?"

"Can women earn that arrogance too?"

He grinned. "A warrior can only hope to attain such a mate."

"Hmmm." Mora glanced away.

It was apparent to him she had something else upon her mind by the way she worried her bottom lip between her teeth. "You have another question for me, wife?"

"Will we ever have need of…assistance, again?"

Tetrik suppressed a territorial growl. "That will be entirely up to you."

"And will the same restriction apply?"

"You mean, no penetration?"

She nodded quickly.

Now that she'd been breached, did she want to experience another man's cock? It wasn't unusual among Kronaki women, but Tetrik felt a pang of anger over her eagerness to experiment. "A man wants to know his children are his own, but there are other places a man can enter that will not cause a pregnancy."

Her eyes slanted back to his. "I could take another man inside my mouth?"

Whose cock did she want to suckle? *Damn, Garion!* "There is another place, too," he said, wanting to shock her into silence.

"Another?" Mora's chest rose as she gasped. "Oh!"

"But, wife, I think I will not permit assistance for quite some time," he said, his words becoming clipped. "There are many acts I will insist I be the first to introduce you to."

"I'd like that," she whispered. "Time to ourselves, to become acquainted."

His anger abated. She was only curious. Perhaps later, say when they were growing gray, he would allow another man into their bed.

Her gaze fell to her hands where they rested on the tops of his shoulders. "Is it true a warrior never loves? Or is that another fairy tale?"

"It is true for most."

"But not impossible."

Tetrik didn't want to hurt her tender feelings, but he also did not want to mislead her. "Kronaki men are hardened to tender emotions. Emotion—whether love or anger—can make us vulnerable in battle."

Her disappointment showed in the moisture pooling in her eyes. "I would never seek to make you vulnerable to an enemy. But I must tell you truthfully that I don't know whether I can accept less from you than your whole heart."

Tetrik grew still, knowing he'd encountered another dangerous minefield he must negotiate. "You have my promise I will never misuse you or lie to you. That I will protect and honor you as my wife."

Her lips trembled, and she drew in a deep breath. "That may not be enough for me. I've settled all my life for seconds—I was second to my sister in my parents' love, second in my people's esteem. I no longer think I can live without being first in my husband's heart."

"What has changed for you?"

She shook her head, her expression so sad, frustrated anger built in his belly. "You wouldn't understand." She drew in another deep breath, one that hitched with a hint of her inner sadness. "I need to sleep now, and you're growing heavy."

Tetrik withdrew from her body and rolled onto his back, his earlier satisfaction obliterated by his wife's rejection.

She wanted him to love her.

Could he convince her to accept what he could offer? Could she be seduced into happiness? Or would planting a babe in her belly be the only way he could force her to remain?

Yesterday, he'd settled on just that plan, convinced a Mellusian woman would never adjust to their ways. Before he'd met Mora, he'd resigned himself to accepting a tepid mate for the sake of improving his people's lives. He'd have fucked her passionless body every night to ensure she could not cry off at the end of the winter, negating the terms of The Promise.

His passionate wife had thrust a spoke in his wheel, shattering his plans for an easy victory. The Promise, though still a primary objective, was not the only consideration now. Even if she conceived and was forced to remain, he wouldn't be satisfied unless she stayed because she wanted him, too.

He would have to earn her love and prove to her that his devotion would be an acceptable substitute for love.

Chapter Seven

Mora awoke alone the next morning, sunlight shining through the narrow window of Tetrik's bedchamber.

She eased out of bed, moving gingerly due to the soreness between her legs that her husband had predicted. She quickly dressed in another suede gown, this one dyed a pale apple green, and fumbled with the buckles behind her back until the fabric covered her appropriately. Then she went in search of her new husband.

As she descended the stone staircase, she felt a little anxious about facing him this morning. She regretted blurting her desires to him last night, and wouldn't blame the man if he stayed in hiding throughout the day.

She hadn't much experience with men, but she knew the raw emotions she'd let surface would make any man, but especially a warrior, uncomfortable—and wouldn't help her in her cause to win his heart. That goal was still foremost in her mind.

In the future she'd school herself not to speak so freely about her desires. The last thing she wanted was for him to be eager for the spring to come, so he could get rid of her. Her pride was strong enough she didn't want him to believe her a clinging or weepy sort of woman.

Mora reasoned he was a stoic warrior, unused to acknowledging softer emotions—maybe not even recognizing them. He would have to be led along slowly, guided by her, to discover how ridiculous his belief that a warrior risked making himself vulnerable to an enemy when he opened his heart to love. It was just another fairy tale.

But how would she approach him today and make him feel at ease in her company? Would her distress over her emotional outburst make her blush and stammer like a simpleton? Just gazing at his hard features and muscular physique had the ability to render her speechless.

Stepping into the hall, she found it empty, save for one young woman who scrubbed a table with a bucket of sudsy water beside her on the floor.

"My lady," she said, bobbing in a quick curtsy. "Breakfast was served hours ago, but I'm sure Agarth wouldn't mind bringing you something to break your fast."

"I don't want to disrupt her day. If you'll point me to the kitchen, I'll help myself. I find I'm famished this morning."

The other woman's expression grew sly. "My lady, may I say how pleased the staff is that all went well for you last night?"

Goddess! Did everyone on this planet discuss her sex life so freely? "Th-thank you," she murmured.

"You hurry along to the kitchen. By the amount of food your husband tucked away this morning, I'd recommend you fortify yourself well."

Cheeks flaming, Mora fled to the kitchen.

Agarth looked up from a table where she stood, her hands kneading dough and a wicked gleam in her eyes. "Good morning, my lady. Get any sleep last night?" she asked, and then laughed.

Mora wondered if her expression was as appalled as she felt. "I slept like a stone," she said flatly. "Thank you, Agarth."

"No, thank *you*, my lady. Garion was quite the beast after we left your room." She wiped her hands on a cloth and indicated a chair at a table next to the great hearth. "Have a seat, and I'll serve your breakfast."

"I'm sorry for the bother."

"Don't be. Your husband told us you needed your rest," she said, with a sinful grin.

Mora sighed and sat at the large wooden table. "So you and Garion—"

"And Serit." Agarth shivered deliciously. "It was incredible. They competed with each other to see who could make me scream loudest."

Mora wondered at the competition, and if perhaps Garion had been feeling the need to prove his manhood. Poor man! He had no idea how inflamed his indiscretion had made her. She wondered if he might appreciate knowing…

She finished her meal as quickly as manners would allow and left the kitchen, following Agarth's directions through the herb garden on her way to the training field.

The herb garden was arranged in long rows of raised beds with graveled paths between the rows. It being winter, the beds were bare of vegetation. A thin, hunched solitary figure worked in one of them, turning the dirt with a shovel, and then sprinkling handfuls of manure to fold into the dark, rich soil.

"Is there a small corner of this garden I might have for my own?" she asked, stepping nearer him.

"This be my garden," the old man said, squinting at her. "I grow the vegetables for Agarth and herbs for Serit's potions. What would you be needing?"

"I need only a small space—one that receives plenty of sunlight. I brought a rose bush that I'd like to plant."

"Do you eat the petals?"

"Oh no! I tended a garden at home—mostly flowers, although I did raise herbs for Gwimmel, our mage."

"I suppose I can plant fewer beans," the old man said, his tone testy. "Do you grind the roots for potions?"

Mora gritted her teeth. "No, I just like to smell the blooms."

He scratched his head and thrust the shovel into the soil, muttering beneath his breath.

With a roll of her eyes, Mora passed through the garden gate and followed the sounds of clanging metal and bellowed orders.

Her husband's voice was of course the loudest. "Dammit, Garion. You're all thumbs today."

"My thumbs aren't the part of me that's growing numb from your ill temper."

Laughter broke from the ranks of men surrounding the two as they sparred with blunt swords in a dirt pit.

Mora crept around the corner of a stone wall to watch the men unobserved. Their rough language and loud laughter didn't bother her much today. Instead of blushing and covering her ears, she smiled and studied each of the men, as she hadn't been able to drag her attention from her husband the previous evening in the hall to take note of anyone else.

The warriors were dressed in close-fitting breeches with fur-trimmed boots that reached their knees. Many were bare-chested and sweating from exertion despite the chilly wind.

They were all tall with well-developed musculature — as this warrior race was famed for. So many broad-shouldered men with trim waists and bulging arms made her a bit breathless.

No wonder her father had turned to them for help when the Graktiles had sent raiding parties in star ships to Mellusia. The Kronaks had made clever use of the mage's portals to move freely behind Graktilian lines. Despite their advanced technology, the Graktiles had been no match for the ferocity of her husband's warriors. In close quarters, the Kronaks had devastated the slighter lizard men in hand-to-hand combat, forcing a withdrawal.

Any one of these men would have overwhelmed her with his strength and sensuality — but she was glad she'd been given to Tetrik. To her eyes, he was the tallest, the strongest, the handsomest. And for the moment, her gaze couldn't drag away from the rippling, flexing muscles of his back and arms, nor the powerful clenching of his thighs and buttocks as he traded blows with Garion.

Last night, all that power had been directed at her to provide her pleasure.

Perhaps her decided preference for her husband was colored by the surprisingly sensitive way he'd handled her fears, prodding her into an anger that had swamped her inhibitions.

She had no doubt that had been a deliberate strategy. He'd assessed her flaws and strengths and known immediately how best to creep beneath her defenses.

He was a master strategist—no wonder he was lord here.

But at the moment her warlord acted a brute toward Garion, pummeling the man with the flat of his sword.

Mora felt a twinge of guilt. Her unintentional praise for the warrior had earned him Tetrik's ire.

"Can I help it your wife exhausted me, my lord?" Garion said, laughing as he dodged another blow.

Mora's guilt-ridden sympathies dried up like a raisin.

"Argh!" Tetrik cried out, his sword arcing toward Garion's head.

Mora's breath caught, and she clasped her hand to her breast. Would her husband really take his captain's head off because of his taunt and her praise?

But Garion feinted to the side and regained his feet in time to charge at Tetrik.

Both men went down in a heap of flailing limbs as the men ringing them began to place bets on which warrior would rise first.

Mora had had enough of their squabbling and elbowed her way through the warriors to stand at the edge of the pit. "Good day to you, too, husband!" she shouted.

"Wha—"

Garion drove his empty fist into Tetrik's side, and then turned to smile at Mora. "Good morning to you, my lady. I'm sure your husband will greet you properly as soon as he regains his breath."

Mora frowned at Garion, whose smile widened at her show of pique.

"I haven't injured him much."

"Garion, shut your yap!" Tetrik said, sweeping his foot beneath both of Garion's to bring him face-first into the dirt. Her husband grunted and rose, stepping in the middle of Garion's back as he strode toward her.

Mora blinked and stared at her dirt-covered husband, whose face tautened as he drew near. Was he angry with her?

Tetrik stepped close and snagged an arm around her waist, raising her so that their faces were level. "Did you get enough rest?" he asked, staring at her mouth.

She couldn't help licking her lips, while below, her body melted like hot wax at being held so close to a steamy, sweaty man. "Slept like a babe."

"Take a nap today, too," he growled, nestling his thigh between her legs.

"Will I need my strength?" she asked, trying to remember how to breathe.

"And ask Serit for a salve—but don't you dare let him apply it."

"A salve?" she asked, her mind already fleeing as her nipples drew to aching points.

"I'll continue your breaching later." His kiss mashed her lips against her teeth and was over far too soon. He set her down but kept his arm around her as she swayed on her feet.

Recovering, Mora turned to leave, having accomplished her mission of breaking the ice between her and her husband. As she stepped away, a hard slap landed on her bottom, and she whirled, rubbing her bruised flesh to gape at her husband.

But his wide-legged stance, with his arms crossed over his chest, set her heart fluttering.

So rather than bellow at the man for the affront—she winked. As she walked away, she exaggerated the sway of her hips all the way until she reached the corner of the stone wall.

* * * * *

Dipping his hand into a crock of herb-scented soap, Tetrik rubbed the soap over his chest and beneath his arms as he showered with the men in the soldier's billets following their day's training. His glance swept over Garion's back with satisfaction at the number of bruises and welts he'd managed to leave on his hide.

"If you continue to look at my ass with that expression on your face, I'll begin to worry over my virginity," Garion said, looking over his shoulder.

"It's still intact?" Tetrik murmured softly so that the rest of the men showering adjacent to them did not overhear. "How disappointing for Serit."

A red flush stained Garion's cheeks. "Now *that* never happened," Garion hissed. "It was just part of the moment…" he spluttered, "…and all because your wife was so damned responsive."

"What you and Serit do is none of my affair," Tetrik couldn't help teasing his friend. "Although by the size of that erection you're carrying between your legs, I'd say *his* virginity might be short-lived."

Garion cursed and turned away to take himself in hand.

Tetrik continued scrubbing his flesh, chuckling at Garion's curse as he spewed cum into the swirling water at his feet. "As it is, I need your advice, Garion."

Garion shuddered and placed a hand against the stone wall as he dragged in deep breaths. "My advice?"

"Regarding my wife."

Garion shot him a puzzled look through glazed eyes.

Feeling foolish, Tetrik scowled as he searched for the words to express his need. "I fear Mora will not be satisfied without some show of deeper affection. I wish to find a way to demonstrate my devotion."

"Shagging her day and night won't prove your regard?"

Tetrik shook his head. "I think her smart enough to know a man can be aroused without feeling any affection. I need to make a gesture."

"Are you afraid she won't consider herself bound to you come spring if you do not prove your fondness?"

"She wants my love."

Garion nodded his understanding. "Then you'll need a very large gesture. Have you determined what she holds dear? Perhaps you can gift her with something precious."

Tetrik realized that other than her surprising passion, he didn't know what else pleased her. He knew nothing of her desires or preferences. "I will need spies to report to me should she mention something she wants. You will see to it."

"I'll engage the staff in this little subterfuge." Garion's gaze dipped and a wide grin stretched across his face. "You'll want to take a few minutes alone to compose yourself, or the men might get a little nervous."

* * * * *

Serit dropped the bundle he'd retrieved from Tetrik's quarters onto the table. "No one saw me take this."

Garion slipped through the door after a furtive glance over his shoulder. "She's at the stables now, and the stable master knows to keep her occupied for a while."

Tetrik untied the drawstring and dumped the contents of the sack—small boxes, a smaller sack tied with frilly pink ribbon and a paper-wrapped bundle of bare roots. "This must be the rose bush she told the gardener about."

"He's still scratching his head over what she's going to use the plant for," Garion said.

"She said she likes the smell," Serit said, his mouth curving.

The men shared smiles at this vagary of the opposite sex.

Tetrik shrugged. "It's a woman thing, I guess."

"What about the rest of this stuff?" Garion said. "We have to be quick about this or she'll find out we're spying on her."

Tetrik grimaced over the depths he was willing to descend to discover what pleased his woman. "Open them without disturbing the contents. We'll need to get everything back to the room without her noticing we've riffled her treasures."

"Treasures?" Garion asked, pulling a polished stone from one box. "It looks like the stones in our streams—not like those gemstones she wore at the wedding."

"Perhaps it has sentimental value," Serit murmured. At their puzzled glances, he shrugged. "Not that I'm any expert at knowing how a woman's mind works."

The rest of the boxes were opened and only added to Tetrik's confusion. No precious gems, no satiny ribbons to adorn her—books, a partially embroidered shift and a smelly bag of herbs. He'd hoped for some hint of what to gift her with.

Tetrik tossed the beribboned bag to Serit. "What do you make of this?"

Serit poured some of the dried leaves onto his palm and sniffed. Then his body grew still, and his eyes narrowed.

"What?" Tetrik asked, his body tightening at the dark shadow that crossed his mage's face.

"These herbs are contraceptive."

Chapter Eight

Mora found her bundle lying in the center of the bed when she returned to the bedchamber. Eager to plant her rose bush, she dumped the contents on the mattress.

Amidst the tumble of plain packages she'd wrapped herself, she discovered the rose bush missing, and a cloth bag with pretty ribbon ties that she didn't recognize. She opened it and peered inside.

Confused at finding dried herbs, she poured them into her palm and sniffed. Shock stiffened her. She recognized the scent immediately, having often helped Gwimmel mix the potion many of the ladies of the court used to prevent pregnancy.

But what was it doing among her things? Then she remembered her mother's odd behavior in Gwimmel's chamber just before she left Mellusia, and the words she'd spoken to Tetrik.

Her mother hadn't been reminding Tetrik of the terms of The Promise. She'd been sending a secret message to her daughter.

Mora's eyes grew moist. Her mother hadn't abandoned her, but had in fact offered her a way to return—if she so chose.

Mora sat on the side of the bed holding the bag, knowing she held her own future in her grasp. She could use the herbs and wait to see whether it was possible for Tetrik to open his heart to her. If she didn't have his love come spring, she could return to her home. Or she could put her trust in the Goddess and let the powers that be determine her fate.

If she took the risk and Tetrik never learned to love her, could she remain in a marriage that would be so one-sided? For she already knew she was falling in love with her warlord husband. Would it be enough to share his life and bear his children? Could she settle one more time for being second to his duty?

Mora poured the herbs back into the bag and retied it, then put it inside her bundle and stuffed it at the bottom of her wardrobe. She'd decide later what to do. For now, she had a bigger problem.

The rose bush was missing. Had someone found the herbs as well? Did they understand their use?

Worried, Mora hurried to the hall where everyone gathered for the evening meal. Taking her seat, she smiled her thanks as a goblet and plate were laid in front of her. She took a long sip of wine to steady her nerves.

No one knows what's in your bag. She took another sip and set down her cup, and then schooled her face into an impassive mask, fearing anyone looking at her now would read the guilt in her expression.

However well-intentioned her mother had been, the herbs spelled another betrayal of trust between her people and her husband's.

Mora fretted. She should just tell Tetrik. The thought of keeping a secret about something of this magnitude—and something that affected him directly—made her feel sick to her stomach.

As soon as he entered the hall through the double doors, she'd tell him. The decision made, she felt her tension ease.

The hall's doors flung open. Tetrik, along with Garion and Serit, entered the hallway. Her palms began to sweat. Their expressions were hard, shuttered. Whatever was on their minds looked more important than any paltry problem she could lay at their feet.

She'd wait until later, when she and Tetrik were alone. She would ply him with drink and seduce him into better humor. Then she'd tell him. Maybe he'd be so far gone with drink and pleasure, he'd not even remember her confession in the morning.

Feeling a little better, Mora summoned a smile as the men approached the dais. "Good evening, husband," she said, and nodded to his companions.

Strangely, Garion gave her a sharp nod, and then took his place behind the table without looking her way. Serit bowed before her, and then paused as he straightened to give her a searching glance.

Mora's smile grew feeble.

Her husband took his seat beside her but turned to Garion to resume a conversation, which presumably they had begun before their arrival, leaving Mora feeling disgruntled and more than a little unnerved at their dismissal.

Sighing, she picked up her fork and stabbed the slice of game on her plate, then pushed it around the gravy in endless circles. When the men halted their conversation, she looked up to find them staring.

"Are you going to eat it or swim with it?" Garion asked, one eyebrow lifting.

Mora put down her fork and pushed back her plate. "I guess I'm not very hungry." She lowered her gaze and played with the suede cuff of her gown. Keeping secrets was extremely nerve-racking.

Tetrik reached across her and gathered both her hands in one of his and placed them in her lap.

She jerked her gaze to his, but he was already engaged in conversation with Garion again.

But he continued to hold her hands.

Mora sighed again, all her anxiety bleeding from her body with just that simple touch. Whether he was annoyed with her fidgeting or trying to calm her, she didn't really care. For the moment, she felt connected — her hands inside his — their skin touching. It was enough for now.

As the meal progressed with Tetrik eating one-handed while she sat still beside him, she began to notice the other diners' curious stares and whispers. "Husband," she whispered.

He glanced over at her. "Yes, wife."

"I think you should let me go, now. People are beginning to stare."

"And you care about what they think?"

"Of course I do. I wouldn't want them to think less of you for my poor behavior."

"You think they stare because of you?" Garion asked.

"Well, because Tetrik saw fit to restrain me when I annoyed him."

"You think I'm restraining you?" Tetrik asked, his brows rising. "You looked nervous, I was reassuring you, wife."

"Oh," she said, heat blooming on her cheeks—this time from pleasure. He'd been aware of her feelings—that was true progress.

"They stare because they're just hearing about your husband's latest project," Garion said with a glib smile.

Mora noted a dark flush staining Tetrik's cheeks.

He aimed a deadly glare at Garion. "I think my appetite's left as well." To Mora, he said, "Would you care to join me for a walk in the fresh air, wife?"

It didn't matter that it was almost freezing outside, Mora nodded, eager to be alone at last with her husband. She let him help her from her chair and lead her through the kitchen and into the garden beyond.

The nearest sun dipped behind the mountain, and light was fading quickly into night, but Mora didn't care as she clutched his arm. The sight of the snowy peaks piercing gray clouds and turning mauve with the encroaching shadows filled her with awe for their majesty.

"Wait, I never think," he said, dropping his arm and shrugging out of his fur vest. "Put this on. I'll not have you sicken."

"But you'll freeze," she protested, pushing the fur back into his hands.

"You will obey me. I've lived all my life in these mountains. This winter is mild. Put it on."

Grateful for the added protection against the wind whipping through the valley, she slipped it over her arms and followed Tetrik as he walked down the row of raised beds.

She noticed right away that something had changed since her visit that morning. A new raised bed, albeit smaller than the others, sat in the middle of the center path. It was octagonal in shape, and one solitary, burlap-wrapped plant sat at its center.

Mora didn't need to peel away the wrapping to know it was her rose bush. "Your new project?" she asked, hating the quiver of emotion in her voice. She'd promised no more outbursts and here she was getting weepy over a flowerbed.

"The gardener provided me guidance, although he's wondering if perhaps you intend to brew the leaves for a healing tea." He tipped her chin up with his fingers. "I know you only wanted it for the pretty smelling blooms."

Mora melted. He might not understand her need for something soft and beautiful in her life, but he'd given it to her anyway. "I plan no use for my rose bush. I suppose it was a foolish thing to bring with me. But I thank you for the planting bed."

Tetrik clasped her hand and stroked her palm with his thumb. "There are flowers that grow wild along the mountainside in the spring. Perhaps you can transplant more blooms to fill your bed. I'll show you where to find them."

Overcome by his offer, Mora stepped close to him and wrapped her arms around his back. "Thank you. It was a very nice gesture." She'd wanted to say "sweet" but knew he'd grimace at such a soft word.

"You are pleased? You are not disappointed that I took the task of building your flowerbed for my own?"

"I'm very happy. Although, now I understand the whispers in the hall," she said in a teasing tone.

Tetrik grunted. "Are you tired yet?"

Mora grinned against his chest. He expected a reward for his consideration. "Are you?"

"I had very little sleep last night," he said, with that growling tone that never failed to make her body weep.

"We can't have Garion rubbing your face in the dirt tomorrow." Mora clasped his hand and tugged him behind her.

Back inside the hall, they were met with broad smiles.

Mora ducked her head to hide her blushes at their teasing glances.

Tetrik paused only to snag a goblet of wine from their table, and after a nod toward Garion and Serit, accompanied Mora above stairs.

Once the heavy wooden door was latched behind them, Mora set about stripping her husband of his clothing, and then struggled with the buckles on her own until he pushed away her hands and completed the chore himself.

Naked, they faced each other with only the light from the brazier to illuminate their bodies.

Mora's gaze swept over him, still in awe of his broad planes and bulging strength. All that masculine beauty was hers to touch and hold.

Her body ripened with desire, her nipples drawing into aching peaks.

Between his legs rose the evidence that he was just as inspired by her generous form. Thick and ruddy as it swelled, blue veins trailed along his length, like the veins that popped up on his arms when his muscles flexed. This particular muscle was the most beautiful and powerful to her mind—the part of him that defined him clearly as a man.

Before he could set the course of their joining, she knelt in front of him on the cold stone floor and grasped his lengthening shaft, stroking his length with her palm, pleased by the satiny texture of the skin that stretched tight around the steel of his erection.

Remembering the way the women had caressed him the previous evening, she encircled him with her hands and licked the soft, bulbous head of his cock, lapping around and around the tip until a small, pearlescent drop of ejaculate beaded from the eye.

Holding his gaze, she stuck out her tongue and took the bead into her mouth, learning the flavor of his pleasure. She inhaled and drew in the scent of his musky skin.

At the heat burning his cheeks and tautening his jaw, she opened wide her mouth and sank on his cock, taking him into the cavern of her mouth, rolling her tongue around his shaft, suctioning softly until she felt the shallow pulse of his hips.

She took him deeper, letting him slide along her tongue until his cock touched the back of her throat. So thick was his sex, her jaws soon ached from the effort of holding them wide to encompass him, but still she suckled him, until the scent of steamy, aroused man filled their bedchamber.

Mora bobbed her head in and out, stroking him with her mouth. Then she remembered the other ways the women had worked his flesh to bring him to completion. She smoothed one hand beneath his cock and grasped his scrotum, rolling the hard stones inside their fleshy sac in her palms until he moaned and his hips pulsed harder into her mouth.

Her other hand gripped the base of his cock and squeezed and twisted, sliding in the moisture from her mouth. By the quickening of his thrusts, she learned how to touch him to increase his pleasure, and soon both hands grasped his cock as her head bobbed faster, her mouth suctioning hard now.

Tetrik's fingers combed through her hair and gripped her hard, holding her still as he pumped faster against the back of her throat. His thighs clenched, his cock hammered, gagging her until she relaxed her throat, humming, and let him gain his pleasure.

Then he groaned, his hips jerking uncontrolled, and a stream of hot liquid shot into her mouth. Mora continued to mouth and fondle him while the storm broke over him, and passed him, her caresses soothing him at the end.

When finally she drew away, she gasped at the stark, naked need she read in his eyes. Mora reached for him again, but Tetrik clasped her wrist, holding her away.

"I'll fuck your body next. Do you need to drink your potion before or after we share sex?" he asked, his words soft and carefully enunciated.

Mora's heart plummeted, and her mouth dropped open in horror. She shook her head to deny the herbs were hers, but the words stuck in her throat.

His face was so taut a muscle jerked at the side of his jaw. His dark, hooded gaze gave away nothing of his inner thoughts.

Fearing his anger, or worse, his disappointment, tears filled her eyes. If she told him her mother slipped the bag into her things, her parents would be damned again in his eyes. He'd wonder, too, why she hadn't disposed of the herbs as soon as she discovered them. She'd be damned, as she should be, because she'd considered using them to prevent the conception of any child of his.

She'd considered her own pride and well-being above the welfare of his people and the alliance. She'd also disregarded him entirely in her decision to keep the contraceptive.

She remained silent and tugged her hand from his grip. Then she rose and went to the cupboard. She withdrew her bundle and upended the contents on the floor, plucking the beribboned bag from the jumble of her treasures.

When she turned back, Tetrik reached for the wine he'd set aside upon entering the room and held it out.

She searched his face for some hint of his emotions, but his expression remained closed and distant. In that moment, she understood her husband was offering her another, more precious gift. The gift of choice.

Mora's eyes filled with tears and she shook her head—he'd put her first, above his duty to his people. She walked to the brazier and tossed the herbs, bag and all, into the fire. With her back to him, she gasped on a sob that set her shoulders shaking.

His arms closed around her waist and pulled her back flush against his body. "I told Serit the bag wasn't yours. You've no use for ribbons and pretty fabric."

Tears spilled down her face. Despite evidence to the contrary, he'd believed in her. She also knew his last comment was not meant to demean—she didn't need adornment to be attractive for him.

Tetrik didn't love her—yet. And he might never acknowledge his love for her in words, but she'd rather have his strength and passion to hold her tight for the rest of her days than sleep with pride for a lack of words.

She caught their reflection in the mirror from the corner of her eye and turned to gaze at their entwined bodies. Her hands slid over his, and she pushed them upward to cup her breasts.

His gaze met hers in the mirror as he pressed a kiss to the side of her neck and aligned his body behind hers to press his erection against her bottom. Already he hardened, inspired by the sight of her body ripening beneath his touch.

How beautiful and perfectly they matched. Her softness to his lean strength. Her softness would be her gift to him, along with the love she'd shower upon him and their children.

Come spring, when her rose bush stretched new branches to the sunlight, and pink buds began to appear, she'd be there to tend her garden.

About the Author

Delilah Devlin dated a Samoan, a Venezuelan, a Turk, a Cuban, and was engaged to a Greek before marrying her Irishman. She's lived in Saudi Arabia, Germany, and Ireland, but calls Texas home for now. Ever a risk taker, she lived in the Saudi Peninsula during the Gulf War, thwarted an attempted abduction by white slave traders, and survived her children's juvenile delinquency.

Creating alter egos for herself in the pages of her books enables her to live new adventures. Since discovering the sinful pleasure of erotica, she writes to satisfy her need for variety--it keeps her from running away with the Indian working in the cubicle beside her!

In addition to writing erotica, she enjoys creating romantic comedies and suspense novels.

Delilah welcomes mail from readers. You can write to her c/o Ellora's Cave Publishing at 1056 Home Ave. Akron, Oh. 44310-3502.

Also by Delilah Devlin

Love Me Tomorrow

Chapter One

"On my mark, wait...steady," Shalene Courers spoke into the mic and flipped the safety switch on her laser pistol from stun to kill. Her heart slammed against her chest, a surge of energy pumping to her head. She took short and fast gulps of air, trying to still the anxiety. Casting a quick glance back at her troops, she gave them a brief nod. They were few, but they were strong. They could do this. She felt their exhaustion, the same weariness settling in her arms and legs.

They'd been out on recon for three days with little sleep and too damn little food. The moon disappeared behind a bank of clouds. Now was the time to move. Confidence in her soldiers coursed through her, steeling her for the confrontation they faced with the enemy. Not just any enemy, but the evil ones that had invaded Earth and taken possession of all she had known.

Anger entwined with hatred and welded into a resolve so deep that sacrificing her own life was no longer a question. It was a given they would all die. It was simply a matter of choosing when and how. And they had made that choice three days ago when they'd decided ambush was their best tactic. Their ultimate final strike.

"Commander?" Abber, the scrappy teenager, spoke behind her. She trained her stare on him, noting the way his six-foot-five frame was hunched over, giving him the appearance of a man half his height. His eyes were hard and cold, like the rest of them.

They had all suffered the loss of their homes and loved ones. Tonight was more than just fighting an enemy, it was revenge in its most base form. Humankind had been reduced to little more than animals struggling to survive a hostile world with renegade bands like hers. They'd hidden in the tunnels carved out all over their planet. It was in the protective secret catacombs that they'd trained and waited for the right moment to extract a little payback.

Defeat of their enemy was a lost dream. The early conviction had been lost when they'd realized so few humans had survived the Rep War. It had been a long and horrendous battle encompassing nearly five years of struggling to defeat the enemy. Her troops had moved underground into ancient secret tunnels and after the last ten years of desperation to survive, had finally resurfaced a year ago to begin the battle anew. Fifteen years of war had changed them all forever. She'd only been twenty when the Demrons attacked Earth. It felt like a hundred years ago.

"Are you all right, Commander?" he asked.

She looked at him. They had survived! Babies had matured and become soldiers. She nodded at the youth. They had grown strong, training in every known artform of physical prowess and mental development. Latent powers had begun to emerge within the underground cities, powers that could very well defeat the enemy, if only the humans were greater in numbers.

She dropped her stare. But they weren't. There were no more than an estimated million people who had survived the Final Coup. Communications were broken. The series of underground tunnels that ran across the planet interconnected in places and in others, nature had sealed them off with earthquakes or floods. The original builders of the underground network were unknown, but it was clear to Shalene that their existence only proved this invasion was not the first time Earth had been ravaged by these putrid vile abominations. The human race had survived then and she was determined to do whatever she could to see it had a fighting chance to survive the current harvesting.

"The moon's behind the clouds, Commander," Abber whispered. "We need to move—now!"

His harsh rasp drew her from the reverie.

"Remember what we've learned these past years. Don't lose focus. Don't let their appearance or size distract you. They're nothing more than overgrown lizards. Don't forget that. They've stolen our world! They have robbed us of *everything*!"

The men and women who were hunched down in the storm drain all mumbled their convictions.

"We've never forgotten and tonight we're going to do something about it!" Shalene nodded.

"Yea!" echoed the restrained chorus.

"We're going to get even! And kick some lizard ass!"

With that she nodded to her team.

"One!" her voice rasped into the head mic she wore beneath her helmet. "Two!" With laser pistol aimed in front of her, both hands supporting the powerful weapon, she stretched it in front of her. "Three!" She stepped from the protection of the large drain and around the boulders, jutting out of the mountainside.

Braced and ready to blast the evil enemy off her planet, her troops rushed into the clearing behind her and quickly hunkered down, waiting and listening. The enemy was cunning and could camouflage itself to resemble anything—a tree, a boulder, even the very sand beneath their feet—but they had trained for this moment. They had honed their ESP and no longer required technological devices for heat sensory detection or, as in the case of their enemies, cold sensory. Their sense of smell had grown with these new powers and surprisingly the reptiles had a distinct scent that overpowered all others. Perhaps it was nature's way of balancing powers.

She squinted and powered up the energy inside herself as she reined it and channeled the electric pulses coursing through her into a clear focus. The brilliant pinpoint of light widened, momentarily blinding her, then popped free, leaving her with night vision. There, that was better.

The terrain was typical earth these days. Dusty and dry with charred stalks of what used to be leafy vibrant trees.

Searing fury threatened to collapse her focus, but she pushed it back. Not now. Now was the time for seeing.

She scoped the hillside, quickly dropping her gaze to the valley below. There! A bright orange, almost red silhouette undulated.

"Human," she whispered.

"How?" Abber asked and squatted beside her.

"Wait," she said, noting the sudden emergence behind the figure. "Lizards. He must be a prisoner."

"I dunno, Commander, look closer," Abber whispered.

She did and quickly saw the laser jet slung over his shoulder.

"A damn traitor!" she spat the bitter word from her mouth. "Okay," she turned to her troops. "Listen up. There's a human traitor among them. I want him captured. Unharmed. Understand?"

"Aye, Commander," the troops mumbled.

"What you going to do with him?" came a low whisper.

"I have a few questions to ask him," she said, pushing a stray dark curl from her face.

"You shouldn't enjoy your job so much," Abber teased in a rasping voice.

"It's our lives, not just a job, Abber boy. We're fighting for our very existence and that bastard is doing everything he can to see we don't have a future."

"Aye, Commander, so let's go kill some reptiles, 'cause suddenly I feel like a real caveman."

* * * * *

"They've moved." Captain Mecah glared over his shoulder at the tall reptilian hunter called Bog.

The scaly creature narrowed its gaze on the boot print just a couple of inches from where Mecah had paused. His dark green face, long and massive, wrinkled in a perplexed frown. Mecah gritted his teeth, fighting the urge to strike the creature and turn on the other reptiles. Were it not that his men would be executed if he seized such an opportunity for freedom, these green lizards would now be dead.

"How can you tell they moved by a mere boot print, Kyronian?"

"Not the boot print, lizard breath, the fire." He gestured to the cold campsite.

The Demron creature lifted his red eyes, settling a piercing glare on Mecah.

He couldn't stop the sneer curling his upper lip as he met the beast's look.

"Hump!" Bog peered past him, lifting the thick greenish scales comprising his facial muscles in what seemed to be a quizzical look.

Who could tell with these toads? Mecah looked away. Bile churned in his stomach as he recalled how he, along with his fleet, had become prisoners of the Demrons. Okay, the lizards didn't call them prisoners, but they were. Mecah and his entire space fleet were caught up in a war they hadn't started and didn't want any part of. They just wanted to go home, but were trapped.

So what if these humans had overrun the Demrons' planet. He glanced around the nightscape. From what he'd seen in the past ten months, the Demrons weren't exactly fighting over paradise. Everything was scorched and seared to the roots or stood as charred reminders of former glory. He didn't give a damn if the humans had destroyed the planet. His Kyronian fleet was trapped into servitude at least until this wretched war was over.

The tall reptilian walked past him with his tongue streaking out of his mouth, tasting the air for smoke residue, no doubt.

"Hmm. Seems the Kyronian is right—again." He turned on thick legs to grunt at Mecah.

"Yeah, imagine that!" His words dripped with sarcasm. Just because he was forced to be this ugly lizard's ally didn't mean he had to pretend to like it.

"So where did they go?" Bog straightened his vest armor and moved his stiff neck to look about them, turning his body to accommodate the movement.

"They went east." Mecah nodded.

"You are certain?"

"Yeah, desert-bait, I am. I can see their vapor trail, remember? Now do you want to keep questioning every damn thing I say, or do you want to just get this over with?"

"I rather enjoy torturing you, Mecah." Bog chuckled and walked past him to look out over the wasteland.

"Captain Mecah to you, Private."

"Oh, do we have to debate this issue again? I'm well aware of your fleet's ranking system, *Captain*. In case you forgot, I'm the equivalent of your Major as it were."

"You're the equivalent of a fucking grasshopper," Mecah spat and gripped his laser rifle, tempted to point it at the lizard that would no doubt be incited to attack him for that last comment. It would be so easy to squeeze off a blast.

Instead of anger, Mecah was greeted with deep-chested laughter.

"You are so amusing to us, alien," Bog spoke between laughs.

Mecah ignored him and headed east, even though the actual trail went north. Stupid lizard would never know the difference. Had Bog been just a tad nicer, he would have directed their party to the underground bunker only ten feet from where they stood and delivered the six humans huddled together in the shallow trench. Lizards couldn't see through the layers of dirt like the Kyronians could. It was the main reason the Demron military had inducted the Kyronians into service. But Bog's arrogance enraged Mecah beyond any level of cooperative assistance. And as a direct result, those six human lives would now be spared.

It was a relief for Mecah to avoid his enforced duty. It was difficult to perform the daily hunts when the Demrons' enemy appeared to be a distant cousin to Mecah's own species. Those damn cold-blooded lizards had to be a cosmic genetic mistake. They should have been cousins to the lizards roaming his home world or even this one.

Mecah tried to give the humans every break reasonably possible now that he realized he'd been wrong about the Demrons. At first, he'd thought an end to their war would mean freedom for his fleet, but recently he'd realized the only freedom they'd ever taste would be the kind death granted.

The one thing he couldn't figure out was why the humans had tried to overthrow the Demrons' planet. And it was one question no Demron would answer. It just didn't make any sense to him. The humans were obviously the weaker race. Somewhere in the back of his mind the question haunted him like a dark shadow lurking in the night. Had the humans' attack on the Demrons been a mistake? Had they underestimated their target?

"Let's go," Bog spoke behind him.

Mecah glanced at him. What would Bog think if he told the green creep what the name Bog meant on Kyro? He chuckled and paused by the burned tree to light a short cigar. Puffing, he drew the smoke into his lungs and expelled it into the night air.

"Put that out!" Bog's voice boomed across the valley floor.

"Keep your scales on." He drew on the cigar once more and blew the smoke in Bog's direction.

Bog sneezed, then began coughing. The three reptiles behind him paused, waiting for the seizure to subside. Satisfied he'd aggravated the lizard just enough, Mecah extinguished the cherished smoke, field-stripping the fire from the remaining tobacco, and returned it to his pocket.

"Do that again," Bog gasped for air, "and I'll kill you with one hand."

"Try it and see if you still have that hand." Mecah started for the tall range of mountains that rose from the valley floor.

The sound of rushing water greeted them just as they entered the clearing. It was rare to find water on this planet. He'd been told there'd been lots of cool clear water before the war. So where had it disappeared to? How could a war stop the flow of water? It seemed odd to him, but then all things about the Demrons were odd, so why should their planet be any different. He bent down to cup his hands into the tumbling stream and drank. The cold water slaked his parched throat, reminding him of the paradise he had left on Kyro. Would he ever see a golden sunrise again? Would he ever ride his horse across the woodlands and into the blue flower meadows of Mangress?

"Your species requires a lot of water. Just like the humans," Bog complained.

"Best damn water I ever tasted." He wiped his mouth with the back of his hand and glanced up at Bog.

"Get up," the lizard ordered.

"Not until I refill." Mecah reached for the cloth flask and submerged it beneath the cold stream.

"Hump," Bog turned to his men.

Their lack of need for water just gave Mecah one more reason to hate them. They didn't perspire and ate only thorny plants. No wonder they could crush an enemy that required frequent water and food.

The night air stirred cooler as the winds swept down the mountain peak into the valley. He shook off the chills and retrieved the flask now swollen with water.

"Turn on your heaters," Bog ordered his men and lifted his wrist, setting his own heater which radiated from the thick armor vest.

Yeah, they appeared undefeatable, but they had that one major weakness. Demrons had no way of self-regulating body temperatures, and relied on their environments during the day and their heaters at night. One day that just might prove to be his best weapon against them.

"They couldn't have gone this far," Bog spoke.

"Well, mega-brain, that's true, they've gone farther." He straightened from the stream and hung the flask onto his belt, but his attention quickly riveted to the glowing red shapes along the valley at the mountain base. Raiders, no doubt. Ten, no, fifteen. The Demrons would be outnumbered. He glared at Bog. And that was a bad thing?

A slow smile spread over his lips. Maybe it *was* time to free himself of these slimy green things. A real ambush, not one staged by him, would be authentic. Perhaps he could do more good for his troops if he were free. If the Demrons believed he'd been taken captive, it just might work.

"What do you see?" Bog stopped beside him.

"A damn big mountain range. Do you think your lizards can stand climbing cold boulders all night?"

Bog released a growl and turned to his men.

"Set up camp. Start a fire before we all die from exposure."

Mecah grinned and retrieved his cigar. Clamping the unlit stub between his teeth, he surveyed the raiding party. Yep, it was going to be an interesting night.

Chapter Two

"Commander, do you see—"

"Down!" Shalene ordered her troops.

They all lowered to the ground, hiding behind boulders.

"We outnumber them."

"That's a human," came the soft female voice. "But why would a human betray—"

"Shut up!" Shalene whispered to the petite brunette who always had more to say than she ever wanted to hear.

"Listen up." Shalene squatted down in front of them. "We're going to be patient. Understand? We wait for them to settle down and fall asleep, then we sneak in and kill us some reps. But don't harm that traitor, he's going to return to base with us and answer some very difficult questions."

"He might be able to tell us where they're keeping the Blue Crystal," the female piped in.

"We *know* where it's being kept, on the mother ship," Abber jeered.

"Oh, yeah, well, maybe he can help us get it back," she sighed.

Shalene considered her for a moment with newfound respect. That might not be such a bad idea. If they could reclaim the powerful crystal, they could finally defeat their enemy! Hope, a faint glimmer against the darkness of years spent in despair, flickered briefly and took hold. It pierced through the depths of reluctant resignation that the fate of humankind was already determined. What if they could retrieve the Blue Crystal? She closed her eyes. It had been a cruel temptation abandoned long ago. Dare she trust the future again? Her troop's muffled whispers fell to her ears.

"Defeat those bastards...win back our home...freedom at last...finally go back home... war over...we could win!"

"Settle down, now," she interrupted. "Abber, come with me. The rest of you stay here. Be ready to move out."

Crawling on their bellies, Shalene and Abber moved closer to the enemy, stopping a few hundred yards along the perimeter of the makeshift camp.

"Do you think we could do that, Commander?"

"Steal the Blue Crystal?"

He nodded.

"It's a big order, Abber." She glanced at him. "How's your mom doing these days?"

"She's busy on a new project. They're trying to develop another virus."

"Well, at least they keep trying," she said, remembering when she'd first met Abber and his mother. Refugees, like the rest of them. Scared, hungry, fleeing the first wave. Shalene had an instant bond with the boy and he to her. As he grew, she had taken him under her military wing and trained him, attempting to pass on all her abilities to him. In many ways, she felt he was like the son she would never have.

"She asks about you every time I communicate with her," he whispered.

"It's been a long time since I was in the catacombs," she sighed. "Someday we'll both pay her a visit." She winked at him.

"Yes, ma'am," he grinned.

The enemy began to settle down for the night. She lay on the desert floor seeking the traitor's heat signature and found him curled up against a large boulder a few feet from the reps, who slept close to the roaring fire. She trained all her power onto the human and searched his mind but was met by a barrier. She frowned.

Had he been schooled in the catacombs of Scotland, too? Only an intimate could block such a screening. She didn't recall him. She probed deeper. He must be an intimate. There were only a dozen of them, she being one, yet how had he come to be a traitor? She pushed the thoughts from her mind and focused harder, probing deeper. Not an intimate. She sensed a different energy. Something new to her. So what was he? A rogue? A lone practitioner? She closed her eyes and concentrated on manifesting a visual of him.

Blond hair, tall, muscular, a handsome face with a lopsided devilish grin, a typical trooper. What else was there? Lilac eyes! She gasped and opened her eyes.

"What is it?" Abber whispered.

"He's not *human*."

"What?" Concern tightened Abber's voice.

"He's not human, Abber. I don't know what he is. But he's not human."

"Are you saying we have a new alien enemy, besides the Demrons?" Panic edged his voice, matching the nervous pitch in her stomach.

"So it appears."

"Oh shit. Excuse me, Commander, what I meant, was, well, damn, this is just great. We'll be going in at a greater disadvantage. We know nothing about this new enemy," he whispered, straining to contain his fear.

"We're going through with this, Abber. We can do it. They appear to be asleep. Signal for the troops to move up," she ordered, steadying her laser on the sleeping reptiles. "And remember, the non-reptile is to be captured."

"Aye, Commander." Abber turned and signaled the troops with a laser flash. "I hope he's not more formidable than the reps."

"He won't be," she assured the youth as they waited for the troops to join them. She lay on the ground, watching the fire flicker shadows over the blond man. It had been a long time since she'd enjoyed summer nights like this one sprawled out on a lounge chair in front of her outside living room. She'd always brought leftovers from her restaurant for late evening meals with her husband. He'd light the outside fireplace and they'd spend a romantic night underneath the stars, eating, sipping wine and planning their future.

After the leisurely meal, they'd lie in the bed swing, make love then hold each other, sharing the day's events, staring up at the stars, talking about the family they would have one day. Shalene swallowed the burning in her throat and pushed back the tears. It had been just such a night when the first strike had hit. She closed her eyes against the bitter memory. Fifteen years and it still felt like yesterday — sometimes.

"All troops in place, Commander. We're good to go."

She dragged herself from the vivid memories and stared into the bleak present. It had been a different life and she'd been a different person.

"Guns set to kill," she spoke into the mic with her voice tightening around the memory's residue. "Remember, the non-rep is to be captured," she reminded and gave each trooper a glance. She was bestowed a nod of understanding. With her hand, she motioned for the troops to spread out and encircle the campsite. Once assured everyone was in position, she signaled the attack.

The sleeping reptiles were slow to react to the laser blasts, but Mecah was on his feet and firing at the attackers, deliberately missing his marks. He watched Bog take a blast in the chest and fall hard on his back. His long scaly tail writhed in the sand then was still.

"Hands up! Drop your weapon. Down on your knees." The woman, dressed in tight leather pants and short bustier covered with a desert-camouflaged military vest, aimed a laser pistol at him.

His gaze traveled from the bluish beam back to the woman. She unstrapped the helmet and jerked it off. Long silky hair tumbled down her back in a long wavy flow, reminding him of a rush of dark water freed from a damn. Tossing the scarred, dull helmet to the soldier standing behind her, she took determined strides across the camp toward him, all the while keeping the laser aimed on his chest.

The moon emerged from the clouds and bathed her in silvery streams of light, highlighting her curly dark hair in shimmering flickers. Her oval face was smudged with camouflage grease and her knee-length boots were scuffed and dusty. Her upper arms, exposed by the vest, flexed as she steadied the weapon on him. Sculpted, feminine muscled arms indicated a trained and disciplined body, and beneath, governed by an equally trained mind.

Overall, she gave the appearance of a capable soldier, yet one thing contradicted the illusion and intrigued him—her aura. Unlike other human soldiers whose auras were usually a mixture of reds and oranges and in some cases blacks and grays, hers was a myriad of colors without the typical dominating hue, giving a rainbow effect of colorful shards that emanated from her.

Her oval face was set in a stern, almost angry expression, with large brown eyes reflecting a coldness that again contradicted her aura of a spiritually evolved being who knew the secrets of the universe.

"What are you grinning at?" she sneered, stopping in front of him. "What's your name?" She lowered the weapon so it was at her hip level and pointed at him. Still kneeling, Mecah looked up into her dark eyes. The air stirred electric and when she moved closer, her aura merged with his.

Encased in her essence, his probing was immediately shoved aside as her barrier walls rose to block him. He pressed harder and his appreciation quickened when he crashed through her shield and found the truth he saw reflecting deep in her soul. Desire surged through his body, responding to her on the basest level while simultaneously connecting on the deepest of all spiritual levels that only Kismet mates could attain. How could it be? How could this alien be his Kismet? His breathing quickened. Dare he believe? It was against all Kyronian laws, but the sensation was undeniable. He'd waited for it his entire life and there she stood in front of him—his Kismet mate.

He slipped past her hatred and found recognition. The same recognition now reflecting in her liquid chocolate eyes. His heart was a staccato beat. She knew they were kindred spirits, too. What would she do now that she, too, knew? In spite of his attempt to control his thoughts, Mecah couldn't help wondering about her. How could it be that he had to travel millions of light-years from his home to find his Kismet mate? The irony was too much and he released the welling emotions in a laugh.

"You find this humorous?" she asked, reinforcing her persona, bolstering her energy against his probing. At that very moment she knew, just as he did—they were made for each other. Designed by a greater purpose to come together at this fated moment.

His thoughts unleashed to explore deeper, needing to know everything about her. Intuitive females who evolved to her level not only knew the secrets of the universe but had a greater appreciation of the art of lovemaking. Orgasms were achieved using their minds as well as their bodies. He'd heard all the legends of such highly evolved women and their abilities to reduce a man to little more than a sex slave. He watched the emotions struggling to escape her rigid control. Oh yeah, he'd gladly be her sex slave. The response to his musings tightened in his crotch.

"Get up," she barked.

Embarrassed by the telltale sign of his arousal, he stood from the blanket. Immediately, her attention was drawn to his erection bulging beneath his tan pants. A slight smile lifted one corner of her mouth.

"You have a strange reaction to being captured, ah…"

"Name's Mecah, Captain Mecah. And what can I say? I appreciate a beautiful woman," he grinned.

Her angry glare hardened under his compliment and radiated from her as a living thing. It sliced through his barriers and plunged deep into his soul, transforming into its true emotion—passion. Deep, wild, unbridled fire excited him beyond any desire he'd ever known. He shook.

"Captain, is it?" she asked, walking around him, as though taking inventory. "And you have no qualms speaking your mind."

"What can I say? I rarely see a woman, at least one that's not a lizard, much less one as gorgeous as you." He shrugged.

The young, heavily muscled teenager standing behind her laughed, and she turned to flash a disapproving look. His amusement choked off and he jerked to attention.

"Abber, make sure the lizards are dead. Stack and burn."

"I'd advise against that, Miss…"

"Commander. Commander Courers." She looked up at him, frowning as though trying to decide something. "Did I ask your advice?"

"You don't want to attract their comrades, do you? We're part of a much larger unit and they'll be looking for us when we don't report in for pickup."

"You don't have a float?"

"Float?"

"Where'd you leave it?" She looked about the nightscape.

"I don't know what a float is."

"It's what the Demrons call their mini cruise ships. The ones used for recon missions."

"Oh those. I understand the Demrons ran out of power crystals for those a few years ago."

She glanced back at her troops, who had the same puzzled look on their smudged faces.

"You didn't know?"

Shalene considered the possibility that he spoke the truth. If the reps had the Blue Crystal in their possession, all they had to do was connect it to their main power source and they'd have enough crystal power for all eternity. Of course, it would also disintegrate them. She smiled slightly. They knew the crystal's power when they had captured the sacred stone. Without the stone, Earth had been vulnerable to the attack. It had always been assumed a human traitor had aided the reps, but now that she was standing face to face with this new alien, perhaps that foregone conclusion had been wrong. In fifteen years, she'd never heard of humanoids with lilac eyes.

"Are you telling the truth?" she asked.

"About the floaters?"

She nodded.

"Just where the hell have you been?"

"I'll ask the questions," she said, leaning forward, slightly tilting her head as she studied his eyes. "What did they do to you?"

"Huh?"

"Your eye color. It's not Demron. Are you a genetic experiment? A mutant human crossbred with a reptilian?"

"Lord of the Wicked, no! I'm no lizard."

"How far back are the rest of your troops?" she pressed.

"A few clicks. But I'm no—"

"Let's get the hell out of here," she ordered. "Abber, take him down."

His pulse spiked in response to her order to execute him.

"Whoa! Whoa! Don't get hasty. There's no need to kill me." Mecah held his palms up in front of him, looking for a way to escape. There were only scrubby plants and rocks too small to offer any protection.

"What?" She turned back to him with understanding glistening in her eyes.

"I said there's no need to take me down. Don't you have something in between the two extremes of life and death? Unconsciousness? Torture?"

She released a deep infectious laugh and turned to the young man she'd called Abber.

"Don't just stand there," she barked at the youth, "take him down."

Chapter Three

To his relief, Mecah learned that "take him down" didn't mean execution. Instead, he was led to a chute that dropped into a large tunnel some ten feet below. The soldiers threw a couple of glow tubes into the hole, then one by one climbed down the rusted metal grips. Once everyone was below, the commander pressed a pad of lights and the opening sealed closed.

He glanced up the chute, wondering how the humans could have created all this in such a short span of time. Perhaps the Demrons had been the creators and the invading humans merely occupied the deserted underground bunkers. He walked behind Commander Courers with the other troops following in tight formation. Light torches illuminated the rock tunnel that appeared to have been carved out of the mountain. That would take some powerful equipment, and certainly the Demrons would have detected the energy signature.

The tunnels had to be old. But who had built them? It just didn't make sense, unless the Demrons had lived underground, yet no Demron had ever mentioned subterranean cities.

His wrists were now tied behind his back with a strip of gagla, a lightweight material as strong as any metal chain he'd ever seen. The Demrons used the material to bind their prisoners. The humans must have found a stash somewhere, he mused as he walked a few feet behind the commander as she led the ragtag band deeper into the earth.

The soldier beside him carried a laser torch. It swayed under his strides, illuminating with every other step the commander's rounded buttocks. He watched the small rounded curves glisten in the light's brilliance and need surged to his cock. Her tight leather pants molded each fetching curve as they descended through the winding tunnel.

He marveled over her long hair swaying under her feminine gait. Her posture was military in execution, but it was definitely female in movement. He sighed heavily, relieved to be out from under the smelly reptilian guard, only he wasn't sure if allowing himself to fall into the hands of the enemy would prove a better fate.

Certainly, watching Commander Courers' ass was far better than ugly reptilians. Male or female, it didn't matter, Demrons were hideous creatures. The sexy human commander, on the other hand, was proving to be more than he'd ever imagined. What were the odds of finding one's fated mate in such a series of random events? It was a strong argument against the theory of randomness. Even if she ended up torturing him, he would prefer to be here than with the Demron Guard. His heart pounded out his desire. On the other hand, a little pain under her hand might be quite pleasurable.

"What are you grinning at?" Abber shoved him forward.

Mecah caught himself and fell back into the brisk pace as the regiment wound its way through the dank tunnels.

Commander Courers swung around, bringing him up short so her face was only inches from his. The torch lights the guards carried flashed around bringing her into full illumination.

"Blindfold," she ordered with her warm soft breath fanning over him. A rough cloth dragged over his eyes and was cinched tightly behind his head.

"Now we're getting into the fun stuff," he chuckled and was rewarded with a sharp painful jab to his stomach.

The wind wheezed from him as searing pain seized his gut. He slumped forward with a nauseating pitch churning in his belly. Painful spasms pierced his insides. He braced himself with both feet spread apart and struggled to suck air into his lungs. The stuffy tunnel closed in on him.

"No more talk." Her voice sliced the darkness, but there was something in her tone that made him mentally probe.

"Stop that!" Her words were followed by another punch, this time centering his solar plexus. The hot streak cut through him, weakening his knees until he crumpled to the dirt floor, with jagged throbs squeezing his insides. The cramping moved down the calves of his legs. He groaned under the unrelenting pain.

"Stay out of my mind." Her hot breath puffed against his ear. "I know how to block and I also know how to do kareé."

"W-What the hell is kareé?" he breathed, drawing his knees to his chest. The pain eased and he relaxed.

"If you know how to mind probe, then you know about kareé," came Abber's voice.

"He's not human, Abber, remember?" she asked. "Kareé's a defense. I'm sure you have it in your culture, just a different name. Our culture calls it 'exploding mind'."

"Oh yeah, like my exploding stomach right now," he said and struggled to his feet with the help of two soldiers who lifted him underneath his arms. They righted him but he swayed slightly while attempting to regain balance.

"Come on. Don't let him trip," Commander Courers spoke and continued through the tunnels, turning off one branch onto another. Boot heels clicked along the corridor, echoing around them. The soldiers sandwiched him between them, assuring he would keep up and not stumble, Mecah squinted and pierced his vision through the cloth and was rewarded with a choice view of the commander's backside. She stood straight and rigid with her back dipping to the curve of her narrow waist, fanning to rounded tight buttocks. Urgent need roared through his blood. This woman was his destined mate. His heart throbbed harder. His *Kismet*!

Suddenly, the air shifted warmer and faint aromas of food grew stronger with each step. His stomach rumbled. Distant sounds echoed and spiraled around them. He focused his vision on the light spilling out into the corridor.

Shalene glanced over her shoulder at the blindfolded prisoner. He was nearly seven feet tall, a good foot taller than she, and had muscled arms that would rival those of any reptile. What had he done back there? He was a prober, but it had been more than a mere mind fuck. He had approached her as a lover—tender, seeking, asking... It didn't matter. She mentally shook herself. It was probably an attack technique. Yet, she straightened her back, squaring her shoulders. She had seen parts of his life. Emotional vignettes of family, love and years of study. And there were other things—seeking, loneliness and pain. She had touched *his* soul. It had been a mutual exchange of energy and had left her wanting more. She cleared her throat. She found herself glancing back at him, needing to reconnect with him. She closed her eyes and opened them, hoping to cleanse the residue of his essence from her, but it would not leave. Just what species was he and why was he a Demron ally? Those were only two of the questions he would soon answer, but first she needed to check in, wash up and get something to eat.

She trained her stare on the pinpoint light ahead. Home. She sighed with relief. Not the kind of home one would normally welcome. A thousand feet below the surface of what once had been a lush tropical paradise. But paradise now stood charred and broken. Anger surged, always lying in wait just below the surface of her calm military persona. She met Abber's dull, empty stare that quickly fired with hatred each time he looked at the prisoner.

Yeah, they all fought the rage lurking just beneath their strongholds. It was the fuel that sustained them. But had they acted strictly on their emotions, the human race would now be extinct. It was by cunning and deliberate actions of extreme patience that they were now strong enough to exact a little retaliation.

She could sense his stare even though she knew he couldn't see her. But his mind was too strong for even a blindfold to prevent him from touching her thoughts. She struggled to resist his mind entering hers, but his essence was exciting and promised great pleasure. The image he created began to unfold and her attempts to push it away weakened. In the thought bubble, he held her close to him. So close she could feel his heart pounding beneath her hand. Her hands rested tenderly against his bare chest. A well-defined chest with hard muscles and warm, tanned skin that quivered under her tender touch. Heat fanned over her and streaks of heated need throbbed to her pussy.

She cleared her throat and attempted to separate from the thought, but he stood in front of her and slowly began to remove his clothing.

I am your Kismet, he spoke in a hoarse rasp filled with burning passion. He freed himself of the shirt and pants and stood naked. His stiff cock was buoyant under his stride as he approached her. *You are my Kismet.* He reached for her, long powerful fingertips brushing an electric trail down her arm. God, how could any touch be so seductive? She lifted her hand to her face, lost in the vision he gave her. His forefinger traced her lower lip, sending excited jags through her.

Absently, she lifted her hand and ran her fingertip over her lip, mimicking his touch. He moved from her and held out his hand. As though under a spell she slipped her hand in his and allowed him to lead her to the pallet on the floor in front of a roaring fire. The scent of gardenias filled her nostrils, so real, yet when she sniffed the dank air, she knew it wasn't real. Still, the scent lingered in her mind. Soft candlelight illuminated a blue décor as he tugged her to the lush velvet pallet with him.

"We were destined to be together." His voice replaced all conscious thought. "We are destined to be one." His lips brushed her slightly.

"Commander?"

Abber's voice pulled her from his embrace. She jerked her stare in the youth's direction.

"Are you okay?"

"Yeah."

The tunnel twisted and the height expanded by some four or more feet. She slowed when they entered the round junction from where ten tunnels radiated like spokes of a wheel. It was a clever design and if one did not know one's way around the catacombs, a lifetime could be spent trying to wind back to the surface.

"Commander Courers." The guard moved from his post and came to attention in front of her. He pounded his fist onto the left side of his chest, then thrust it forward with his index and middle finger forming a V. It was a salute that had quickly replaced the more formal one of the old military. She'd never been accustomed to any saluting or military protocol. Not until that horrid night.

"Private, as you were."

"Aye, Commander, I see you have a prisoner. A traitor?"

"Something like that. Where's General Jacob?"

"In the officer's mess."

"Dismissed, Private."

"Commander." He returned to his post as the recon party passed him. She ducked into the darkest tunnel and her troops followed, pushing the prisoner's head lower so he could enter. It was a good illusion, because instinct would drive the enemy into a larger tunnel. The cramped space only extended ten feet then grew wider as they neared the next exit where it dumped into yet another circular chamber. This one was smaller with only five tunnels radiating from it.

She motioned for Abber to take the prisoner into the tunnel behind her.

"I'll be there in ten."

Abber gave her an askance look.

"Get Doc Henson to examine him. I want to know just what kind of an alien we're dealing with."

"You *could* just ask me," the blindfolded prisoner spoke with deep sexy amusement edging his words. "I'm a Kyronian. Ever hear of Kyro? Nice little planet tucked away in a parallel universe—"

"Get him out of here, Abber." She turned away, motioning for her troops to draw closer. "Listen up." She watched Abber lead the prisoner into the far tunnel. "You all did good! We not only bagged a few reps, we got a prize. So you've earned three days of R&R. Stay smart!"

The weary troops mumbled a low cheer then trudged off through the tunnel leading to the barracks.

Shalene considered the Kyronian as she walked briskly down the long corridor that led to the mess hall. The smell of stew greeted her long before the light and heat emanating from the large room at the end of the hallway. The floor was solid rock, just like the walls, all neatly carved out of the earth by people they had nicknamed *cavers*.

She entered the noisy chamber and immediately her senses were assaulted by loud laughter, chatter, metal cups and plates clinking and the wonderful smell of hot food. The luminescent pigment paint they'd sprayed onto the walls gave a pale violet illumination to the room and was just one of the latest inventions from their science team, along with glow lanterns, comprised of a natural glowing compound they'd discovered in one of the tunnels. Eventually all tunnels would be sprayed with the paint mixture.

Letting her stare sweep the crowded room, she quickly found the general in the corner with two of his aides. Her boot heels clicked faster as she made her way across the expanse, feeling the hungry stares following her. They thought she didn't know they watched when she passed, and they had no idea she knew what they were thinking. Each and every one of them. There was a shortage of women in their regiment and more than one of the male soldiers had been thrown in the brig for unwanted advances. It was unreasonable to expect the men and women not to have sexual relationships, but the laws of harassment had not changed. At least some of them had found companionship and solace. A burning lump settled in her throat. She had lost her husband, Kade, the night of invasion.

"Commander." General Bourne Jacob nodded and his aides stood to attention. She returned their salutes as they excused themselves.

"When'd you get back?" General Jacob, a typical cave soldier — tall, brawny and muscular — was around her age but always seemed older. He'd lost his wife and children during the first strike.

"Just now, sir. I wanted to report in before I got cleaned up."

"Cleaned up, hell, how about some real food?" He leaned back in the white plastic chair. "Private?" he called to the youth dressed in a stained apron.

"Get the commander here a plate of chow and something cold to drink." He turned back to her with fire sparking in his brown eyes.

She steeled herself, knowing he would rein his lust, but nevertheless it was unsettling to know her commanding officer had the hots for her, especially when she knew she was dusty and weary-looking after three days out. His reaction bespoke the desperation of their overall living conditions. In pre-Rep times, the sexy, dark-haired general would not have given her the time of day, much less those devouring glances.

She bowed her head and ran a hand through her hair, but stopped when her fingers met a wad of tangles.

Shalene, don't leave me in the cell to rot. Mecah's voice intruded, sounding so real, she glanced over her shoulder to make sure he wasn't standing behind her. *A locked cell will not keep me from your mind.*

Get out of my head! she demanded.

"You look damn tired, Commander. Did you lose anyone?"

"N-No sir." She looked up as the private plopped the bowl of potato and carrot stew in front of her. She breathed in the aromas and her stomach growled, but the sound was lost in the ever-present din.

"Excellent!" He sat back in his chair and stared at her as she sipped the soup.

"But," she spoke between mouthfuls, "we did kill three reps." She willed her hand to stop shaking.

"Hot damn!" The general was on his feet with his fingers between his lips. The whistle pierced the room and silence followed in its wake. "Commander Courers' troops encountered enemies on their recon. We now have three less lizards on our planet!" His deep voice boomed across the high-vaulted room.

The response made her ears ring with shouts, banging of cups and the slamming of knife hilts against the long tables. Pleased, the general fell into a chant with his arm pumping over his head and was soon joined by everyone in the mess hall.

"Death to reps! Death to reps! Death to reps!"

Chapter Four

Shalene lifted the spoon, balancing the slice of potato swimming in the thick broth, and shoved it into her mouth. She savored the heat and texture, wondering how she had ended up being a commander instead of being in charge of the mess. She washed it down with icy cold water, another luxury they had in abundance underground. The reps had siphoned most of the fresh water streams, and each time it rained their spacecrafts would hover over the pools of runoff and rob the world of fresh water, dumping it into the ocean. Fortunately, there were pools of water in the underground caverns. Beneath the network of tunnels, water, probably older than when dinosaurs walked the earth, flowed free.

"There now! See what your recon did for morale? Each time a successful mission returns, we regain a little more of ourselves." General Jacob sat down across from her, smiling at the troops, nodding occasionally to a soldier who let out a whoop of victory.

She glanced up from her meal, noticing how the men were growing louder and louder. When a couple of female soldiers entered the room, the dog whistles broke out. She lifted an eyebrow in the general's direction and shook her head.

"At ease, gentlemen!" His voice boomed over the rowdy catcalls and the men settled down.

The two women soldiers jeered at them having been reprimanded, then sat down beside them. Shalene glanced from the couples to the general.

"They're just blowing off steam, Commander," he whispered.

"General, there's steam and then there's *steam*. You know the issues we face in keeping them at bay. We need our women soldiers to fight, not bear babies. Not now."

"We also need to rebuild the human race."

"Fine, then get some volunteers to be breeders, just don't mess with my female troops."

"Excluding female troopers, we have about two hundred women candidates and they're either medical personnel or scientists."

"So let them bear smart babies to help find a way to stop the reps."

"But we need soldiers. Lots of soldiers."

"In all due respect, sir, we've had this conversation before, I'm not having it again. I'm in charge of all female soldiers. You placed me in that position and I take it very seriously. One hundred percent of them want to fight the damn reps, not bear children."

"But they have needs too, don't they? Don't you?"

"Excuse me?" Anger bristled up her spine. She gritted her teeth against the words pressing to be voiced.

"I apologize. I'm out of line, Commander. Just think about it, again. Talk to them once more. Maybe some have changed their minds."

"Are you talking about raising a family or are you talking about using them for breeders? The latter would make them prostitutes."

"That's not fair, Shalene. We're in a crisis. My men are restless as hell. We've only had about a hundred children born over the last ten years, and most of those were born in the first couple of years with no births since. What does that tell you?"

"That the women are smart."

"Meaning?"

"They're using birth control."

"If you don't do something voluntarily, the Council's going to issue a mandate. I'm just trying to spare your gender from enforced breeding. Choose now while there's an option."

His warning jarred her to the core. Being forced to mate with someone chosen by a lottery was worse than dictatorship — worse than war.

"General, these women have trained to be soldiers. Would *you* want to give all that up to play nursemaid to a kid?"

"That's different."

"Is it? The reason they're using birth control is because they don't want to bring a child into a rep world!"

"Just take it under consideration. Be warned, the pressure is on. These men want willing mates, not just sex partners. They've gone to the Council. It's instinct to want to create a family."

"The female troops will rebel if forced into anything. The old days of family building are long gone, General. You've trained them to be warriors, not mothers. If you press this issue, you'll end up with more than the reps to fight." She glared at him.

"Stand down, Commander," he ordered and leaned back in the chair.

Shalene shoved her plate toward him and sat back in her chair, folding her arms over her chest. She knew what this was about. It was about him, not the men. He wanted her to be his mate. He'd all but come out and asked her several times. He was not the one destined for her. That man had yet to appear in her life. As much as she had loved her husband, she'd always known he was not her eternal mate. Her thoughts turned to the prisoner and his claims of Kismet. Her pulse throbbed harder.

"This is damn pointless," the General spat.

"It is. We're all going to die one by one until there's no one left to bear children," she argued.

"Shut your damn mouth." He leaned forward with his voice low and restrained. "You're not to speak that way again. Understood?"

"It's pretty fucking bleak and it just got bleaker last night." She leaned forward, resting on her forearms. She strained to keep from calling him an asshole because sometimes he was just that.

"What happened?" Concern transformed his face into hard lines.

"The reps have recruited another alien race to fight for them."

"What?" The color drained from his face, leaving him a sickly pallor.

"We captured one. He's down in holding."

"And you're just now telling me?"

"I was hungry." She tipped the cup to her lips and let the wonderful cold water roll around her mouth then down her throat. Just plain water, something she'd taken for granted before the reps had invaded Earth.

"On your feet. I want to see this creature. What does he look like?" He pressed his hand against the small of her back, urging her through the mess hall faster than her normal pace.

She paused to look up at him.

"He looks a lot like you, sir."

"What?"

"Human. Only *he* has lavender eyes," she grinned, and led the way.

The guard pushed him into the small dark room. Mecah stumbled and came up against the cold wall. He turned to his jailer, prepared for the beating he knew would come as the natural beginning of his imprisonment.

Instead, the guard keyed several numbers into an illuminated pad on the opposite wall. Blue and white light streams filled the space until a wavy force field vibrated over the wide opening.

"Thinking of escape?" The guard tossed a piece of paper into the invisible shield. It ignited and burned, with ashes scattering into the air.

Mecah frowned and plopped down on the cot, leaning against the cold, stone wall. How long would he have to wait until she came back? He crossed his legs at the ankles, folding his arms over his chest, and waited.

He'd just dozed off when the sound of boots marching down the tunnel startled him awake. His heart pounded heavier, but instead of jumping to attention, he closed his eyes and waited.

"On your feet, an officer's on deck!" A light flashed against his closed eyelids.

"On my planet it's sacrilege to interrupt meditation." He swung his feet over the side of the cot.

"And just where is this planet?" The man dressed in dark military garb stood over him, staring into his eyes.

"Don't let the color be of concern, General. I assure you, I'm not a mutant rep," he said, glancing up at the commander. "Although I was accused of being such an abomination." She was just as sexy as the last time he'd seen her. Maybe more. He cleared his throat.

"Your species has purple eyes?"

"Sometimes rather plum or even darker depending on my mood. But usually pale purple. As I told Commander Courers here, I come from a parallel universe. If you've got a stellar chart—"

"Stand up." The general looked to be about thirty-odd years of age and, from what Mecah had seen of humans, rather tall for his species, standing well over six feet, although still shorter than Mecah. The general's eyes were dull and his skin a pasty white—probably from living underground for nearly fifteen years, if he were like the rest of the humans and had escaped underground after their first attack on the Demrons had failed. Cowards! Except for her. He glanced at the comely, very athletic Commander Courers, who was bursting with vitality. Her tanned face clearly revealed someone who lived aboveground. Her face was still streaked with camouflage oil, telling Mecah she'd gone straight to her CO with her news of the alien capture.

Mecah stood slowly, unfolding his full height to tower over them. The general moved closer to the invisible wall.

"You were right, Commander, he does look human. He could pass for one of us, except for those eyes."

"Some corrective lenses…" she said, letting her gaze travel over Mecah.

"Assuming they could get hold of colored contacts."

"I'm sure they're on the black market. We've discovered all kinds of commodity stashes throughout the underground cities." She looked from the general back to him.

Mecah met her probing gaze, sensing her arousal. A lazy grin slipped over his lips. She knew they were Kismet.

She stiffened her spine. He could see the heat leaching from her body, filling her aura with red streaks interspersed with pink. Mecah tilted his head and smiled. Instantly the pink and purple flashes increased. Her sexual arousal reflected in her aura as pinks and deep reds. Oh yeah, she not only felt his desire, she was struggling to control her passion.

If they can disguise themselves, then they could infiltrate our troops, Shalene thought. "There's been talk of doing that, but presently we're more valuable as hunters. Search and destroy human targets. The Demrons seem to enjoy ferreting out your underground bunkers. S and D's almost a game to them," he said, noticing the surprised looks on their faces.

"So you're a telepath," she said and moved closer. "What other abilities do you possess?"

"Oh, I have many I'd love to demonstrate to you, Commander." He enjoyed the way her aura vibrated with new streaks of pink.

She struggled to block him from reading her mind, but he'd struck the most vulnerable area—her femininity. It was the one part of herself she denied more than any female warrior he'd ever met.

"Why are you aligned with the Demrons?" she asked.

"It seemed like a good idea since they were going to torture and kill my men."

"How did you come to be so far away from home, Mecah?" she asked.

"*Captain* Mecah. We were caught in a rogue wormhole and came out the other end, unfortunately to this hellhole."

"It wasn't a hellhole before the Reps."

"What's that supposed to mean?" he asked, meeting her stare, knowing her façade was purely for the benefit of the general. Her heat was rising and her pulse was a wild drumming. It was more than mere physical attraction. They had made a connection when she'd probed his mind. A deep connection! His heart hammered out confirmation. A shudder ripped down him. Involuntarily, he jerked from the electrical shock piercing him. Mecah narrowed his stare on her.

There it was, glinting in the depths of her eyes. She'd felt that, too. At long last, he had found his Kismet mate! The sensations were beyond anything he'd ever experienced. His knees weakened. With a mixture of disbelief and awe, he fell onto the cot. After all these years of waiting until the day when his Kismet would stand in front of him, after seeing it happen to everyone but him, Mecah was unable to rationalize that his Kismet was an alien female.

Had his fleet not been sucked into a wormhole and delivered to this world, he would never have met Shalene Courers. He would never have fulfilled his destiny and met his mate. His mind whirled with the ramifications of every small, seemingly insignificant act. He looked up at her again. Dare he believe it true? He probed her mind quickly and the same force of electricity greeted him.

Her hands tightened into white-knuckled fists and she physically appeared to be bracing herself, resisting the current flashing between them. She knew, just as he did. Mecah seized her stare.

"What's wrong with him?" The general frowned at her.

"I have no idea, sir, probably something alien." She spoke with such control, Mecah closed his eyes and searched their connection just to reassure himself it was there. He sighed. It did indeed live.

Get out of my head! She mentally shoved him away. Her angry glare pierced his heart as surely as a knife blade had been plunged into him.

"Look, something's going on here between the two of you. Is he like you? A prober?" The general's voice was strained and his aura sparked dark yellow with shards of white. Definitely an angry man.

"I'm not sure," she lied.

Mecah continued to stare at her, wondering why she lied. Was Kismet not sacred to her race? Such a revelation would be cause for great celebration on his planet. Of course, having Kismet with a suspected enemy could put a damper on the joy. He smiled at her, knowing her uncomfortable inner squirming was because of him.

"I want answers, Commander. Get them for me by this evening." The general turned and left.

"Aye, sir," she mumbled, her energy still focused on him.

"How dare you mind fuck me! That's mental rape in my society."

"I wasn't trying—I had to know."

"Know what?"

"If you were a mentalist."

"A what?"

"You know, mind reader, empath—your general used *prober*. And you definitely are one."

"Where did you train?" she demanded.

"I was trained from the moment I was born as are all Kyronians. Can we forgo this nonsense talk?"

"I don't know...it's up to you." She crossed her arms over her chest.

"Then I assure you, we can." He ran his hand through his long blond hair, letting it fall over his back, knowing her attention was momentarily captured by the seductive gesture.

Her aura was a fusion of reds, pinks and purples. She was connected to him but insisted on feeble resistance. What was wrong with this woman? Why was she shielding her feminine side so strongly?

"I want answers," she spoke.

"What are the questions?" He sat back down on the metal cot.

"Why did you align with the Demrons?"

"I told you, we were caught inside a rogue worm—look, Commander." His stare entwined with hers until their energies were sealed together. "We're not fighting by choice. We were on patrol along the outer rim of my homeworld galaxy when this wormhole appeared out of nowhere and my fleet was drawn into it and plopped out the other side to this hellhole of a place. What I'm trying to do is keep my troops alive until my science officer can figure out a way back home. I don't give a flying shit if you cave dwellers win or lose. I'm merely buying time for my fleet." He watched the pink splotches on her cheeks darken.

"I see you're a man of great conviction and principle," she sneered.

He stood and walked over to the barrier as close as he dared.

"See here, woman, you don't know me, my morals or my motives. And stop that frail attempt to read my thoughts. You can't. I'm stronger."

She seemed to bristle at being found out. He didn't want to put her on the offensive any more than she was, but neither was he going to allow her to stand in judgment of him.

"Let me explain one more time. It's simple. The Demrons enslaved my troops. We do as ordered. Right now it's to S and D all humans. That's what we do to stay alive until—"

"You can return home."

"Exactly."

"And you don't care that you fight on the side of the enemy?"

"Whose enemy? Yours? Why should I care?" It was his turn to get angry.

"Because you have morals, Captain?"

"Way I see it, Commander, you humans are getting what you deserve."

"How...do...you...surmise that, Captain?" The fire in her aura jettisoned into brilliant flames, but it was not the red of desire but rage. "Just how do we deserve to live underground like rats?" Her fists were tight balls by her side.

"Maybe because you tried to take over the Demrons' planet? Killed off all their plant life save a few scrubby bushes and, oh yeah, turned it into a fucking desert! I'd say your race should damn well suffer living in the hell you created."

Her look blazed with fury. He'd struck a nerve for sure.

"You are so misinformed, Captain—"

"Why don't you show me exactly how misinformed I am, then," Mecah baited, wanting her to step closer to the barrier and order it lowered so he could probe her mind fully. Mind-linking was the ultimate test of Kismet. If she were his fated mate, then a melding would allow them to be one mind. Once linked, they would remain connected even after death.

"Haven't you ever probed a human? Asked about the war?" Shalene restrained the rage quaking in her.

"We don't take prisoners. I never had a need to probe a human." He pierced through her attempts to block him.

Let me see the truth, he insisted mentally, and at last she submitted, dropping her resistance.

"Get out of my head," she spoke between clenched teeth.

"I can be very persuasive," he teased, raising one eyebrow slightly. "Do you have someplace where we can be alone?"

Shalene glanced at the guard and then back at her prisoner. There was something here that demanded further interrogation. If this alien was who he claimed to be, then he might be convinced to help them fight the Demrons.

I might be convinced to help you fight the lizards. It just depends, he smiled, enjoying her discomfort over him reading her mind.

She glared at him. How did he do that without her sensing his probing?

It's how my people communicate. We don't need voice. But we've used voice since our enslavement by the Demrons. I find your voice very sexy, Commander. His pupils waxed a deep red. He was aroused. She looked down and quickly saw the bulge below his waist. When she met his gaze once more, he shrugged with a lopsided grin tracing his handsome tanned face.

"Escort the prisoner to the interrogation room," she ordered.

"Now we're going to have some fun," he whispered, leaning closer to the invisible shield. "You're going to be very happy you agreed to this."

"I've agreed to nothing, Captain Mecah. This is not going to be a pleasurable experience for you. I assure you."

She watched his expression, expecting concern or at least anger. Instead, his grin widened. A burning need to feel his touch shocked her. Shalene turned sharply on her heel, nearly colliding with Abber.

"What is it, soldier?"

"It's about Captain Mecah. I think you better come see for yourself."

She glanced back at the prisoner, then fell in beside Abber.

"Can you not just tell me?"

"No, ma'am, you have to see this."

Chapter Five

They trekked the long distance to the control room that housed all of the equipment, monitors, radar and the uplinks to several satellites the Demrons had confiscated.

The huge room was noisy with a buzz of activity. Abber led Shalene through the maze of desks and consoles. She nodded greetings to some of the officers on deck and followed him to the general's cubicle.

"Commander. Lieutenant Abber, you're dismissed." General Jacob glanced from the holographic screen.

"Sir." He saluted and left.

"What's going on, General?" Shalene asked, always on guard when alone with him.

"That's what I want to know, Commander. Look at these satellite photos of the site where you captured Captain Mecah."

The images flashed onto the screen above the console. She stared at the bodies of the dead reps.

"Sir? I don't understand. What's the problem?"

"Wait, look at the time-lapsed pics coming up."

She watched the series of pictures display in sequence of the three human-size lizards lying in the desert where they had killed them. The last picture flashed onto the screen.

"What happened?" She leaned in to examine closer. "Where'd the third one go?"

"That's what I want to know, Commander. You reported all three were dead."

"That's correct, sir."

"Well, something or someone removed one lizard, unless he wasn't dead and walked away."

"He was dead, sir."

"Did you run vitals?"

"My troops know the procedures, sir." She bristled at having her competency questioned. She was weary of his games. Sometimes she was tempted to accept his advances to be free of his harassment. But, she frowned at him, nothing was worth that price.

"And you didn't burn the bodies?"

"No, sir, Captain Mecah informed us there was a column in the vicinity and smoke would alert them."

"And you believed him?"

"I did, sir."

"I just sent a scouting party to locate the third lizard. I shouldn't have to be cleaning up after your team."

"Understood, sir, but it was an unusual situation and my team's never had a single incident."

"There's a first time. Isn't there?" His sarcasm scraped against her last thread of control. Her earlier rejection had only fueled his anger. Clearly he wanted to get back at her for his bruised ego. He'd always managed to overcome the embarrassment, but perhaps after so many rejections, the general had finally had enough. She tried not to probe his mind, but his thoughts were so angry, she couldn't help but read them. Her heart quickened. He was planning something. The thought twisted away from her. If he were smart, he'd realize pissing her off was not the way to win her acceptance.

"In case Captain Mecah is lying, I want you to extend your *interrogation.* Can you do that?"

"I don't understand." The thought flashed in his mind again.

"Forgo the typical interrogation, Commander. I want you to use the opportunity to probe his mind."

"He's stronger than I am, General. I don't think I can break past his barriers."

"I'm trusting you'll find a way to *persuade* him, Commander." He smiled slightly.

She bristled under the innuendo, not needing to probe his twisted mind to know what he was ordering her to do.

"Are you familiar with the Fated Reclamation Prophecy?"

"Somewhat."

"It speaks of an alien man captured in the company of two lizards. Of course, growing up I always thought it meant two earth lizards, not the two-legged Demron kind."

"It's an old legend." She tried to dismiss.

"Or a real prophecy. If so, Captain Mecah could be the one prophesized who will help defeat the reps, then it's important you do whatever's necessary to discover the truth. The seers believe Captain Mecah is the fated one."

"The ancients described a being descending from the heavens to deliver the world from lizards and snakes. It was an abstract story used to illustrate a moral about redemption, not to be taken literally," she reasoned.

"Our world has changed. News of Captain Mecah has spread. There's renewed hope. To the point the Council has mandated you undertake this mission."

"Th-the Council? And how did they come up with such a ridiculous idea? I protest, sir. My duty does not mandate I—"

"Your duty is to obey all Council directives. I don't need to remind you that we're fighting for our very existence, Commander. Nothing is too great to ask of a soldier. Nothing! The ultimate sacrifice has been requested of you. It's your obligation as a soldier and an officer to comply." His eyes danced with the excitement of power. He thought he had broken her. If she would not be his, then he would force her to be with the alien and the meaning was clear. He could force her to be with anyone he chose by abusing his command and declaring the need before the Council.

Hatred burst in her and she restrained the urge to slap the smirk off his face. How dare he demand she use sex as part of her interrogation? Granted, she'd been trained in the art of sexual stimulation for interrogation tactics, but she'd never been ordered to perform it.

"Have I made myself clear, Commander?"

"Will there be anything else, General?" she asked.

"I've had the interrogation room sprayed with ore residue and had the alien moved there."

"Sir?"

"It should prevent him from attempting to contact his troops if he is indeed as telepathic as he appears."

She knew the properties of the special spray would block all telepathy from entering or leaving the room, but it couldn't protect *her* from Mecah's probing. Dread weighted her. It would be just the two of them in the secured room. His mind was stronger than hers. How would she maintain control over the interrogation?

"That's all, Commander. Report back first thing tomorrow morning."

"Tomorrow morning?"

"Well, I don't expect you to get the information quickly if you're going to try to be subtle, Commander," he grinned, enjoying her defeat.

"Won't the Demrons be searching for him? It's a risk we don't need should the reps send out a search team."

"What are you proposing?"

"I don't think an entire night is necessary."

"Well, I do, Commander. The reps have no way of tracing him. We both know they're lousy trackers. They'll just assume he was taken prisoner and is being tortured. Once your interrogation is completed, you'll know if the captain is telling the truth or lying. You must find out all there is to know about this Captain Mecah. The entire base's security is depending on you being successful. Dismissed."

"May I say one last thing, sir?" she asked, determined he would not have any satisfaction from this order.

"Sure, what is it?"

"I just want to thank you, sir."

"Thank me?" A sickly pallor washed over him.

"Yes sir. I know Captain Mecah is a suspected enemy, but, well, sir, based on what the Council has ordered me to do, I feel it is now safe to admit to you had I been ordered to torture him, I'm afraid I wouldn't have been able to do perform my duty. I'd have been greatly conflicted.

"There's a powerful chemistry between the captain and myself. This mission I'm about to undertake, well, compared to other missions, this will be the most enjoyable. So thank you, sir. Thank you so much. I truly appreciate this," she smiled widely, reading his thoughts that the order was far from punishment. Rage consumed him. His face darkened and the look in his eyes fired under his outrage, looking as if he could explode.

Shalene saluted and turned on her heel, knowing she had pressed all of his buttons at one time. Let him simmer with that for the night. She couldn't stop the grin from spreading wider as she marched across the room.

Abber was waiting for her outside in the corridor.

"Commander?" His eyes were wide with concern.

"Abber, boy, it'll all be worth it just to have that image of the general in my mind for eternity."

"Commander?"

"Nothing."

While the general had planned the assignment to be more than just demoralizing, she now had the upper hand in their ongoing struggle. He was no doubt hoping she would fail so he could strip her rank and reduce her to begging him for leniency. Perhaps in his twisted mind he thought that the ploy would ultimately wear down her resistance and she'd accept him as a mate. She would play this game and she would be the winner!

"First thing I want you to do, Abber, make sure the interrogation room was actually sprayed with an ore shield."

"I oversaw the project. They did a good job."

"I need a new helmet then, one that has—"

"An ore lining?" He sidestepped her and ran into the office off the side of the hall and returned with a helmet. "Had it waiting for you."

She took the helmet and placed it under her arm, feeling confident that combined with her own mental blocking, Captain Mecah would not be able to read her thoughts or place suggestions in her mind. She'd control the session.

"Where's the prisoner?"

"The general ordered a shower and fresh clothing. Isn't that odd treatment for a prisoner?"

"Yeah," she spoke, managing to keep the anger from her voice. She would not disobey orders, but she had a few maneuvers even General Jacob didn't know about. She turned for her quarters, dismissing Abber.

The luxury of showers was the only good thing about living underground. With a wealth of springs, rivers and even lakes within the underground city, rationing was not an issue. The warm spray fell over her, washing away the layers of desert and the charred smell of once-vibrant forests. Working the lather into her hair, she rinsed and let it fall down her back, plastering against her wet skin.

She was an officer, a proven warrior, and yet General Jacob had managed to reduce her to the basest of values, a seductress. And knowing he'd done it out of vengeance only cemented her resolve to best him at this game.

Her thoughts turned to Mecah and what he'd said about her being his Kismet. If he was everything he'd claimed, then he could become an ally. She took a deep breath and steeled herself against the possibility he was lying. But the overwhelming question remained. Why did she feel such an attraction to him? Could his mind-control abilities be so adept that he could implant emotions, making her believe they were her own?

If there truly were such a thing as a Kismet mate, did that mean the ancient prophecy of fated reclamation was at hand? Could the being destined to save Earth really be Mecah? She stepped from the shower, wrapping the towel around her, and picked up another to dry her hair. The long mirror betrayed her inner conflict. Her face was drawn and her eyes dull as she combed her long dark hair. It was difficult to recall what it felt like not to be a soldier. Her more feminine side had been displaced by hatred and a need to fight. And it had been a long time since she'd felt like a woman. She always blocked and discounted the advances of men, shielding her mind from their thoughts and hiding behind her rank when things began to get too hot for comfort. But when Mecah looked at her, she didn't want to block those emotions or the hot fiery sensations tingling her pussy alive. How could she have forgotten those feelings so easily?

She changed into a clean uniform, donning a fresh pair of black boots. If she was going to seduce him, then she needed to allow herself to enjoy it. Didn't she? It was a direct order. She was a good soldier and did whatever she was ordered without hesitation or question. She squared her bare shoulders, looking at her reflection.

Strong arms were exposed from the tight bustier vest. Her breasts rose high and full above the leather lacings. The matching leather pants clung to every curve, and she knew with the high-topped boots, in another time, she would have looked like a dominatrix. All she needed was a whip. She laughed at herself and turned from the mirror.

She reached for the canister of brandy, noticing how her hand shook. The glass was cold against her sweaty palms. She poured the golden liquid into the goblet, letting the bottle tilt longer than normal, until the glass was full. That should bolster her enough to seduce Captain Mecah. It would be easy. He was a willing partner. But was she? Could she do this? It had been fifteen years since she'd been with a man and while it was her choice, it was still something she missed. Would she find, after years of abstinence, her ability to control her passion foolproof, or would the ever-present longing for the feel of a man overpower and dominate her?

The alcohol shot through her, fanning in warm layers, dulling her mind and giving her a relaxed buzz. That felt good. She picked up the helmet, feeling giddy and school-girlish.

Chapter Six

Abber waited outside Shalene's door.

"The prisoner's demanding food. I ignored his request. I figured food would be part of the...ah..."

"Torture?" Her boot heels clicked faster as she hurried down the corridor with Abber a few paces behind her.

"The general ordered me to get some extra things, so I need to see about it."

"What things?" She halted and turned on him, her rage seething just below her façade of control.

"Ah." His face rushed crimson. "Wine, music, candles, ah—"

"You have to obey the general's orders, Abber. Don't worry about me. I can take care of myself." Her heart tugged for the pained look centering his eyes. "While you're about it, grab a plate of chow for the prisoner and bring it to the room."

"Aye, Commander." He saluted and practically ran to the mess hall.

Her hatred for General Jacob flamed at the thought of him using Abber. He knew how close the youth was to her. She balled her hands into hard fists, standing outside the metal black door, dreading what she had been ordered to do. She was a soldier and a commander. In spite of all attempts to accept the order, her anger toward General Jacob grew.

So be it! She'd not give Jacob any satisfaction. Donning the helmet, she stiffened her spine and took a deep breath. She would do this her way and to hell with Jacob! She keyed in the passcode and shoved the door open. Mecah jumped from the mattress, not even attempting to hide his excitement over seeing her.

"Commander? I've not had a leisurely shower in a long time. A plate of warm food would make this close to utopia."

She noticed he'd plaited his blond hair into a single braid that fell below his shoulders. His strong, muscled body filled the military-issue pants and T-shirt, highlighting the raw strength of years of disciplined training. As a warrior she could appreciate his body, but as a woman she appreciated it more. She cleared her throat, trying to disentangle herself from the unwelcomed sensations fluttering in her stomach.

"We're afforded baths because there's plenty of water down here." She noticed he had shaved and was surprised by the compelling desire to trace his square jawline with her fingertips. Instead, she tightened her hands into hard fists by her side.

"Plenty of water? Then we have something to bargain with."

"What would that be?"

"Water in exchange for information."

She looked away from his intense stare and pushed the helmet down tighter on her head.

"I thought something was wrong since you were gone so long. Had I known you were showering—" He sighed appreciatively and sat down on the edge of the bed, resting his forearms on his legs. "What's with the helmet?" he squinted. "Oh, I see, ore lined. Just so you know, it won't stop our minds from reconnecting. Once the initial contact's made, it can't be severed. Now, I do like your black leathers, and a lace-up bustier vest always makes me hot." His gaze swept over her.

Shalene felt as though she weren't wearing any clothes.

"Do take off that helmet, love, so I can see your silky hair. Frankly, had I known you were grooming for me—"

"Please don't flatter yourself. I've been out on recon for days. And my delay was due to a very boring and typical debriefing. It certainly wasn't in preparation for you. And you will address me as Commander or Commander Courers but never as 'love'. Are we clear?"

"Do you really mean *never*?"

"Are you going to make this painful or painless, Captain?"

"Is that an invitation, Commander?" He flashed a devastating smile and she looked away, attempting to shield herself against his disarming magnetism, but his smile ripped a need through her that startled yet aroused.

"Interrogations can become very unpleasant, as I'm sure you know." She closed the door behind her. The automatic lock jarred her pulse into an erratic throbbing. She glanced at the wall mounts where cameras had once been suspended. The general would not be playing voyeur. Perhaps Abber had removed them on his own. Relief washed over her.

"I only want to indulge in pleasure where you're concerned, Shalene." He took a step closer.

"I will remind you only once more to address me as Commander or Commander Courers." She squared her shoulders and took a step forward, all the while studying the way the corners of his lips turned up in a very sexy grin.

A sudden urge to feel those lips pressed against hers overpowered all reason. She halted mid-stride, fighting against the impulse. Had he inserted the very desire into her mind without her knowing it? She fought the quivering heat slipping down her spine to her pussy and willed the aching need to leave her body. Instead, it burst white-hot in a passionate urgency to feel his mouth claim hers. Was he right? Was the ore-lined helmet useless?

"You feel it, don't you?" His voice invaded her protective barriers, storming through her defenses as though they were mere vapor.

"What?" Her voice shook in spite of her attempt to keep it unemotional.

"Kismet. I feel it too. Do you have it in your culture?"

"Do you mean fate?"

He nodded with eyes turning dark plum. His look seared her skin in a fiery path as it dropped to her lips then wandered to her breasts. She knew the bustier pressed their fullness high above the leather lacings. With each rapid breath, the soft leather stretched against her nipples, creating erotic sensations.

"W-What are you saying about fate?" She leaned back, flattening her hands against the cold door for added support.

"There's a Kismet between us, Commander Courers. *Shalene.*" He stepped closer.

The way he spoke her name sent excited goose bumps up her arms, followed by electrical jags of heat and desire racing to her pussy. Her heartbeat thumped harder. He was moving closer and with each step, her pulse pounded harder.

"I don't know what you're talking about." Whatever was going on, she clearly had no control over her own body. She stepped across the room in front of him, feeling his stare follow her, slipping down her back to her ass. She knew her body was in strong physical shape from training, yet had never felt such delight in a man's appreciation. She braved a look in his direction and her gaze was immediately captured by his intense stare.

"You can deny. You can try to resist, but Kismet has its own *agenda,* as your people say. It won't rest until it is appeased."

"A-And just how is it appeased?" she challenged.

"The only way any hunger can be sated." His laughter was deep and infectious.

Shalene swallowed back the lashing fire that threatened to consume her. Was it his passion or hers coursing through her? How could she discern?

"Stop trying to understand it. There's no understanding. There's no avoiding it. When Kismet declares itself to a man and woman, the only solution is submission to its power."

"You're a talented mind controller." She turned her back to him, focusing on anything else that might break the connection with him.

"Like I said, there's no stopping it. We can play this game forever or you can take that helmet off and sit down with me so we can talk."

"You're my prisoner, in case you forgot. I'll decide when we sit." She crossed her arms over her chest.

"Have it your way." He sat down in one of the plastic chairs but continued to stare at her.

Scenes, unbidden, flashed in front of her. He stood over her as she lay naked beneath him, enjoying the way he looked down at her as she moved her hands over her body, spreading the lips of her pussy wide so he could see her better. His excitement charged her, sending a frenetic rhythm undulating to her hips.

Shalene squinted against the vision.

"Stop that!" she yelled.

"I didn't give you any vision you didn't want. I merely summoned your deepest desires. They did the rest." He paused. "Care to share what you saw?"

"I'll ask the questions."

"The first being? What do I want?" He smiled.

"Exactly."

"Aside from you? I want the same thing you do, Commander. The Demrons destroyed."

"And so to accomplish this, you fight by their side killing my people?" She inched closer to him.

"I explained what happened to my fleet."

"And why change sides now?"

"I met you." His tanned face beckoned her touch.

"Right, your Kismet." She clenched her jaw.

"*Our* Kismet. It's sacrilege to mock a declaration of Kismet." His tone grated harsh. The look in his eyes transformed from playfulness to sternness.

"That may be true where you come from, but not in my world."

"If you'll just give me a chance to prove Kismet, then we can get on with the real fun and eventually how to destroy the Demrons and free both our people."

She considered him for a moment.

"How do we do that?"

The knock on the door was loud, startling her. She hurried over to the keypad by the door. Pressing the series of numbers, it clicked open.

Abber entered with a metal tray. Balancing the bowl of steaming soup and bread, he quickly surveyed the room. The aromas floated into the room, filling her nostrils. Mecah perked up.

"Set it down on the desk in front of him," she ordered. Abber did as ordered and quickly left the room. The door clicked locked again.

"You feed your prisoners?"

"We aren't barbarians. I assume you can eat our food."

From what she'd been able to read from his thoughts, he was not a threat. Misguided about who was the enemy, perhaps, but his responses so far had been made with resounding truthfulness. He intrigued her with his claim of Kismet and the onslaught of such unique sensations she felt in his presence — strong sensations not easily dismissed. The possibility that he also spoke the truth about their destinies panicked her yet excited her beyond caution. She needed to know. And the Council had ordered her to do whatever it took, especially seducing him.

It was difficult to discard protocol, but Shalene knew from the first time she'd seen Captain Mecah there was some kind of connection between them.

He devoured the food, moaning his pleasure as he ate. Her body responded to the seductive tone, the tingling making her nipples hard.

"How long has it been since you ate?" She stood a few feet from him, watching.

"Hot food? Since arriving. We've conserved our ships' power any way we can, especially water usage. Cold meals or showers. We're limited to sink baths at best."

"How much power do you have left?"

"We have ten transports the Demrons commandeered for their own use—those will lose power in a couple of months. My biggest concern is the fleet. I have five carrier ships and half of them are near end cycle of their fuel cycles. The fighters were depleted within two months of our arrival. The Demrons are consumers of everything."

"I know."

"When the fuel cells go, we'll need to transfer the crews onto the other ships. Doubling the weight and life support requirement will quickly drain our fuel sources. Eventually, the Demrons will relocate us to the planet's surface."

"What is your fuel source?"

"Hydrogen. If the Demrons' planet had plenty of fresh water, we'd have no fuel issues. But we've kept this knowledge from them. They've yet to unlock our technology. You know, they aren't a very creative race. Resourceful, yes, but they don't understand fuel and energy exchanges. We've been careful about what we've revealed to them. They don't know about our telepathic abilities or much of anything else. They've assumed we're much like humans, especially since we aren't from this star system."

"Okay, first of all, the Demrons are the ones responsible for the lack of fresh water, not us. And second of all, it's not their damn planet. It's ours."

He pulled a chunk of bread from the loaf and crammed it in his mouth.

"Well, it's your planet *now*."

"Our planet always. The Demrons attacked us! This planet is called Earth. We'd never heard of a Demron until the night they appeared and began blowing up my world."

"You have proof of this?"

"I don't need proof. It's the truth." She folded her arms over her chest.

"See? If you'd just let me do a mind link, we could get through all this much quicker."

"What do you mean?" She moved closer.

"A mind link is like a bridge from my mind to yours. We become one mind and share our thoughts, memories, everything."

"Everything?"

"It saves a lot of time and assures mate compatibility."

"I'm not your mate." She straightened her back.

"Yes, you are. You just don't realize it—"

"So say I agreed to do this link," she interrupted, not wanting to hear his theories about why she was his mate. "How would we do it?"

"Very slowly," he grinned.

Heat swept over her. Visions of making love to him flashed before her again. A nervous tingling raced to her clit.

"See, that's the very reason I can't trust you, Captain Mecah. You have this devilish streak in you."

"What's devilish mean?"

"Evil."

"Oh… I think you're jesting, aren't you?" His teasing expression tightened into stern lines to crease his forehead.

"What are the risks of a mind link?"

"Risks?"

"Yeah, residual effect, side-effects."

"Nothing negative. We could do a short one first if you like. A selected memory, like the beginning of the war. That way I can verify your claim that you are merely defending yourselves." He winked at her, then spooned the soup into his mouth.

His gesture sent her heart pounding harder, and in spite of her attempt to control the giddy sensations his smallest tease created, they continued to unnerve her.

He shoved another spoonful of stew into his mouth. His lips closed around the spoon and she wondered what it would feel like to have them close around her aching nipples. She cleared her throat.

"What would I need to do?" She surprised herself agreeing to such a dangerous submission. What if he had malicious intent? If she gave him access to her mind then —

"Don't second-guess yourself, Commander. I won't take advantage of you. Just sit down beside me. I can do it from here." He lowered the spoon and pushed the tray from him.

She felt numb. Her knees buckled under her and she landed onto the chair harder than intended. Mecah turned sideways, shifting his long legs so she was sitting between them.

Her cheeks flashed hot. He reached for her hands and held them between his large warm ones. The contact sent delightful shivers over her.

"Just relax." His words drifted over her like a protective blanket. "Let me remove your helmet. I can read past the ore lining, but I want to see your beautiful hair."

"If you can read past it, I'll keep it on." She didn't want to do anything to arouse him further, even though she longed to feel his hands threading through her hair. She straightened in the chair. If his magnetism was this overwhelming, how could she allow him inside her head?

"Just relax. Take a few deep breaths," he coaxed.

She willed her body to relax so he could gain access to her mind. It was not easy letting a stranger, a sexy stranger at that, have free entry into her most intimate thoughts. It meant being vulnerable in the most intimate way. Yet, she knew he wanted only one thing and should he decide to snoop around, she could toss him out. Hopefully. She focused on bringing the memory to the foreground.

Chapter Seven

Mecah closed his eyes and allowed his mind to enter hers. He paused and pushed past the anger and multiple tragic memories. He passed the memory of her husband, respecting her privacy, but was unable to avoid the deep sorrow attached to the memory of his death. He moved past it, recognizing the cell he sought where it waited, glowing red. He sensed the rage and fear. Placing himself in a protective shield of light, he entered the memory and jerked involuntarily against the blast of hate.

Quickly, he separated the emotion from the unfolding scene. Nocturnal sounds encased the scene with a cooling breeze drifting from the nearby mountain range. She lay with a man, her husband, beneath a full moon, staring at the brilliant canopy of stars. An open fire crackled in front of them as she snuggled deeper under the blanket, molding her body to his, relaxing after a delicious dinner.

Mecah could taste the succulent flavors of the meal they'd shared. The fullness of the red wine she'd sipped while he'd gone inside to get coffee and dessert filled Mecah's nostrils. She luxuriated in the moment of contentment. Her thoughts slipped from the day's events to the conversation she wanted to have with her husband. The news was exhilarating. She was pregnant!

She had planned the entire evening, waiting for this exact moment to announce it. The sound of the sliding door announced his return. Her heart pounded harder. She ran a trembling hand over her flat stomach, envisioning how it would feel in four months, five, seven...

"This cheesecake is your best." The tall man set the tray beside the suspended bed.

She turned onto her side and smiled.

"You sneaked a taste." Her laughter filled Mecah with love and warmth. He longed to have that smile bestowed upon him.

Suddenly, the night sky flashed with colors. White, blue, red. For a brief moment, darkness burst to brightness, then flashes faded to darkness again. At first she'd thought it was lightning, but a second flash mocked the first, soundless, until the loud boom a few miles away.

"What the hell was that?" The man turned to look out over the dark valley. Another flash, and then an explosion from the valley floor was followed by distant screams.

"Lightning?" Shalene was on her feet, standing by her husband as they peered from their mountaintop haven to the town below. Buildings exploded and nearby homes burst into flames as streaks of light flashed from the dark sky.

"Run!" he yelled as the flashes hit a nearby house only a few feet away. He grabbed her and threw her to the ground, shielding her with his body as their home splintered beneath the powerful laser torpedo. Fire consumed the mountainside.

"Do you see?" Her trembling voice broke his concentration.

His eyelids flew open and he was staring into two liquid pools of pain.

"You speak the truth."

Shalene stood from him. Her palms were clammy. She wrung her hands together, twisting them against the memory, willing it back into the dark recess of numbness.

"I-I had no idea. We've been so wrong to believe the Demrons."

"Did you never question?" she murmured, still in the midst of the memory, trying to distance herself from the resurrected pain.

"We were outnumbered and outarmed. In the beginning we questioned everything, but their methods are extreme. The Demrons threatened to blow up one vessel for every hour I refused to order my troops to surrender. After the first carrier was destroyed, I gave the order. I had the lives of my entire fleet to consider. If we were to die, then it wouldn't be as sitting targets for Demron laser torpedoes. We bide our time until the wormhole returns."

She spun from him, not feeling at all like an interrogator. He came up behind her and slipped his arms around her. Trembling, she tried to pull free, but he turned her around in his embrace and held her. His tenderness stripped Shalene of all resistance. Heated streaks of excitement quaked through her, leaving an intense want in their wake. Desires, long held in rein, suddenly unleashed. She ached for his touch, needing to taste his lips, longing to feel his embrace.

"War means we haven't the luxury of time to woo or seduce according to your race's courtship. But I know you feel it, Shalene." He lifted his hand to brush his fingertips over her lips ever so lightly.

Nervous pulses throbbed in her pussy, setting her clit aching with a frantic need to feel his fingers pressed into her moist heat.

"It lives between us. Ever since that first moment when we met."

"This is insane." She gasped for the breath his nearness stole from her.

"I never thought I'd find my Kismet mate. I've known others who have found theirs. And how I envied their passion. I watched how once their Kismet was acknowledged, it carried them to great happiness. Every aspect of their lives together flourished. I longed for it." He moved to cup her face between his hands. "Eventually, I grew to understand that for me there would be no Kismet. I was resigned yet built a life, a military career, and excelled even without my mate. Unlike other Kyronians, my life was to be a solitary journey. And it has been a good life, granted unfulfilled in the way of Kyronians, but nonetheless a good life—until we were swept into the wormhole."

Her breathing quickened with his scent, a mixture of soap and what must be his own delicious musk filling her nostrils. Like incense, it seeped into her pores and claimed her.

"These past months I've felt remorse. Admonished, even blamed myself, for had I found my Kismet then none of this would have happened. I would not have dedicated myself to a career. Instead, I'd have devoted the energy to my mate and family as I'd expected. My career would have held second place in my life and I would not have been leading the fleet that doomed day. And then I met you." He pressed her against the wall with his hard body.

"Standing there with your laser pistol pointed at me, giving orders and looking so tempting in your leather. A woman warrior, equal to me in every way. A human, yet one trained in the ways of a prober. It was too unique to be circumstance. At that moment I knew I had been wrong. I had not been denied the most basic expectation of all Kyronians. Indeed, my Kismet mate had merely been awaiting my arrival. I was destined to journey through that rogue wormhole just so I could find you—"

"This is crazy!" She pushed against him, but he tightened his embrace.

"Don't you understand? I've waited for you all my life. Now that I've found you—"

"How could you possibly say such a thing? We just met. You know nothing about me." She shoved against him again, and once more he didn't budge under her attempt. Her mind clouded. She couldn't maintain control over her body, a body that wanted only to be possessed by him.

"I know you, Shalene. You let me inside your mind. There's no more intimate an act between two people than the sharing of minds. And when it's accompanied by the sexual act—it's perfection."

"Please stand aside." She attempted to block the overwhelming emotions pouring into her, like waters released from a dam. She'd guarded her heart for so long, not daring to be tempted by the many advances and displays of unwanted affection by fellow survivors. She'd lost everything. She dared not risk finding it again only to lose it a second time.

Mecah tightened his embrace, reveling in the alluring scent rising from her. He inhaled the sweet floral and leather mixture. It had been a long time since he'd been around a woman, especially a prober. The thought of her being his Kismet mate excited him to the edge of self-control He wanted to take her without finishing this game she insisted on playing. Once he'd made love to her, melded with her mind, then she'd know he was her destiny.

"Please." She pushed from him and this time he relented, releasing his grip. She moved across the room with his stare slipping over her tempting curves. Heat pumped in his chest. He needed to touch her, feel her writhe beneath his strokes.

"I thought we'd reached a genuine meeting of the minds. I was looking forward to a little melding later on." His willed his voice to pull her from her fears.

"You're very confident."

"As are you." His thoughts were sizzling with images of her naked lying in his arms and his fingers stroking the hot moistness of her pussy.

"I'm all business, Captain Mecah. Don't think for one moment I'm undertaking this task with any pleasure." She paced in front of him, keeping her stare centered on him.

"Well, damn, you know how to wound a man's ego," he smiled. She met the knowing look in his eyes.

"I thought you were a Kyronian, not a man."

"We call ourselves men and women. We aren't that far apart on the evolutionary scale."

"You think not?"

"God, I sure as hell hope we aren't," he sighed, feeling the sexual energy exude from him. It was not something he could control even if he'd wanted, and smiled at the uncomfortable arousal squirming in her. Her pace quickened.

"I want to talk about the Demrons for a moment." She wrung her hands together. "Tell me about their mother ship."

"Ah…" He paused, taken off guard by the sudden change of topic. He knew she was trying to distract herself and him. "It's a big ship with many functions. What kind of information do you seek?"

"Everything. How many reps are onboard?"

"Close to a million on the mother ship. Probably three times that on the planet's surface."

"My God. I had no idea it was so huge," she said, stealing a glance in his direction.

"They have about fifty thousand human slaves onboard."

She bowed her head, not wanting to think of the plight of her fellow humans captured by the reps.

"They use them for sex."

She put her hand over her mouth as the churning bile rose up her throat.

"Demrons attempt to arouse their prisoners sexually and seduce them. Their seduction techniques turn very sadistic. They also use humans against other humans. Coerce information from new prisoners."

"Stop! I don't want to hear anymore."

"And I guess it's hoping too much that you'll be administering some of their techniques," he asked.

"On the contrary, my orders are to interrogate you thoroughly by whatever means I choose. If our new Rep Training program had undergone final testing, I would activate the program and really torture you," she smirked.

"Voice activation recognized," the computer voice interrupted.

"Oh shit," Shalene realized she'd inadvertently started the new training program.

A hologram of a reptilian soldier flashed in front of her and in spite of herself, Shalene drew her weapon.

"This is pretty damn good. I had no idea you had such advanced technology. Not bad for a bunch of cave people," Mecah laughed. "So how does this work?"

"It's voice-activated and password-driven. Our science team just developed it to prepare the troops in case of capture by the Demrons. It's scheduled for a final test run tomorrow."

"Looks like that scheduling has been changed. I'm familiar with their torture. First they attempt to manipulate you. This is done by giving pleasure followed by deep pain. They condition you to these responses. When you answer their questions correctly, you are rewarded. Is that why you activated the program?" he grinned widely.

"I'm not sure what activated it. Computer. Disengage training module."

"Cannot comply," the female mechanical voice responded.

"Discontinue training module, command code 5354."

"Silence, human!" The Demron hologram, dressed in military armor, carrying a whip in one hand and a laser gun in the other, turned on her.

"Is there some kind of kill switch?" Mecah started toward the panel by the door.

"Shut up," the hologram drew back its arm and struck at him.

Mecah punched at the rep hologram in a reflex reaction.

"Die, you son of a bitch!" He kicked at the hologram's head.

"*You* will die, human." The Demron image punched at Mecah.

"If only it could be more realistic," Shalene chuckled as Mecah struck several martial arts-type blows at the rep. She watched his strong arms bulge in muscled power and release fierce blows to the hologram.

"We use holograms for training in secret. Our holograms manifest enough energy to pack a punch with their blows," he explained.

"Perhaps you'd be willing to share that technology with us later on."

"Perhaps." He sidestepped the Demron's attempt to strike him and stopped in front of her. "I'm more than willing to move past the Demron aspect of this interrogation."

"Computer, heed command code 8959. Disengage training module."

"I'm unable to comply with your command, Commander Courers. Authorization code invalid."

"Perhaps we need a little assistance, Commander. Is there someone you can summon?" He placed his hand on her shoulder.

Delightful sensations tingled where he touched her.

"Get your hand off my slave, human," the rep struck at him.

"Just ignore him." Even though Mecah stood several feet from her, she could feel heated puffs against her ear. How was that possible? Had he mentally thought it and she'd felt it?

"Computer, unlock door."

"Door magnetically sealed. No entry or exit will be allowed during program runtime."

The bulky lizard towered over her.

"Get undressed." The rep hologram folded his arms over his chest.

Heat rose to her cheeks.

"I said strip, slave."

"Computer, skip section."

"Unable to override."

The hologram moved toward her.

"Computer, pause program."

"Unable to comply."

"Computer, reset program."

"Unable to comply."

"I said take off your clothes, slave." The rep suddenly wielded a whip and it sliced through the air, cracking inches from her head. She knew it wasn't real, but it sure sounded real.

"Computer! End program. Code 848898."

"Please repeat."

"End program, verify code 848898," she said, with her voice pitching higher.

"Code not recognized. Please try again."

Mecah burst out laughing. She glared at him and the rep turned on him.

"Do you think this is funny, human?"

"Yeah, I do and I'm Kyronian, fish bait."

"Your insolence will soon be dealt with." The hologram reared back and threw what would have been a powerful blow had he been real.

"Computer, override code 97556," she said, trying the main password.

"Code not recognized."

"I said get undressed." The rep turned to her once more and the jagged slicing of the whip cracked inches from her face. She jumped.

"I want you naked in three seconds."

"Me too!" Mecah laughed.

"Damn it, Captain, you're not helping matters any."

"I'm eager to help. Why don't you do what the program requests? Let it run through to the end."

"Are you serious?" She tapped her COMLink. "Abber, come in."

"Strip!" The rep struck his whip at her again.

Chapter Eight

"Abber? Respond." Static crackled over the headset. "What's going on here?" She walked over to the door and jerked on it.

"Get away from the door."

"Fuck you. I'm not taking off my clothes."

"Then what are we going to do? How long will it take for someone to come looking for you?" Mecah reasoned.

"I'm afraid no one will bother until tomorrow morning." She bit her lower lip.

"And to think I was afraid you were going to leave soon," he said with hope rising in his eyes.

"You're not supposed to think, slave. You do as I command."

"Oh, shut the fuck up!" She struck at the rep.

"Maybe you ought to at least try to appease the command so we can move forward with the programming.

"Computer, end program."

"Unable to comply."

"Damn it." She sat down on the bed.

"Strip first. Then lie down and spread your legs, so the prisoner can see your wet pussy."

"Oh God!" She blushed, having no idea how graphic the program was or what else to expect.

"I like this guy. Please do comply," Mecah groaned.

"Unable to comply," the computer droned.

He burst into a fit of laughter.

"Take off your clothes, slut. Show the prisoner how your nipples have hardened with desire. Comply now!"

She bowed her head, unable to stop the fierce blush covering her body.

"Just take off your vest. That should stimulate the program to move on to the next module. It's worth a try."

"Strip!"

Shalene tapped her COMLink again. "Commander Courers to central. Do you copy?"

"Unable to copy. Please rephrase command."

"Just take the damn vest off," Mecah begged.

"Strip, slave."

She tugged against the lacings of her bustier vest and slowly unlaced them. The leather bustier slipped apart, revealing the deep cleavage of two creamy mounds rising and falling. His stare seared a path between her breasts. She sensed his held breath, knowing he expected them to tumble past the final constraints, but her breasts were fuller than they appeared and pressed against the loosened bustier.

"Continue to strip," the hologram groaned.

"This is getting us nowhere." She flashed a harsh look in Mecah's direction.

"Just try it." He ran his tongue over his lower lip. She was more beautiful than he had imagined. "Oh, come on, you know there's only one way to shut him up. I don't want to spend the next hours listening to him. Do you? Just go through the motions. Maybe he isn't programmed so much to know what you are taking off as how many articles of clothing."

She looked about the room. He followed her gaze to the towel he'd tossed over the bed. She grabbed it and walked over to him.

"What are you doing?" The bulky lizard lumbered toward her.

"If I have to go through this program in order to get it to stop, then you're going to sit there with this over your head." She motioned to the chair. He plopped down and let her pull the towel over his head.

"Uncloak the prisoner now." The rep turned to her.

"I can either strip or uncloak, your choice."

"Strip."

Mecah's laugh was muffled.

"Do you see the female standing in front of you? Do you long to feel her breasts in your hands, suckling them with your lips?"

"Oh yeah," he groaned with liquid fire coursing through his veins to his hardened cock.

"Code alert!"

"Access denied."

"Remove your bra and continue stripping. Music!" the hologram commanded and the slow undulating instrumental droned from the speakers in the ceiling.

"Oh yeah, now that's what I want." Mecah peered through the material, watching her walk over to the door.

She raised her fists and struck against the metal door, but the absorption steel prevented any sound.

"Didn't anyone ever think to install a failsafe?" he asked. She turned to face him, unaware the bustier had slipped and one of her full rounded breasts was now exposed. His breath caught in his chest. Lust and months of abstinence gripped him. Hard.

She planted her hands on her narrow waist, fitting them against the curve of her hips.

The bustier angled with a wider gap and her breast teased him with its dark rosy areola and hardened nipple. He ran his tongue over his lips, longing to capture the sweet nub between his lips and suck it into his mouth, licking and teasing with his tongue.

"Damn it, Computer, end the program."

"Unable to comply."

"Damn this new program. I have no idea how it activated itself."

"Well," he choked, his entire body captivated by her sexy pose, "it does have a few bugs."

She took a step forward and the slight tinges of areola-pink emerged along the gaping bustier. His cock throbbed with a fiery need growing hotter with each movement she made.

"I said to strip, human. Cooperate or I'll see that this lashes against your flesh instead of near your ear." The rep popped the whip over her head.

"Oh, fuck off!" She kicked at his head with her boot, thrusting through the hologram.

The movement freed her other breast and Mecah leaned forward as though the very breath had been knocked from him. He clasped his hands in his lap, longing to touch the two soft mounds and lower his face into their sweetness.

"I said to remove your clothes, slave."

"Damn it!"

"So why not do like he says? Let's get this over with. My head is covered and he's just a hologram." His cock pulsed faster. The need to be inside her quaked in him and he tightened his hands together.

"Slaves don't disobey commands." The whip sliced the air again.

"I've had enough of you."

"Dare you talk back to me? Kneel before your conqueror."

"I'm going to kill Abber and whoever helped him program this module."

She jerked off the bustier and tossed it to the floor. Her nipples tightened against the cooler air and she stared at Mecah. His breathing was labored. Her breasts heaved with each angry breath. He longed to cup the rosy-tipped breasts in his hands and capture the erect nubs between his lips. Closing his eyes, he groaned, almost able to taste their sweetness in his mouth.

"Now the pants." The rep hologram turned and leered at her.

"Please, take the towel off my head, lizard-man," Mecah begged.

"Shut up." The lizard slammed an invisible punch at him.

"Take off your boots and then your pants, now!"

Mecah heard the loud crack of the whip and the sound of her weight on the cot. Once more he pierced his vision beyond the material and was rewarded with a vision that set him scorching. Liquid heat pumped through his body. The need to fuck her was stronger than any need he'd ever experienced.

Watching the two boots fall to the floor, his pulse sharpened. It was agonizing to just sit there so he closed his eyes, willing himself not to look. Seeing through a towel was child's play to someone who could see beneath layers of earth. If she knew he had such an ability —

"Now remove your pants," the hologram demanded.

The sound of the zipper ripped through him, carrying visions to his mind, and in spite of his vow to not peep, his eyes flew open. She stood by the bed, her full breasts perfect, needing to be suckled by him. Mecah licked his lips again.

She slipped her hands beneath the waistline. His breath was hot against the terry-cloth. He watched as she slipped her hands deeper inside the pants and slowly pulled the black leather down and over her hips. Shifting in the chair, Mecah clasped his hands until white-knuckled.

Slowly she wiggled and pushed the pants down her long slender thighs. The dark tuft between her legs sent his pulse throbbing. He tried to resist but his stare traveled the path of the neatly trimmed thin center line that stopped just above the slit of her pussy.

His cock pounded with the building need, aching for release. Still unaware he could see her, she stepped from the pants and stood with her hands planted firmly on her narrow waist once more, this time affording him a full frontal view of her strong body. Her long legs were contoured and slender. He groaned. His erection ached for her touch. The foreskin stretched and pulled down his shaft as his cock tightened and pressed against the material of his pants.

"Yes, you are very beautiful naked," the hologram moaned.

"Oh, this is too gross. Just shut up!" She folded her arms beneath her breasts, lifting their white softness higher, tempting Mecah beyond control. He closed his eyes, blocking out her naked beauty. Sweat broke out along his spine and rolled down his back.

"Lie down."

Mecah heard the bed give under her and lifted his head again, despising himself for stealing glances at her but unable to resist the temptation. It had been so long since he had seen a naked woman, much less made love to one. Holograms could satisfy only so much. He released a ragged breath.

"I will now lash your wrists and legs. Spread them."

She lay with her arms angled from her body toward the bedposts and slowly spread her legs. Mecah bit the insides of his mouth to keep from groaning out loud for he sat directly across from her.

She opened her legs slightly. He fidgeted in the chair with his heart hammering out his excitement. She spread wider, revealing a shaven pussy. It glistened in front of him, a perfect rounded mound, tempting him as nothing else in the universe could tempt him. The tender slit opened more and his breath lodged in his chest. He twisted his hands together, struggling to keep from jumping from the chair and taking her.

The lizard hologram moved over to her and reached down to stroke her pussy.

"See, human, I can have her anytime I want. You, on the other hand, can only watch."

The scaly hand moved up her body to her breasts where his ghostlike hands attempted to squeeze a nipple.

She was quiet and lay looking at Mecah. Was she probing his mind? He quickly activated his mental shields. It was a struggle to drag his attention from her pose to protect his thoughts.

"I am the one who will fuck her, human. Not you." The lizard unwrapped the leather kilt about his waist and freed his large erection.

"That's enough!" Shalene slid from the bed, moving through the lizard. "Computer, abort program."

"Command recognized."

"What?" She spun around, unable to believe the command had worked.

The hologram faded.

Disappointed that the drill was over but relieved he didn't have to watch the lizard hologram violate her, Mecah sighed. He'd have taken her if for no other reason than to keep from having to watch the Demron.

"What happened?" Mecah asked, reaching for the towel.

"No. Don't remove it. Not yet," her voice trembled. Guilt seized him for having violated her, watching her without her knowledge.

She hurried over to the edge of the bed and grabbed the sheet, but stopped a few feet from him. Her stare dropped to his lap. Lifting his head, Mecah looked up at her. She stood naked in front of him. Her breasts heaved as realization washed over her face and she snatched the sheet, wrapping it around her.

"What are you doing?" she glared at him.

"Waiting for you to tell me when I can remove the towel."

"You...have other abilities...don't you, Captain?" she asked.

"Like what? May I remove this towel?" He didn't wait for her approval and jerked it off, tossing it to the floor.

"Like the ability to see through solid matter?" she glared at him.

He tilted his head and jerked a nod, feeling her embarrassment as his own.

"I apologize. It wasn't intentional. Well, at first it was."

"You're no better than the rest of them." She hung her head.

"You're right. I'm not. I'm besotted by you. I don't blame you for hating me, but didn't you…I mean, wasn't there a part of you that knew? Suspected?"

"That you were actually watching me undress and spread myself before you?"

He nodded and stood from the chair. His erection tented his pants as he walked over to her. She turned, but his hand closed around her wrist.

"I just want to talk."

"Do you think peeping at me like that is something I find arousing instead of violating?" She clutched the sheet tighter.

He gathered her into his embrace, but she pressed her hands against his chest.

"It's not like you think it is, Shalene. I tried to explain it to you earlier and you scoffed at me. But I know you feel it too. You do."

"Kismet?" she jeered.

"You will see." He whispered in her ear, letting his lips brush the delicate tender skin as his heated breath fell down her neck.

"Leave me alone!" She pushed against him, and this time he released her. "You don't have any women in your crew. Do you?"

"No. But that wouldn't matter. Not just any woman would do. It has to be you."

"Save it for someone who'll believe your poetic words." Her legs were weak-kneed and threatened to collapse beneath her. He was a stranger! An alien! What had she been thinking? Rage replaced confusion.

She would get dressed and leave. She had all the information she needed. There was no getting through the rest of the interrogation when all she could think about was the way his body felt against hers and how he'd been watching her. She tried to will herself someplace else. Her embarrassment was greater because she'd wanted him to see her spread herself in front of him. Somehow the pretense that he could not see had steeled her to do the thing she longed to do most.

"Our ways are simple when it comes to our mates. We believe each of us has one person destined to be our mate for life. As I explained, I never found mine. I sought her. I could feel her. All my life I felt her presence, out there, somewhere, but she never showed up. Until—"

"Until you saw me?" She couldn't keep the sarcasm from dripping from her words.

"Why do you find that so difficult to believe?"

"It's convenient. Don't you think?"

"For what?"

"For infiltration. For spying."

"For what purpose?"

"To turn us over to the Demrons."

"And were that my intent, would I not have done so by now? What would have prevented me from communicating with my ships and sending attack coordinates? This ore sprayed on the walls? It might work for human probers, but not for Kyronians."

She didn't answer.

"If you really want to know the truth, Shalene, then do a mind blend with me."

"H-How?" She surprised herself. Could she really do such a thing?

"Before when you allowed me to seek the truth about the beginning of the war, you granted me access to one memory."

She nodded.

"With a mind blend, our minds will meld together as one mind. It's painless, but it's intense. It's the only way you'll fully believe my sincerity, and during the process I will be unable to block you entry into any of my memories or thoughts and vice versa."

She looked up at him, taking in his handsome face and plaited blond hair. Hesitancy pulsed from her, encasing him.

"It's all I can offer as proof of my sincerity."

Chapter Nine

Shalene knew he had respected her privacy during the mind link and believed him trustworthy in spite of watching her strip.

"Let's do it," she agreed.

"Good." He lifted his hand to stroke the curve of her face.

"Let's sit on the bed, facing each other." He sat down, crossing his legs with his hands poised on his knees. The cot was hard as she sat down, mimicking his posture.

"First you must remove this," he reached over and before she knew what he was doing, removed her helmet, tossing it onto the bed.

Her hair cascaded past her shoulders and down her back.

"You are so beautiful." He sighed heavily and closed his fingers into a hard fist, then resumed the meditative position. She sensed his longing to touch her hair. His unmasked arousal made her blush.

"Match my breath," he instructed, holding her stare captive with his fiery, dark plum eyes.

"Slower," he took a deep breath and held it. She copied him.

"Now lift your hands in front of you, palms facing me."

He lifted his in front of hers. The tingling sensation along her fingertips grew. His hands emanated an energy field similar to opposite magnets repelling each other.

"Slowly, allow my hands to touch yours." His hands were strong and rough. She marveled at the way his flesh felt. Good. Familiar. The current shocked through her like a jagged bolt of lightning. His fingers interlaced with hers and the surge of energy increased.

"Open your mind, Shalene. Allow me entry." His voice was deep and soothing.

She struggled to lower her mental shield just as a brilliant light struck her third eye, opening it wide. Streams of purple light entered through the opening and filled her mind.

Vignettes of landscapes, a lake-house, children playing, music, aromas of freshly baked bread, all filled her to overflowing. She saw him as a child, strong and curious. And as he grew, felt his constant longing. Others got married and Mecah watched, longing for his own mate. The clothing reminded her of medieval and yet held a flare of futuristic styling. Celtic-like knots adorned sleeves and hems, even furniture. Suddenly, she was onboard the starship. Mecah stood at the helm, staring into a black hole that had emerged from nowhere. It turned blue and whirled as it gained strength. She heard the shouts and orders. She sensed overwhelming confusion as one by one the ships were dragged into the powerful field of energy and then silence. Earth lay before the ships and the orbiting Demron mother ship was attacking.

Emotions bombarded her as she moved through the months with Mecah, knowing his every thought. And then she saw herself, through his eyes as she stood over him in the camp. The sensation struck her like a thunderbolt. Just like ancient tales of love at first sight, only this was more. It was Kismet!

She released his hands and slid from the bed, running her hand through her hair. The air latched in her lungs. She needed fresh air. She needed distance from him.

"What is it?" he asked, coming to stand beside her, drawing her into his embrace. "You're shivering." He drew her tighter against him.

"It was too intense, Mecah. Too much information. Too many emotions."

"But did you see the truth you sought?"

"Oh yes." She lifted her face to his. "I saw you, Mecah. You were telling the truth." She reached up and touched his face.

"It truly is Kismet, Shalene," he whispered and lowered his face to hers, letting his lips brush hers while his hand cradled the back of her head.

The taste of his lips against hers was exciting and yet at the same time comforting. She needed to taste more of him and ran her hand over his blond hair and down the tight braid. Her fingers longed to free his hair from the plait, but instead she trailed her fingers to his neck and drew her arms around him. She pressed her lips harder into his. Her mind filled with his silent words of endearment. Could this be true? Could he be the man fated to be hers? She broke from his kiss, searching his face. His eyes opened wide and she found the truth in their depths, once more.

"I never thought it possible," she murmured and slipped back into his kiss, spreading her lips to receive his tongue. She greeted his entry, lashing her tongue around his, moving in response to his feverish passion, allowing herself to fall deeper into his possession.

"Shalene," he whispered against their kiss and lifted her into his arms, carrying her to the bed where he lowered her, pressing kisses against her throat.

She moaned, wanting to feel him inside her. His hands were warm and strong as he undid the folded sheet, pulling it open. She lay fully exposed to his slow appreciative gaze. His hands traveled over her smooth skin, cupping a breast, massaging it, rubbing her nipple with the tip of his finger, then pinching it tenderly. Jagged streaks of hot pleasure throbbed to her clit each time his fingers squeezed against a nipple.

She moaned against their kiss, kneading his back with her fingers. His lips slipped from hers and he trailed kisses down her neck to her breasts. The taste of her nipples between his lips sent him into a frenetic need to free himself of his clothing, yet he was under a spell and could not break free. He wanted to touch her, taste her, make her his. Forever. Her hands moved over him, freeing him of the shirt. Gentle strokes massaged his chest and moved to trail lingering strokes down his muscled back.

"Hurry please," she whispered in his ear.

Incited, he wasted no time ridding himself of the trousers and pressed kisses against her ivory flesh over her abdomen to her wet lips that begged for his kisses. She moved her hips, positioning her pussy for his touch.

His fingers parted the slit and his mouth covered her mound, sucking and drawing her clit between his lips. She gasped and moved her hips in a frantic rhythm, needing more, demanding more. Her heat flexed and her juices rushed between her legs, preparing her for his penetration. Instead, he flicked his tongue and lashed against her hardened clit, drawing her hips higher to meet his touch. His tongue teased her opening, probing and pressing into her.

Slowly, he lifted from her to stare down at her. Her eyes were glazed with passion.

"You belong with me now, Shalene. You are mine." He lifted his hand and plunged his forefinger and middle finger into his mouth, then slipped them into her pussy.

Do you enjoy watching me, she thought.

Most definitely, he sighed. "Let me in your mind." He moved closer in her thoughts.

She moaned as he finger-fucked her, lowering his mouth to suckle her wet heat. She moved against the rhythm of his tongue, moaning as the jolts of pleasure shot through her. The walls of her pussy clamped around his fingers, gripping him deeper inside as he flicked his tongue over her clit, sucking in her juices as she came in hard, gripping spasms. She cried out in her release and he lifted from her, pulling his fingers from her opening, only to plunge them deep inside again. He watched her writhe under his strokes. His heart swelled with a joy unchallenged by any memory. To this point in his existence, he had lived in a fog, seeking the other half of himself. He trailed his hand up her abdomen to lightly brush her breasts, then dipped over to capture a cherry nub between his lips, sucking and nibbling just enough to draw a soft groan from her.

Looking up from hooded eyes, Shalene watched him. He held his cock in his hand and stroked the scorching need. He could read her thoughts, feel her arousal as fire burst and raged to her pussy. She wanted to feel him inside her. The thought excited him. She writhed under him as he mounted her and slipped his cock into her soft heat, slowly at first until she wrapped her legs around his waist and grabbed his buttocks, pushing herself against his cock. He must have her! She ground her hips faster, undulating and meeting each thrust as he fucked her harder and harder.

He pressed his hands onto the mattress and pounded his cock into her pussy. The slapping of his balls against her echoed in the stark room and her passion burst with the pulsing of her clit and the clenching walls of her pussy around his large cock. He thrust deeper and drove her beyond the orgasm to another height of renewed passion.

Frenetic, urgent excitement pushed her hips into him and ground her need as she drew against his length and forced her hips higher. She rocked with him, digging her fingers into his muscled shoulders as he pounded his cock into her. She gasped for breath as the new surge of hot edgy need consumed her. She showered his face with kisses, nibbling his forearm, circling her tongue in teasing patterns around his shoulder and arm. She knew his taste, knew his touch.

Anticipation snaked up her spine and lingered, rising higher, retreating, then rising higher once more. His sweat mingled with hers. His back grew hot with beads of sweat popping over his skin. She cried out. Intense pleasure carried her to the very edge of orgasm and lingered, tempting her and fleeing from her attempts to come. She gripped his back and thrust her hips into each new plunge of his cock.

Shards of heat and bliss broke free and she jerked against the powerful orgasm, clenching his cock inside her until he groaned, shuddering as he came at the same time. His heat spilled in a rush. He captured her lips once more as he thrust one last time, long and deep with his cock throbbing inside her. She sighed, feeling more complete than she knew was possible.

"Listen to me, my new love," he whispered in her ear with his breath searing against her flesh. "You are my Kismet. Nothing will ever change that. You and you alone now own my heart from this moment forward."

"Mecah." She grasped his tanned face between her hands and kissed him tenderly at first, then harder. Her fingers trailed the length of his blond plait.

He lifted, pulling her head onto his chest as he settled onto the pillows.

"I know your pain, my love. You're afraid to allow yourself to believe love could find you a second time." He placed a tender kiss on her forehead, stroking her head, losing his fingers in her thick curls.

"I've never dared believe there was a man fated to be with me."

"And here I am," he chuckled, nuzzling her hair. She shifted to lie on top of his chest, resting her chin on her hands to stare into his face.

"So you are," she whispered.

He held her face between his hands and planted short, gentle kisses on her lips. She giggled and drew her arms around his neck, turning and pulling him back on top of her. He supported himself on his arms and scattered kisses along the column of her neck and to her breasts.

His lips closed over a tightened nipple and sucked it into his mouth, flicking his tongue over the rosy nub. The fiery urgency to fuck him stoked within her again. She lifted from the bed and pushed him onto his back. Kneeling between his legs, she held his cock between her hands and massaged with hard strokes, lowering her mouth to his shaft. She took him inside with lips gripping and tongue flickering over his tip. She quickened the strokes, tightening her lips around his cock as she plunged him deeper into her mouth and out again. She couldn't taste him enough, feel him enough.

His hands grabbed her head and held her firm to receive each thrust. With one hand, she tightened her fingers around the base of his cock while cupping his balls, massaging gently, letting her forefinger find the tender spot just behind them. His groan was one of deep pleasure and she massaged harder.

It was true. Her heartbeat pounded in her ears. He was her Kismet!

She slipped his cock in and out of her mouth, feeling the heat surge in his body as she drove him beyond all control. Feeling him move with each lash of her tongue against his cock sent shivers of excitement through her. She quickened the rhythm. He grunted and looked down at her, then reared back.

She drew the foreskin over the top of his cock, only to pull it back with a rapid stroke. The creamy white seeped from the reddish slit and she lowered her mouth to lap his come. This incited him. He grabbed her by the shoulders and lifted her by the hips, setting her down onto his erect cock.

She quickly guided him into her and met each thrust with one of her own. His hands cupped her breasts as she rocked forward, lifting her hips slightly and pulling the length of his cock, teasing, then lowering onto him until his length plunged into the depths of her hot pussy. His fingers bit into her flesh as he held her down, as though afraid she'd dismount. She rode him, pulling his cock in and out of her pussy with each titillating movement.

"Shalene," he moaned and quickened his thrusts. Pressing her hands against his chest, she traced imaginary circles through his auburn chest hair. His breathing was hard and short. His muscles tightened and his coloring darkened as he pumped his cock into her.

His fingers slipped over her abdomen and found the warm, creamy moistness and pressed harder into the fierce melting sensation.

She rolled her hips and rocked against him, grinding into his urgent thrusts, clenching the walls of her pussy around his steel cock. Never wanting to let him go. He gripped her hips and his body went rigid. She felt his release as though it were her own, sensing his pleasure in the orgasm. He groaned and liquid heat burst inside her, filling her with his come. Hot air rushed between his clenched teeth. Spasms racked his powerful body. His cock pulsed inside her.

His cream pumped inside her. The edgy need for release throbbed to her clit. She wiggled against him, willing the energy to snake up her back and beyond the teasing tip of orgasm. Inching heat rose higher, then retreated, then rose again with each movement until it shot past the teasing rhythm and burst into pleasurable spasms, writhing her body in brilliant climax.

She sat on top of him, shuddering, enjoying the undulating throbs raking her body and his. Their stares locked. He drew her deep into his thoughts. Warmth and love welcomed her as she slipped into his mind and found herself waiting as though having been there always, but unrecognized. The moment was endless, yet new. He drew her down onto the mattress with him and held her, planting kisses over her face.

"There's something I need to ask you," she whispered, her breath fanning in hot puffs against his neck.

"What is it?" he asked.

"During our mind meld. I bumped into a thought, well, more of a fear."

"Yes?"

"You're concerned that to love me is sacrilege. There's a law that states if one claims Kismet with a non-Kyronian, then you'll be disowned by your family and exiled from your world.. Is that true?"

"If you're a purist and believe there's only one way to happiness and one way to Kismet."

"And what way is this?"

"The right way," he chuckled.

"Is it against the law of your people?"

"You are not to worry."

"But if your people believe this, then once we've defeated the Demrons, your people will live here, in my world, and to do so will mean they must accept our Kismet."

"And as with all things in life, change is inevitable, my love."

"That's nice, but it's not practical. Is it?"

"Perhaps not." He rested against a pillow and gathered her into his arms once more, cradling her and stroking her hair. "It doesn't matter to me, Shalene. Do you understand? Kismet is sacred. It's a birthright for all Kyronians to find their Kismet mate. No one can tell you who that mate is. Kismet does.

"I've been an enigma to my own race, my very culture, until now. I'd given up all hope of ever laying claim to my destiny and then you showed up, dressed in your leather pants, pointing a laser pistol at me, and I was thunderstruck. At long last I knew what others had experienced, what they had found. It required crossing over a million light-years of galaxies to find you. Do you think I'd allow anything to prevent me from claiming you as my eternal mate?"

"It's just…well, it's all happened so fast, Mecah."

"What is time's relevancy to destiny when you recognize the soul you meet? It's all you need to know. To know you will love me now and tomorrow is all the truth there is in my universe. Anything else are merely restrictions placed upon the soul by those who believe control is the remedy to distrust. They believe control balances all things, but that belief is an illusion."

She snuggled against him. If only she could be so clear about things.

"You have been trained that relationships take a certain course, a certain amount of time. Your culture has rituals such as courtships, dating, and many more that my culture does not practice."

"But what about our immediate problems? How do we handle our Kismet in the midst of a war?"

"We handle it by not handling it, Shalene. We let it be what it is and do what we must. It's very simple."

"I don't know if I can compartmentalize my life that way."

"It is not compartmentalizing. It's acceptance that all things are connected and all things are destined to be what they are. It's a simplistic approach to life, but one based upon profound truths. Promise you'll try it?"

She nodded.

"Now, tell me, what did your general hope to gain by my seduction?"

Chapter Ten

A bleeping sound pierced the room and it took Shalene a moment to realize it was the door.

"That's Abber." She climbed out of bed, dragging the sheet with her, and pressed the wall intercom.

"Leave it outside the door, Abber," she called, feeling the rush of red flashing over her face.

"Is everything okay, Commander?"

"Yes, Abber. I don't need anything further. I'll see you in the morning."

"Are you sure?"

"Yes." She clicked the intercom off and rested her head against the door, feeling embarrassed and overjoyed. She wanted to tell Abber how wonderful love was, yet at the same time worried what he would think of her. It had not taken an hour to crush her resistance. And yet in that span of time, so much had been revealed. She didn't feel like the same person.

"What did he leave by the door?" Mecah asked from where he lay in the bed.

She glanced back at him. He lay poised with one leg bent, supporting his arm. She let her stare move slowly over him, taking in his sexy body with the appreciation of a lover. The pose he'd unconsciously struck with his long legs with well-defined thighs, revealing a warrior's strength. His cock lay against his thigh, and even in repose made her eyes widen. How had she taken such a large cock into her? Her pulse and her breath quickened.

Needing to distract herself, she hit the series of numbers and the door opened. She stared at the metal cart of food, feeling absurd, reminded of a life destroyed forever when room service and vacations were commonplace. She pulled the cart into the room and slammed the door, the automatic lock clicking into place.

"What's this? A feast?" He swung his legs over the bed.

"Wine." She held up the bottle. "Do you have it on your world?"

"We call it nectar." He walked over to her.

"Hmm. I like that." She reached out and let her fingertips brush his chest. The patch of fine hair tickled her fingers as she traced the narrow line to his waist and cock. She wrapped her fingers around him and he moaned, nuzzling her while encircling her with his arms. "Shall we eat?" she asked.

"I would rather eat you," he whispered in her ear.

She lifted her lips to his kiss. Again, his mind opened and received her inside the safety of loving thoughts. It was unlike any experience she'd ever known. She longed to feel his fingers massaging her clit and no sooner had she thought it, his hand trailed down her back and cupped her buttocks, then glided across her thigh to her pussy.

Her sharp intake of breath fanned against his kiss.

You see how convenient it is to know your mate's thoughts? he asked.

I am discovering just how much, she thought.

He slid from the kiss, leaving a small peck on her lips and held her at arm's length.

I love you, Shalene. His eyes pooled with tears and she heard his thoughts, *I love you, I love you, I love you! So long I have waited to find you so I could tell you.*

Oh Mecah. She lifted on tiptoes to kiss him, drowning in the pool of warm sensations.

I love you, too, my sexy spaceman.

He chuckled under her kiss and pulled away.

"Spaceman?"

"Yeah, *my* spaceman."

"Perhaps I should reveal my special lovemaking talents to you that only a spaceman knows."

"Hmm. That sounds divine."

"Do you have an antigravity chamber on the base?"

"No," she frowned, feeling deprived of what sounded like an exciting experience.

"Never mind." He picked her up and Shalene thought he was taking her back to bed. Instead, he spread her legs and pulled them around his hips.

Heat and steel scorched her belly and she glanced down at his erection.

"Spaceman seems ready for takeoff." She nuzzled his neck.

"There's no time for a countdown."

Take my cock and put it inside you, he thought.

She slipped her hand around him. He was hot with juices trickling around her fingers as she moved her hand up and down his cock.

"You're a tease," he leaned over and flicked his tongue against her ear.

"And you're a very virile man, Captain." She glanced up and met his lustful stare. Fire scorched a path to her pussy. She guided him into her opening, lifting her hips so he could slip inside.

She moaned and clasped her hands behind his head, locking her lips to his once more.

You belong to me, forever.

Shalene wasn't sure if it was his thought or hers and ground against him.

I can't wait. I need you now. He supported her in his arms and carried her to the cot. His cock slipped out of her as he lowered her on the edge of the mattress.

Lift your legs.

He grabbed her by the ankles and pulled her legs over her head, exposing her pussy to him as he bent over her, ramming his cock into her. Urgency drove him, and Shalene locked her ankles around his neck as he pounded his cock into her pussy, driving her to the edge of climax with each thrust. Her fingertips trailed over her abdomen to her pussy, and she stroked her clit, pressing her fingers deeper into her flesh, rubbing faster, keeping tempo with him.

"Ah…" Mecah groaned. His body went rigid against the ejaculation, pumping hot come into her. Spasms gripped her and her pussy throbbed, clamping around his hot, pulsing cock.

"We call that a quickie," she whispered and unlocked her ankles, bending her legs so his broad shoulders were sandwiched between them.

"We use the word mad to describe someone who is insane," he propped himself on rigid flexed arms.

"So do we."

"Then you shall understand our term for your quickie. We call it the mad burn." He leaned down and captured her lips in a deep consuming kiss.

* * * * *

The pounding crashed around them.

"What is it?" he asked, rising onto his elbow, slipping from her.

"Commander Courers!" The shout sounded from the other side of the door.

"Awake, my love," Mecah stroked her hair from her face and she squinted up at him.

"Commander Courers!" the voice boomed and instantly paradise faded, replaced by the dread of facing her troops. They would know how she had spent the night—

"It doesn't matter, love. It's Kismet," he handed her the bustier and pulled on his pants just as another bang resounded.

"Open up the damn door!" General Jacob ordered. Her pulse spiked and she swung her legs over the edge of the bed. Retrieving her pants, she struggled to pull them on while realizing she needed to lace the vest.

Mecah slipped the T-shirt over his head.

"He sounds angry," he laughed and came over to help her lace the vest. His nimbleness surprised her. As she zipped her pants, he finished the last lacing, tying it in place.

"There, now let me see your beautiful face." He tilted her chin and planted a wet kiss on her cheek. "You're good to go, Commander." He ran his hand through her hair and turned her toward the door, giving her ass a playful smack with his hand.

She giggled and walked to the door with bare feet slapping the cold floor.

"Commander Courers, are you okay? Commander?" The general's tone seemed genuinely concerned. Served him right.

What had he been thinking by putting his top officer in a sealed room with the enemy?

Surprised how clearly she heard his thoughts, she glanced over her shoulder at her sexy captain. He stood with his arms over his head, plaiting his long blond hair.

"I can do that for you," she sighed, longing to feel the strands in her hands.

"Answer the door. All his guilty thoughts are giving me a headache." He frowned and finished the last few twists.

Shalene retrieved an elastic band from her pants pocket and caught her hair into a ponytail.

"Commander—"

"One moment, General, I was asleep," she yawned and cast a worried look at Mecah. He held up his thumb and sat down in the nearby chair.

"Open this damn door now, Commander," he ordered, his voice edged with anger.

She smiled slightly, hearing his thoughts of worry that she had done exactly what she had done last night. Keying in the code, the door clicked open and she stepped back as it swung open.

The general stomped into the room, red-faced and huffing with his narrowed glare flashing from her to Mecah. The look in his eyes mirrored the thoughts rambling in his mind. He knew what had happened when he looked at the rumpled bed.

"Grab your gear and both of you meet me in my office." He turned on his heel and stomped from the room.

"Follow me, Captain. My general waits to speak with you," Abber spoke from the hall.

"Abber," she greeted him, sitting down on the bed to pull on her boots.

"Do you need any assistance?" Mecah winked at her.

"No, thank you. Go ahead with Abber. I'll join you directly."

* * * * *

When she entered the general's cubicle, she found Mecah seated across from his desk. He stood when she entered the room. The general's scowl darkened at the obvious change between them.

"Join us, Commander." He motioned to the chair.

Mecah remained standing until she sat down. The general's irritation shone in his eyes and he looked away from her, motioning for Mecah to retake his seat.

"You're in a unique position, Captain Mecah," General Jacob spoke, but anger bubbled just beneath his stern expression.

"How is that, General?" He settled back into the chair.

"You have knowledge of both the reps and us. That places us at the disadvantage and you in a place of control."

"I don't have any need for control."

"The reps deceived the Kyronians into believing we invaded the Demron home-planet, General. The Kyronians are biding their time until the wormhole returns." Shalene met General Jacob's angry glare.

"My people want only one thing — to return to our home world."

"Then perhaps we can assist you in accomplishing that."

"How could we do that?" Panic seized her, cutting off the air in her lungs. Mecah leave? She hadn't thought it possible. She flashed a worried look at him and he reached out and clasped her hand. The gesture seemed to provoke the general and he cleared his throat.

His thoughts were a mass of shouting and cussing. She could barely understand him and forced his thoughts from her.

"Our scientists could assist the captain's science team in secret."

"That's very generous, General. Perhaps we could stage my escape and when I return to active duty with the Demron S and D squad, I could assist you in your sabotage."

"If they'd believe your escape to be real," Shalene spoke up, and regretted it when Mecah glanced at her. Allowing him entry into her mind had made her vulnerable to him and weakened her ability to be objective. He was stronger than any prober she'd ever met. And yet, she longed to embrace him, allow him access to her mind and feel his presence inside her, always.

"I don't read you, Commander," he smiled, letting her know he could in fact hear all her worries and concerns.

"Reps are known for their distrustful nature. They don't even trust each other, so you'll be subjected to interrogation to ascertain the truth of your story."

Your interrogation is the only one I want. He smiled.

"They have their ways, but I'm stronger-minded." He turned so only she could see his face and winked at her.

Shalene gritted her teeth. He apparently felt there was no need for professional decorum between them since he'd walked around inside her mind and spent endless hours making love to her. Well, he would quickly realize that was not the case. She lifted her chin slightly and squared her shoulders, purposefully ignoring him and directing her comments to the general.

"I don't doubt that Captain Mecah has incredible abilities, sir. My point is that even strong minds like Captain Mecah might need reinforcement. I'm offering my services when the time comes for him to escape. I'll avail myself to a mind bond to help boost his defenses."

"Is that possible?" the General asked Mecah, ignoring her completely.

"Yes, sir, it is," she spoke, not waiting for Mecah to respond.

"That's a very generous offer, Commander, but I have an entire fleet of probers. It's as common to my species as breathing is to yours. So if I need a boost, I have my entire people to give it to me."

Why you ungrateful alien! she seethed.

Hey, no need to get nasty. I appreciate the offer, but I'm not willing to risk your life.

Oh, you're pissing me off now! I'm a warrior, not some babe you need to protect.

"Commander?" The general's voice pierced their mental tête-à-tête.

"Sir?"

"What of the escape plan? Can we assure Captain Mecah's safe return to the mother ship?"

"Yes, sir." Her mind whirled.

"I'm anxious to get a plan in place so we can get started," Mecah grinned and mentally kissed her on the forehead.

Glancing up at the general, she ignored the obvious question in his eyes. She didn't owe him any explanations. Her heart skipped a beat at the thought of Mecah. Her Kismet mate. She bit the insides of her mouth to keep from smiling from the overwhelming joy that burst through her.

I love you. His voice sounded as though he were whispering in her ear.

"I'd like permission to accompany Captain Mecah."

No! Mecah shouted mentally.

"What?" The general came to his feet. "Are you insane?

"Please hear me out, General. I have a plan, a way to regain the Blue Crystal."

He tilted his head to one side and considered her request.

"That's daring, isn't it?"

"I've been thinking about this plan for some time, General. I will return with Captain Mecah as his prisoner. He and his men will help me recover the Blue Crystal, steal me off the mother ship and transport me to the Guardian Temple. Once I replace the Blue Crystal in its proper place, the enemy will be destroyed. It shouldn't harm the Kyronians."

"That is a complicated plan, Commander, and would require great coordination."

"Listen to me, General. This plan will work."

"What guarantees do you have that the Kyronians, that Captain Mecah can protect you long enough to allow you to accomplish all this?"

I won't agree to this! Mecah shouted.

"There are no guarantees in anything, sir. This is what I want to do. We won't have this kind of opportunity ever again. I'm qualified. I know what the Blue Crystal looks like and I know how to activate it."

I will not risk you, Shalene!

"Please, General, it could mean the end of the war! The end of the reps. We could reclaim our planet and begin rebuilding." She avoided Mecah's look and blocked out his mental shouting.

"It's tempting, but it's a foolhardy mission, at best. If the Kyronians don't agree."

And we won't!

"They will. Captain Mecah already has assured me," she lied. She would convince him later. Right now she needed the general's permission.

"Captain Mecah? Do you believe there's a chance of success?"

She looked at him, mentally pleading with him.

"I don't agree with the risk to Commander Courers."

"It's not up to the captain. It's my decision and you have the final say, General. It's our only last hope of regaining our planet. You have to say yes."

Don't do this, my beloved, Mecah pleaded.

I would not ask you to stay here if you had the opportunity to return your men to their home world. Don't ask me to give up the only chance to save mine. You said it was simple. Our Kismet remains and we do what we must, she countered.

"Very well, then, what do you need?" the general asked.

* * * * *

Mecah watched the way her hips swayed slightly with her gait. Everything about her made his heart pump harder. She was the embodiment of all he'd ever sought in a female. She glanced over at him and he grinned widely, leaning in to whisper, "You have the cutest little ass." He enjoyed the way her cheeks splotched red as she strapped on the helmet.

"Your training program has a few bugs in it, Abber," she said as they headed toward the chute.

"What kind of bugs?" Anxiousness grated his words.

"Oh, just that it started on its own and wouldn't respond to command. And locked us inside the training room."

"Oh no," he blushed. "What did you do?"

"We went through the entire program, Abber, that's what we did." She smiled at the rush of red that raced over his entire body.

"See that you fix it," she nodded.

Mecah zipped up the camouflage vest and turned to smile at her.

Her spirit soared when she met his gaze.

I wish you'd change your mind. He mentally pulled her into his arms and planted a teasing kiss on her lips. A kiss she could almost feel.

I have my orders and I will proceed with or without your help.

I don't doubt it.

He stopped in the tunnel and jerked her around to face him.

"The Demrons kill their prisoners but only after hours of torture, and it won't be the sexual game we played," he whispered as the team continued up the chute.

She jerked free of him and took brisk strides through the gate. "I'm counting on you and your men to keep that from happening."

"We can't." He was by her side, stopping in front of her to block her path.

"Please don't make this difficult."

"I can't let you do this, Shalene. I didn't just find you to turn around and lose you."

"I'm counting on that." She lifted her hand and stroked his cheek, letting her fingertips brush the length of his strong jawline. "How closely guarded is your ship?"

"Pretty damn guarded. All departures and arrivals go through the Demron mother ship before being transported to the fleet."

"That's perfect."

"The hell it is."

"With your help and that of your men, my plan will work."

"The hell it won't. This plan is crazy! Let me go back and gather information. Together we can present a solid front and then plan this mission of yours, whatever it is."

"There's no time. This is a perfect opportunity. There won't be another situation like this where you can take me onboard as a prisoner."

"I don't care."

"Mecah, don't you see what's going on in my world? We're dying. We can't spare the woman power to have children. The human race is going to die unless we upset the balance of power."

Are you all right, Captain? the stranger's voice blasted in her head.

I'm well, Lieutenant, stand by, Mecah replied.

"What was that?"

"My lieutenant. You can now pick up on our wave as a result of our mind blend."

"So is this like a collective consciousness?"

"Sort of."

She grabbed the first rung of the chute, but Mecah grabbed her by the waist and pulled her into his arms, slamming her against his hard body.

"Please, my love, don't go through with this. Don't endanger your life so callously."

"It's not callous. It's war and the one great hope to save my world. If you delay returning to the Demrons, they'll never believe your escape story. We need to do this now."

He stroked her face and tilted the helmet back on her head so she could receive his kiss. His lips melted against hers and the need to feel his naked body against hers surged hot.

"Mecah, no. I have to be on guard," she panted and pulled from him. "Please don't fight me. I need your help," she panted and hurried up the chute.

Shalene emerged into the hot glaring sunlight, still trembling from his kiss. Mecah followed her and they moved toward the exit of the natural archway. Peering out, she scanned the scene.

"Nothing," she said.

"Agree," he nodded.

"Here's some gagla, bind my wrists."

"I still think this is a bad idea."

"And it doesn't matter because I am on an official mission. Tie me up," she insisted.

If only you'd said that back when we were in the interrogation room.

You don't need anything to keep me by your side, Mecah.

You know I can't resist being near you. All I want to do is kiss you and make wild hot love to you, he breathed.

You can make love to me tomorrow. But today we have to do this, she said, not believing her own words. She knew it was a suicide mission at best.

He let his hand fall to her shoulder, trailing his fingers along the length of her arms to her wrists where his fingers encircled. "Reading your thoughts during lovemaking was so exhilarating," he breathed.

"That's not what I was thinking."

"But I was."

"Can you try to focus just a bit here?"

He slipped the gagla over her crossed wrists and pressed the release. The limp binding hardened.

"Too tight?" he asked and slipped his fingers from beneath the steel-hard substance.

"Thank you for the extra room."

"You're going to need it when you break free."

"When will that be?" she asked.

"Just before we jump the mother ship."

"No. I need access to the Demrons' ship. Our intel says that's where the Blue Crystal is being kept."

"What exactly does this crystal do?"

"It's the catalyst for our global defense system. With it in place, no alien force can penetrate Earth's atmosphere, much less invade. There's a lot of speculation how it was stolen. Once I've retrieved it and placed it back into its rightful place inside the Guardian Temple, it'll automatically reactivate the system."

"How does it work? Something so powerful must—"

"Global security prevents me from telling anyone without security clearance. I can tell you that once it's back in place, anyone who is an alien hostile will be vaporized."

"What? How can a crystal ascertain if someone is hostile or not?"

"Trust me, it works. That's why the Demrons had it stolen before their attack."

"But you know for fact it works that precisely?"

"I do."

"But how could you?"

"My h–husband created it. I know everything there is to know about it."

"And all the more reason why this is an insane plan for you to become a prisoner."

"No, all the more reason I have to do this. It's the only thing that has kept me going since this nightmare began." She held his stare with hers, pleading for him to look into her mind and see. He entered her thoughts easily and she knew incredible comfort.

"All clear," Abber's voice crackled over the COMLink. She peered around the rocks at her team a hundred yards away.

"Copy that," she tapped the COMLink.

"Please, Mecah. I need you to be onboard with this." Her heart pounded when she met the pain in his eyes and heard his mental cry.

"Then let's go retrieve that crystal. I'll alert my men. Perhaps our science team knows."

"We'll need a way off the ship and transportation to the Guardian Temple."

Chapter Eleven

It was not easy allowing herself to be taken prisoner, but Shalene trusted Mecah to be the man reflected in his thoughts and his lovemaking. She knew he would not betray her and would lay down his life for her. If they failed, she'd would be tortured and eventually sacrificed to the Demron god, Moketai.

"I'll not let that happen to you," Mecah whispered as they walked toward the freighter. "That's one of my ships."

She looked at him, wondering what that had to do with anything.

Captain?

Go ahead.

The wormhole appears to be opening again. It could be days, or it could be hours. We believe the power of the wormhole will be stronger than the force field of the Demrons and will break us free so we can ride it back to our world.

Disappointment struck her hard in the chest. She gasped for air. What had she expected? How could she compete with his entire world? His family? His troops? It didn't matter, she told herself. He had explained it all to her. They had to continue their work, regardless of how they felt about each other or if it meant being separated. However bittersweet, they'd shared a powerful night and the memories of it would see her through whatever she must do.

So you'll leave without warning? she asked

There shall be a burst of energy just before the wormhole opens. I promise we'll have plenty of time to restore the Blue Crystal. I won't abandon you or your planet. The Demrons will be defeated.

I pray it will be so.

Trust me, Shalene.

Those were the words that steeled her for their arrival onto the Demron mother ship. As the Kyronian freighter approached the massive reptilian ship, her heart pounded harder in her chest. Huge was a misnomer for the size of the ship. She had only seen rare photos of the ship in the early days and the floats used to carry troops to Earth had held nearly two hundred reps. It was no wonder they had overtaken the planet.

Everyone knew their part and the Kyronians set about the docking. Dread settled in the pit of her stomach as she watched from the helm with Mecah by her side. Holding the laser pistol aimed at her back, they emerged down the wide ramp into the belly of her enemy. The temperature was hot and the air stuffy inside the megaton vessel.

"Practically their entire race is onboard this ship. They depleted their planet of its natural resources thousands of years ago. They've gone from one star system to another until all viable resources are exhausted. They're consumers and know nothing of sustainable living, and they have huge appetites," Mecah said.

She nodded as he led her down a hall. She knew he was chattering in an attempt to calm the panic gripping her, threatening to paralyze her. The metal floor and walls echoed each step made. Panic threatened to override her conviction, but she took a deep breath, determined she would remain strong regardless what happened.

Remember most of my fleet can now pick up your thoughts if you do not direct them to me only.

And how do I do that?

Simply say my name before thinking. That should block all others. Unless they are – "

As gifted as you?

Yes.

"What have you brought us, Captain Mecah?" The reptilian's question slithered across the room and snaked up her spine in a rush of dread. Her breathing was rapid, in spite of her attempt to remain calm. It was instinct to fear them, and just as base as the need to kill them. She focused on her hatred for the Demrons and allowed the anger and rage to build inside her, bolstering her against the terror of being in the heart of her enemy.

"I've captured a human soldier. She served as my hostage during my escape."

"Your escape? How resourceful of you, Captain." The reptile turned back to the console and punched a few buttons.

"It wasn't easy," he lied and nudged her forward, further into the center of the helm deck. Massive viewing windows encircled the bridge and she looked out onto her beloved home world. Thousands of spaceships orbited Earth, with a constant flow of cargo carriers moving back and forth to the planet's surface.

"And Bog and his men? What about your S and D team?" The reptile looked up.

"Dead. They were killed in a night raid and I was taken prisoner," Mecah said, meeting the intense stares. The one who appeared to be in charge clasped his hands behind his back and paced in front of them.

"If Major Bog and his two gunners were killed, how did you escape?"

"They thought I was a traitor and took me prisoner, then realized I was not human."

"And of course you didn't tell them anything about your mission or why you were there."

"I did not."

"Good, Captain. You have exceeded our expectations. Isn't that right, Major Bog?" He turned slightly.

"The captain always had good plans and this was his finest. Congratulations, Captain, you appear to have had a very successful mission." Bog stepped from around the far corner.

What? Panic replaced her bravado. Suspicion grounded her to the stark reality facing her. Mecah had lied? Had he orchestrated it all and infiltrated their underground base? He had betrayed her. All of Earth would pay for her mistake of trusting him. "You bastard." She lunged at him, slamming her body against him. How could she have allowed herself to be fooled by this handsome, charismatic man?

"I see she believed you, Captain." Bog moved closer with his long scaly tail slithering behind him. "You look as if you just found out your lover has betrayed you, my dear." He lifted his clawlike hand to her face.

Shalene tried to jerk from his touch, but he grabbed her by the back of her head and pulled her to him.

"Is it any wonder your people lost the war to us?" He lowered his huge face to hers. "Such a gullible race. And the Kyronians are such charmers." His dog breath filled her nostrils. Her stomach pitched from the obnoxious smell.

"You lying bastard!" she seethed.

"Yes, he's all that and more." Bog pulled her by the hair and she cried out.

They are testing us. It's good for you to react this way, but don't believe them, my love, Mecah finally spoke. *Say nothing more.*

"Take her to my quarters," Bog ordered and pushed her from him. She slammed into the hard chest of another rep and stumbled from him, but the guard came up behind her and grabbed her by the arms.

"This way," the rep hissed and shoved her in front of him.

Shalene glanced back at Mecah.

Mecah stood helpless as they took her away. He tried to connect with her mind, but her outrage and anger blocked him. The door closed behind her and he turned to face Bog.

"I do not trust your claim of escape, Captain Mecah. Regardless of the woman's demonstration. And why don't I?" Bog moved around him.

"I have no idea, ole snake," he jeered, refusing to reveal anything to his enemy.

"While I lay wounded in the camp that night, I heard your exchange with the human raiders. I don't believe you have been quite honest with us about your loyalties."

"Oh hell, sure I have. I never pledged loyalty to you, Bog, or your minions. You know I hate your green guts."

Bog glared at him, then laughed.

"You play it to the end, Captain, I give you that."

"I want to know how you survived and got back to the ship," Mecah spat.

"It was not easy. Restrain him," he barked.

"Hey now." Mecah raised his hands in front of him and took a step back.

"I overheard you, Captain Mecah, while I lay on the ground, presumed dead." Two guards approached him.

"Then you should be very grateful to me."

"Why is that?"

"Because I convinced them not to burn your smelly body, that's why. Would it have been better to have been burned alive?"

This brought Bog up short and he tilted his head slightly.

"I will give counsel to this, Captain, as I decide what to do about you. In the meantime, you can wait in the holding area."

"Hey, that's not fair. I saved your fucking life and you're going to throw me in prison? What kind of gratitude is that?"

The Demrons lashed a strip of gagla about his wrists and moved to stand on either side of him.

"I will deal with you later," Bog hissed and stomped over to him. "Take him to the lower cells. I will be in my chambers." He turned on his heel.

"You leave her alone, you smelly bastard," he yelled as they dragged him from the deck.

* * * * *

Shalene's heart pounded as she was led down the long passageway, around several decks of the ship and finally inside Bog's chambers. It wasn't what she'd expected. Rich in velvets of deep purples and greens, the oversize furniture and enormous bed were shadowed in candlelight. Real candles appeared to flicker along the wall, but upon closer examination she realized they were holograms.

"So you thought you could fool an old trickster?" Bog entered and removed his armor vest, plunking it down on the table.

"I didn't attempt to trick anyone."

"Indeed." He moved over to the aquarium and picked up one of the mice by the tail. He lifted it in front of him and stuffed it into his mouth.

She looked away, but the sound of crunching bones made her stomach pitch.

"What to do with you is the question, Commander Courers."

She gasped that he knew her name.

"Yes, I know you. I glimpsed you as I lay on the ground, bleeding."

"I just regret the laser didn't find its mark more accurately."

"There are so many wonderful ways I could go about your torture." His split tongue glided over his profuse lips. "I just have to decide which is going to be the most arousing for me."

"You're sick even for a lizard."

"But I'm the one in control." He moved over to her. "You are a very beautiful human specimen. While I do enjoy watching, it would be such a shame to waste you on some slave."

"Go fuck yourself," she spat, knowing the lust she saw in his eyes meant extreme torture for her.

"Now that's a very unique saying. One I've yet to understand how it would be done." His forked tongue slithered from his mouth and this time lashed against her neck. She took a step back, but his arms wrapped around her like steel bands.

"There now, I think we can do this without all the bravado. I know you're frightened and frankly, that's the way I want you. The more fear you feel, the better I will enjoy taking you."

He picked her up and carried her to his bed. She fought against his embrace and he dropped her on the thick mattress. She scrambled to the other side, but he overpowered her. Cutting her wrist binders, he lashed new ones and secured her arms to the bedposts. He spread her legs and lashed each one to a post. She struggled against the binders, knowing it was futile but refusing to make it easy for him to rape her.

"There, now. That 's how I've fantasized about you ever since you shot me."

"I didn't shoot you! If I had you'd be dead!" She jerked against the gagla.

The sound of a knife scraping from its sheath paralyzed her. Slowly, he lowered the blade and touched the razor-sharp steel against her face. The cold metal chilled her skin and she tried to pull from the wicked blade as he guided it down her neck and toward her vest. He dipped the blade beneath the leather lacing of her vest and rotated the knife in his hand so the blade's edge now pressed against the laces.

A loud blast sounded from the hall, followed by another.

He jerked and the knife sliced through the leather. Her vest fell open with her breasts tumbling free. He groaned with his beady-eyed stare widening on her.

"Major Bog," the intercom shrieked. "Captain Mecah has escaped."

Chapter Twelve

"Damn that Kyronian." He stomped across the room just as the door whooshed open.

"How did this happen?" Bog bellowed and shoved the reptile against the wall.

"I-I don't know, sir. The guards were found unconscious. I've sealed off all exits, but the signature on the transport stream shows his. It appears he returned to the planet, sir."

Mecah had been imprisoned? That meant he'd been telling her the truth. Relief washed over all her anguish. He had not betrayed her!

Shalene? His voice rang in her head.

Mecah! Where are you?

I'll be there soon to free you. Are you unharmed?

"Get a patrol ready to follow me. I'm going after him."

"Yes, sir, what about her?"

"She's not going anyplace. Now move." Bog yelled and turned his fury on her. "Prepare to die, Commander. When I return I'll have my pleasure with you for as long as you entertain me, then I will kill you." He picked up his armor.

"Fuck you!" She tried to rise, but the tethers held her down.

Strapping on his armor, Bog stomped from the room.

Shalene writhed under the gagla binding, but eventually tired. She lay with arms and legs spread wide, waiting.

Mecah? Where are you?

The door opened and closed quickly. She strained to see if Bog had changed his mind and returned to kill her.

"Oh baby, you didn't start without me, did you?" Mecah's voice sent a warm flush over her, filling her with relief.

"Untie me before he comes back."

"Oh, he's gone, sweet love, down to the planet," he spoke with a husky lust expanding in his voice. "In fact, no one is going to come into this room. Bog is down on your planet looking for me."

He moved around and stood in front of the bed.

"You are indeed the most beautiful female I've ever seen." His gaze traveled over her.

"Enjoying yourself?" Her breasts heaved with each excited breath. The heightened danger fanned her desire to feel him.

She should be outraged and demand he set her free, but instead she longed for his touch. She needed to feel his lips travel over her and his tongue flicker over her clit, taking her to new heights of pleasure and sensations.

"I've located your crystal."

The seduction fled.

"Where is it?"

His gaze never left her as it traveled over her rounded breasts. Her nipples seemed to beg for his fingertips to squeeze them and his lips to suck them.

"Please free me," she swallowed.

"We may never have this opportunity again," he whispered and let his fingers trail over her leg. She jumped under his touch and found herself arching to meet the tips of his fingers as they brushed against the leather pants shielding her pussy.

"You're insane. We're on the enemy's mother ship. They're going to execute both of us. We should escape."

"We should, but there's no way off this tanker. The transporter stream was a hoax. No one left the ship. It's just that our technology is better in some areas. They'll never detect the false reading. Right now, they're scratching their scales still trying to figure out how I escaped."

"How did you?" she asked, panting as his fingers slid over her stomach toward her pussy.

"I didn't. I merely cloaked myself. They opened the door to check the cell and I slipped out."

"You have all these powers and yet the Demrons overtook your fleet. How?"

"Outnumbered and outweaponed. We slid through the wormhole and they were waiting for us. They ensnared us in their force field. Unfortunately, we've never been able to imitate our natural cloaking ability for our vessels. Each time we board this ship, we're held within a force field until we are transported back to our vessels."

"But you can read minds. You can make yourself invisible. Surely you could have defeated the reps."

"We tried. But then we never really needed to defeat them, just bide our time until the wormhole returned. Of course, that's assuming the wormhole will be stronger than their force field. This is the first time I've been out of the transporter area." His fingers caressed her breasts, pinching her nipples tenderly. Pulses of heat shot to her clit. "I had to do a little investigating, gather data for my science team. That's why I was delayed getting to you. God, you are so beautiful."

"We don't have much time, please untie me." She swallowed the dryness in her throat. Wet heat rushed between her legs.

"I love the way you feel." He leaned over, letting his fingers slip beneath her pants and gliding down to the slit of her pussy, wet and hot. Her clit throbbed beneath his touch, and Shalene moved her hips, unable resist him.

His lips covered hers, tender at first, then demanding as his fingers moved firmly against her clit, driving her into a hard and fast arousal. She moaned and opened her mouth to his kiss. He moved his hand faster and she arched into the rhythm, her climax rising higher as he pressed his fingers into her moist heat. She jerked against the sudden release as shards of bright light exploded with delightful spasms raking her body. He slipped his hand from her and tugged on her pants, sliding them past her hips, unable to budge them further.

"What are you doing?"

"I'm going to fuck you—hard," he breathed and freed his cock from his pants. "Danger always heightens a mad burn."

"You like me tied up, don't you?"

"I like you anyway I can have you."

He twisted, trying to enter her, but the leather pants prevented him. He pulled something from his trouser pocket.

"What's that?" she panted.

"New Demron mini-laser." He flashed a wide smile and aimed the beam at the post. The gagla melted and freed her leg. She moaned as he pulled the pants lower to her ankle. It was awkward, but he managed to position himself between her legs. She rolled her hips to meet him and his large cock slipped into her moist pussy. She was tight from the orgasm, and he moved slowly, gently, until the walls of her pussy relaxed around his hardness. He bent over her and captured a nipple between his lips, sucking it into his mouth.

"This is so dangerous," she breathed, moving with his thrusts, the fire licking at her senses.

"I love you." His voice was low and full of unbridled hunger. He moved in and out of her, drawing her higher and higher toward climax.

Frenetic pulses throbbed, melting into heat and need. Her hips undulated and met his thrusts. She could hear his thoughts. His love for her drew her deeper into his mind until she melted and joined him as one person. One thought. One love.

"Oh God!" she cried out as the rising fire lashed and ebbed until bursting in spasms and such intense pleasure tears poured from the corners of her eyes.

Mecah groaned and reared back, plunging his cock deeper. His passion moved through her, blinding her to her own thoughts. Sweat rolled down his back beneath her hands as she kneaded his muscles, lost in the pleasure of his cock slipping in and out of her pussy. She clamped her muscles around him, driving him into a frenetic pace until he groaned between clenched teeth. His body flexed rigid, with powerful muscles glistening with sweat from the intense climax. His body spasmed and spilled his come into her womb, slowly grinding his cock into her, burying himself deeper, luxuriating in the hot liquid afterglow.

He leaned down to capture her lips and sucked them into his mouth, then released her. His lips slid over her cheek to her ear, where his tongue flicked wild drummings against her ear.

"God, I love you, Shalene," he panted and set about untying her.

She let him draw her into his arms, still drugged by his lovemaking. Should the enemy barge into the room, she would not be able to defend herself. Her mind screamed for her to get up, get dressed and prepare to fight, but all she wanted to do was lie in his delicious embrace. It was unimaginable that she had just made love while in the midst of an escape. It was insane. She'd heard of arousal during great times of danger, but until now she'd never believed it possible.

She had been in mourning ever since the Demrons had invaded her planet and now, of all times, she had found love with an alien who was set to return to his own universe through a wormhole. Her eyes widened and she sat up, pulling from his arms.

"What's wrong?"

"I-I think we need to get dressed—"

"They won't be back for hours. We have time for more." He tried to pull her back onto the bed, but she shifted from his embrace and rose unsteadily to her feet. Drawing her pants up, she zipped them and set about looking for her bustier.

"I'm lying on it and refuse to give it up until I get a kiss," Mecah teased with renewed passion stirring in the depths of his eyes.

"Please, Mecah. This was a great risk."

"You didn't enjoy it?" He flipped one of the leather lacings in front of him.

"I loved it, Mecah. Too much. I love you. Too much!"

He grabbed her hand and drew it to his lips. His tender kiss melted her heart.

"You love me?" He looked up at her.

Shalene sat down beside him and caressed his cheek with her hand.

"I love you more than I've ever loved anyone and that's why I'm worried. We need to get dressed and find the crystal."

He frowned and shifted his weight, pulling the bustier from beneath him.

Shalene took it but his hand closed over hers.

"Just know that what we've shared is only the beginning. It will get better and better."

Excited prickles inched up her arms. A lifetime of such intense pleasure with him? It was too wonderful to be long-lasting.

"But it is long-lasting, my love. It's forever," he swung his legs over the bed and sat in front of her, drawing her into the space between them. He buried his head into her breasts. Firm teasing lips mingled with hot breath as his hands cupped and guided each nipple to his mouth. He kissed one nipple then the other, catching it between his teeth. He nibbled and sucked, drawing each rosy tip into a hard nub. Jagged pulses flamed to her clit. She tried to pull from him, but his hand closed over her ass, tugging her closer.

"Just one more time," he groaned and stood with his pants still down around his ankles. His hard cock pressed against her belly.

"I want to, but I'm worried Bog will return. We must find the crystal before he does." Shalene was a confusion of extreme emotions.

"There's time." He cradled her face between his hands and tilted her head to receive his demanding kiss. His lips moved over hers with his tongue pressing against them until she relented and open her mouth.

"No!" She jerked away and turned from him, pulling the bustier vest over one shoulder. "You spin such an erotic web around me I can't even think straight. Your thoughts tumble through my mind and I'm left wondering which are mine and which are yours." She pulled the vest together and began lacing it, refusing to look at him, standing there with his cock hard and throbbing. If she looked up, her resolve would crumble.

"It's part of the blending, my love." He grabbed his pants and pulled them up, righting his shirt before walking over to her.

His hands covered her shaky ones and he finished lacing the vest.

"I love you, Mecah." She traced the strong line of his jaw. "But I don't want to love you. You're leaving."

"But you can come with me."

"I can't. I have to return the Blue Crystal to the Guardian Temple."

"We'll do it together and afterwards return to my ship. You'll love Kyro. It's paradise."

"I can't leave my planet. Don't you understand? If we're successful, then it'll be time to rebuild. I will be needed. Every human will be needed. I can't abandon my people. My race."

"I won't leave without you." He cupped her face between his hands and stared down into her eyes. "I won't be without you." He leaned in to kiss her, but she pulled from him.

"We must hurry, Mecah. We must find the Blue Crystal."

"There's no hurry," he confessed. "It's not here."

"What?" she choked.

"Bog has it. He keeps it with him at all times. We must await his return."

"How-how do you know this?"

"When I was cloaked and on the departure deck, setting up the bogus activation. I watched him and saw him take it out of his pocket to inspect it. It was a blue prism crystal about six inches in length. I've seen it before, only I didn't know what it was. I thought it was a religious icon since he was always fingering it when we'd make camp."

"And you failed to tell me about this because...?" She planted her hands on her hips.

"I tried to warn you. To tell you it was hopeless, but you insisted on doing this. I had hoped to find a way to steal it from him and transport us to the Guardian Temple."

"You can use the transport?" Her mind whirled.

"I can transport us to any grid on Earth."

"Where did you send Bog?"

"To the Chinese region. Why?"

She paced the room.

"How many can be transported at one time?"

"Their technology is limited. They can only transport two people at a time, that's why they use our freighters."

"How many men did Bog take with him?"

"Three. What are you planning, Shalene?" A worried frown creased his forehead.

"Can you pick up Bog's signature and transport him to the Guardian Temple?"

"I see what you are planning, but if I do that, it means he will arrive before us and we will be ambushed."

"Not necessarily. How exacting is the transporter?"

"It has limitations."

"But if we transport him so he must travel to the Guardian Temple then we can buy some time."

Captain Mecah? the voice interrupted them.

What is it?

The information you retrieved from the Demron computers is not enough. We need access codes to initiate the release.

"What does he mean?" she asked, having heard the communication too.

Copy. I'll retrieve and send to you in five minutes.

"Mecah?" she asked.

"The wormhole draws closer, Shalene. Once I was certain Bog had left you, I did some exploring before I came to rescue you. I found the control mechanism for the Demron force field. I will only be a few minutes, then we will transport Bog within visual range of the Guardian Temple and then we'll follow.

"We'll arrive cloaked," he grinned. "I can cloak you as well."

Hope sprang in her, renewed and full of power. They had a chance. A good chance.

"First we get the codes for my crew, then we transport Bog. Hold on to my hand. As long as we are joined, you will be cloaked. If you break from my hold, you will rematerialize. The only way to regain cloaking will be for me to rematerialize and to repeat the process. Understood?"

She nodded and clasped his hand. She didn't know what she expected when he cloaked them, but there was no physical sensation. She could still see him and her hand clasped in his. Were they really cloaked? she wondered as he pushed open the large door leading from Bog's chambers.

The metal corridor glistened with holographic lights. Footfalls sounded behind them and she moved to dart into an alcove, but he held her against him, pressing them into the doorway.

Several Demron troopers stomped toward them and she panicked, certain his cloaking had malfunctioned. She shifted, but his grip tightened on her hand.

Easy, love. They cannot see us. His thoughts calmed her frantic heartbeat...

The lizard troops marched past them and she sighed in relief. It had worked. The soldiers turned the corner.

"This way," he whispered, and they ran down the long corridor. Mecah pulled them up short just outside two large doors, polished to a high gloss. She marveled that they did not cast any reflections. Later, when they were out of danger, she would discover the secret to this ability.

The two doors opened and a rep stomped through them. Mecah led her around the bulky creature and paused just inside the control room. He seemed to know his way around and led her past several workstations. She held her breath, still unaccustomed to being invisible and expected they would be discovered and killed. Her hand was cold and sweaty in his warm dry one. Her admiration for his ability grew when he stopped behind the rep keying in data to the main computer.

"Bog to command," the voice crackled overhead.

"Report, Major."

"There's no sign of the captain in this sector. Request retrieval."

"Are you sure? We cannot afford to have him escape a second time. Perform another sweep."

"As you command," Bog growled.

"His arrogance increases every day," the officer mumbled to the other one at the COMLink station.

"As long as he controls the Blue Crystal, we have no choice."

"Perhaps. But what if something happened to Major Bog *and* the crystal?" the other one spoke so low Shalene had to strain to hear the words.

"It could be arranged," the other rep nodded. Both of them chuckled.

Even his own people despise him, Mecah thought.

Captain, do you have the codes? The energy field is increasing. We're running out of time.

Understood.

How are you going to retrieve the right codes? Shalene asked.

First I find a free workstation. Over there. He dragged her toward the far corner.

Using one hand, Mecah keyed in the main password and the panel lit up. She glanced up and swept the room to make sure no one had noticed the sudden activity.

The screen flickered and darkened. A series of numbers rolled in front of him.

He repeated them mentally, reading off the long series.

"What's going on over there?" A nearby rep shuffled over to the workstation. Mecah pulled her out of the way but continued to read off the numbers.

"Who did this?" the rep bellowed across the room.

"What is it?"

"Someone has accessed the code panel."

"Who? No one is over there."

"Has our system been compromised?"

"Checking."

8743 03923 02934 23 04 23042 112 03 93 09 2392 4023 20394… That's it, Mecah said.

Got it, Captain, now get out of there. The wormhole is projected to reappear in ten minutes.

Are all personnel on board?

All but you, Captain.

There's no time, she said. *You must return to your fleet.*

Prepare to transport me on my command, lock onto my chip.

Done, sir.

I'm transporting to the planet, start the tracker now.

Affirmative.

Chip?

We have a chip implanted in each of us at the time of birth. Makes for easy retrieval.

She nodded.

"Find the source!" the rep's voice rang across the room.

"Send someone down to security and check the workstation there."

"On your command, sir!

They jumped out of the path of the rep as he ran for the door. When the door opened, they slipped between the metal doors.

The transporter deck was vacant as all hands were ordered to conduct a security sweep. That meant her escape would soon be discovered.

"I need you to be my other hand," he said. "You key the numbers on the left pad."

"Copy."

"What are the grid coordinates?" he asked.

"Yours are 92 03 54 788. I'll key in my side."

"Locking on Bog's signature and sweeping for the closest to him. Activate," he ordered.

She pressed the orange, lighted button and a burst of energy surged from the panel. The grid screen revealed two green dots within the grid square.

"Complete," she sighed.

He squeezed her hand and planted a small kiss on her forehead.

"Now us, remember as soon as we arrive move to the right. Don't hesitate."

"I won't," she squeezed his hand.

Captain, ETA is now eight minutes and counting, the voice rang in her head.

"We have plenty of time, Shalene." He keyed in the coordinates and she reentered hers. Mecah pressed the green panel button and tugged her from the station, running toward the corner platform. She stopped in front of the large mirror, unsure what to do.

"Just step through it. That's all you have to do, and make sure to hold on to my hand."

She nodded and stepped through the frame with him. The mirror was liquid and the space around her began to break up into tiny pixels. Magnetic surges coursed through her and she feared her hand would slip from his and tightened her grip.

"Hang on," he called as the transporter powered up. Her ears rang and the world washed from her. The sensation of flying unbalanced her.

"Don't move," Mecah spoke. His voice soothed her and the sensations began to disappear. The world darkened and solid matter reappeared beneath her feet.

"You will die!" Bog's voice boomed and she moved to the right, squatting down, still holding onto Mecah's large hand.

The blast whizzed inches from her head and burst against the monument behind her.

"Did you think I actually believed the false signature you left in the transporter? I merely waited for your escape. Show yourself, Captain!"

Mecah pulled her behind a statue and crouched beside her, drawing his pistol from his belt.

Let him come to us.

Footfalls ground against the temple floor as Bog circled behind them.

Mecah shoved her out of the laser's path. She fell spread-eagled into the open space. Lifting her head, she met the green, scaled feet.

"Well now, what have we here? I'm impressed. Is this a new talent for humans? Or is it a carefully guarded Kyronian ability?" Bog jerked her from the floor, holding his arm behind her neck as she struggled to free herself.

"Let her go." Mecah emerged from behind the large statue with his pistol aimed at Bog.

"I'm going to taste her first, then once I'm sated, I'm going to kill her while you watch."

"No!" Mecah disappeared.

Bog blasted a round of lasers in his direction while holding Shalene trapped with one arm. He jerked around searching for Mecah, aiming his pistol at the vacant air.. A sound drew his attention to the far side and he squeezed off a couple of rounds, shooting at nothing.

Something hard pressed into Shalene's ribcage and she touched the bulky shape beneath his breast armor, immediately recognizing it. The Blue Crystal! Her body trembled. Freedom was so close her mind reeled. If she could remove the crystal and get it to the altar. She looked about the pink marble temple and quickly found the black marble altar across the vaulted chamber. The grove that housed the sacred crystal was deep and empty.

Mecah, distract him. He has the crystal in his armor.

"Over here, desert breath!" Mecah's voice called in front of them and Bog growled, shooting wildly into the air. The lasers impacted a few feet away, shattering chunks of marble from the wall onto the floor.

She worked her fingers into the space, groping for the crystal.

"What's the matter, Bog? Can't aim straight?"

Mecah materialized and lunged for him.

Bog yelled and shifted, but Mecah slammed into him, sending all three of them to the floor. Shalene wrapped her fingers around the crystal and pulled it free just as she slammed onto the hard floor. The force jarred the crystal from her grip. She cried out. It slid across the black marble floor, coming to a stop at the base of the holy altar.

Mecah pounded his fist into Bog's face, the sound of impact made her wince, but she took advantage of the moment, stumbling to her feet. She hurried across the temple her full concentration on the crystal. Strong arms lifted her from the floor. She yelled as she was hoisted into the air and tossed across the room as if she were a limp rag. The impact against the wall crushed her. Pain streaked through her body. She fell to the floor and lifted her aching head just as the rep stomped toward her.

Bog's face broke into a wide grin.

"Now you die, bitch!"

She looked around for Mecah. He lay on the top step of the altar, motionless.

"No!" she cried out and moved toward her beloved, but his voice stopped her.

Shalene, get the crystal. Throw it to me.

She scrambled toward the base of the altar, groping for the sacred crystal, and closed her fingers around it just as Bog reached her.

Captain, the wormhole has opened. Prepare for transport.

Shalene looked up at him. Her gaze locked with his. *Don't leave!* She drew back her arm and pitched the crystal in his direction.

Mecah had pulled himself up onto the altar and lifted his arm above his head in a desperate effort to catch the crystal.

Bog roared and turned from her, taking long strides up the steps in Mecah's direction.

"Mecah!" she cried out as the lizard leapt to the second landing.

She watched as though life moved in slow motion. Prisms of light reflected from the Blue Crystal, creating rainbow streaks against the walls and ceiling of the temple as it sailed through the air toward Mecah. His hand opened wide and the crystal landed in his palm with a loud smack.

"You will not return the crystal to the altar!" Bog took the steps two at a time, his tremendous weight crumbling bits and chucks of marble from the slabs.

Mecah strained to pull himself up the last height to the altar. Bog's clawlike hand clamped around his leg.

"Mecah! No!" Shalene screamed, running toward them, scaling the steps as fast as she could, knowing she'd be too late.

The sound was unmistakable. It was the sound of freedom as the crystal locked into the hollow space.

Transporter initialized.

The hum burst through the chamber like a bomb's wave, rolling past the door and into the world as the brilliant blue light radiated from the altar.

Bog held his hands to his head, yelling as the Blue Crystal's power penetrated his body.

"Look away," Mecah called out. "Shield your eyes."

Activated.

"Mecah!" she screamed as his body began to disintegrate under the transporter's beam.

"You bitch!" Bog lunged for her. Light pierced his body, cracking through his scaly shape. He yelled as the blue light opened jagged edges throughout his body and ripped him apart, leaving charred ashes to fall along the steps.

"Mecah!" she screamed, scaling the rest of the steps to the altar. Tears streamed down her face as she frantically searched for him. He was gone!

"Mecah!" she wailed. Her very heart felt as though it were breaking.

My Shalene. His voice sounded as though it was beside her. Could they still communicate even though he was millions of light-years away?

Goodbye, Mecah, my love, she sniffed.

Shalene. He materialized in front of her.

"Mecah?" she screamed and threw her arms around his neck, clinging to him, unable to believe he was really there.

He cupped her face between his hands and covered her tear-stained face with kisses.

"I thought you had gone home."

"*You* are my home, Shalene." He cupped her face between his hands. "Do you think I could ever leave my Kismet? Together, we shall build a new world and start a family. You have my love forever. And we shall always have tomorrow." His lips covered hers.

~ *End* ~

About the author

A native North Carolinian, Sally lives with her husband and cat, Bow, in the Blue Ridge Mountains. Her daughter is a recent EFTHN (Escapee From The Home Nest).

Growing up just outside Charlotte, NC, Sally spent summers playing on the beaches of the Carolinas and learning to "shag" — a form of beach dancing.

Born in the South and into an Irish/Scottish family meant storytelling was as natural as breathing. Everyone had their own repertoire of jokes and stories and growing up in North Carolina, famous for its ghost stories, meant scary ones, too. Sally knows a lot about ghosts since she's lived with them all her life, very much like the film, "Sixth Sense". Invited to participate in a three-year paranormal research project she at long last embraced her Celtic seer heritage and even runs an online paranormal workshop featuring paranormal research professionals.

Trained in commercial art, she discovered writing fulfills her creative energies, especially Romantica™. When not writing, she can be found tending to her flowers and jungle of houseplants, studying all kinds of subject matters, and setting out on new adventures with her soul mate husband.

Sally welcomes mail from readers. You can write to her c/o Ellora's Cave Publishing at 1056 Home Ave. Akron, Oh. 44310-3502.

Also by Sally Painter

All I Need

All I Want

Secrets of the Wind

Chapter One

Major Chastain Neff was tired, hungry and covered with a thick layer of mud. She was hunkered down beside a dead body watching a fourth-class medical examiner's mate doing his thing. The sight of the yawning body cavity where once a chest had been didn't faze Neff, but the smell of burnt flesh from the phosphorus blast that had taken out that chest made her a bit queasy.

"Is he Storian?" she asked.

"Well," the fourth-class med ex drawled, "I don't see any markings to say he was, but until I get him back to the shop, I won't know for sure."

"Sure as hell fought like one," Chastain remarked. She ran the back of her dirty forearm under her chin to catch the drop of sweat that had been hanging there precariously.

"He stinks like one," Chastain's immediate superior Colonel Brock commented.

Chastain got wearily to her feet. "How's the target doing?"

Brock looked around. "Still puking," he replied with a snort. "I don't think he's accustomed to someone getting ventilated."

"That's understandable."

"By the way, the general would like to see you," Brock told Chastain.

Chas frowned. "Don't tell me he's got another assignment for me this quick," she said and winced at the whine of complaint she could hear in her voice.

"We're down two operatives," Brock reminded her. "We do what we have to, Neff."

Sighing heavily, Chas hung her head. Her hands were on her hips as she shook her head. "I am due for leave, Colonel. I *need* some leave."

"Everyone is overworked, Neff," Brock reprimanded her. "I'm sure the general will give you extra time off after the next one."

Knowing it would do her no good to argue, Chastain lifted her head. She looked over at the target for a long moment then walked over to where he was sitting.

"Can we get you anything else, Councilman Jost?" a med-tech asked the shivering man as Chastain joined them.

Councilman Jost pulled the thick wool blanket tighter around his shoulders and could barely speak for his teeth were clicking together. "N-no. I'll b-be all right." He glanced up at Chastain. "Thank you, Major. If it hadn't been for you…"

"There's no need to thank me, Sir," Chas told him. "I'm just glad everything turned out okay."

"If I hadn't hired you to protect me, if you hadn't been with m-me…"

"Another Guardian would have been, Sir," Chas cut him off. She could tell the man was going into shock and caught the eye of the med-tech.

"He was going to kill me, wasn't he?" the councilman asked, his teeth chattering.

"Aye, Sir, he was. He would have taken your money then he would have taken your life. You were wise to get us involved in this extortion plot, Sir."

"Let's get you to the clinic, Councilman Jost," the med-tech suggested. "We've put in a call to your family and they'll join us there."

Chas stepped aside as the med-tech helped the councilman to his feet. She nodded at his grateful look and gave him a tired smile. "Take care, Sir," she said as the shivering man was led away.

"Go get cleaned up and get something to eat, Neff," Colonel Brock ordered. "I'll let the general know you'll be in his office first thing this afternoon."

"Aye, Sir," Chas replied.

Walking back to the runabout in which she had brought Councilman Jost to the place where he had been meant to die, Chas felt a brief respite from the bodily aches and pains she knew would be ten times worse when she turned in that night. She always felt a rush of healing adrenalin course through her body when she'd performed her job well and the target lived.

The Storian—if indeed the assassin had been of that nationality—had fought well. He had gotten in a few lucky punches and even one well-timed kick before going for his phospho firearm. That he might have had the weapon turned on him, and his massive chest blown apart in the ensuing struggle, had more than likely never occurred to him. Then again, he had not counted on his opponent being a Riezell Guardian, either.

Going through the start-up procedures without thinking much about it, Chas settled back in the form-fitting command chair as the mighty engine roared to life. She sat there feeling the runabout vibrating beneath her rump and smiled at the nearly silent power encased in the titanium hull.

The runabout belonged entirely to Chas. It had been awarded to her a year earlier by a grateful target and his family. Top of the line, state-of-the-art, the runabout was one of the most sought-after models at Tappa Industries. Only a handful of high-ranking officials within the Riezell Conclave could afford a Fiach model runabout. Not even General Siri, head of Fleet Command, had such a sweet machine at his disposal, for the retail price of the craft was upwards of one-point-five million credits.

Buckling herself in the command chair, Chas tightened the safety harness, took a look at the proximity screen to make sure no unsuspecting body happened to be within range of the propulsion tubes and engaged the throttle to twenty percent. Beneath her, the runabout lifted with a wash of thick white clay dust spiraling up from beneath the sleek black matte belly of the craft.

Those at the crime scene shielded their eyes as the runabout climbed fifty feet into the late-morning sun, nosed to starboard — the propulsion engine heat pointed away from any humans on the ground — then took off like a rock from a slingshot.

"That's one awesome piece of work," the fourth-class med ex said with a sigh.

Colonel Brock nodded as the runabout disappeared from view. "Aye," he replied. "She is, and one of our best operatives. If I needed protection, Chastain Neff would be the RG I'd want assigned to my ass."

It was obvious the med ex had been commenting on the expensive piece of machinery that was transporting the Riezell Guardian, but he made no comment to the colonel's remark. Everyone there knew how the colonel felt about his operative.

* * * * *

The bath had cleansed away the dirt and a twenty-minute power nap had cleared away the fog that had permeated Chas' tired brain. After a bowl of high-protein chips and an energy shake, she dressed in the silver-gray uniform with its bright copper anchor insignia on the shirt collar that marked her as a Principle Riezell Guardian. Checking one last time to make sure she was properly attired, she left her quarters and took the elevator to the eighteenth floor of Command Central.

The guards at the door to the general's complex snapped to attention as she passed, the bases of their phospho lances thumping in unison upon the polished marble floor.

"At ease, gentlemen," Chas said as she entered the door they were securing. Immediately, the guards shifted their legs apart in parade rest.

"He's expecting you, Major," the general's secretary told Chas.

"Any news yet?" Chas inquired.

The secretary shook her head. "No, Ma'am. Not yet."

"No news is good news or so they say," Chas reminded the young woman.

"So they say," the secretary echoed.

"I'll light a candle for his safe return."

Miriam Quillan smiled. "Thank you, Major. I appreciate it."

Chas tapped twice with the back of her index finger knuckle upon the wall beside the general's open door and smiled as she entered the man's office. "You wanted to see me, Sir?" she inquired.

"Aye," the great man answered. "Close the door, Major."

Chas' left eyebrow arched upward at the order but she made no comment as she did as she was told. When she turned around, the general told her to take a seat.

"They've found him?" she asked softly as she sat.

"About half an hour ago," the general replied. "At least what was left of him. I just haven't had the heart to tell her."

Chas felt a tug at her heartstrings, and she asked if the general would like her to inform Miriam that her husband of less than a year would not be returning.

"No, I'll tell her," the general said. "I just have to find a gentle way in which to do it."

"This internecine war has destroyed many a life, hasn't it, Sir?"

"Too many, Major. Far too many."

There was a long moment of silence then the general leaned back in his chair. "I was very pleased to hear the Jost situation has been successfully resolved. Good work, Chastain."

"Thank you, Sir. I wish we could have taken the Storian captive, but one less rebel assassin is better than nothing."

"It is definite, then? He was Storian?"

"I had a message on my Vid-Mem when I returned to my quarters. He had the mark on the sole of his left foot."

The general winced. "A primary," he noted. "Thank the Goddess you were able to take him out."

"He could have given us much-needed information had I been able to capture him alive, but he didn't give me any choice," Chas confessed.

"Well, at least you survived the contact." He eyed her carefully. "A few bruises and a scrape or two seems to be the extent of your injuries."

"I was lucky," Chas maintained.

The general waved away her modesty. "Luck had nothing to do with it, Major. You are good at what you do."

Chastain smiled, the compliment being one that was rarely extended to an RG. "I take it you have a new mission for me?"

A dark scowl spread over the general's face. "One demanded of us by the Caitliceachs."

Chas' eyes widened and General Alphon Morrison grinned mirthlessly. "Surprises you too, eh? I never thought the Council of Cosaint would ask for our help, did you?"

"No, Sir. Never in a millennia," Chas said slowly. "What do they want us to do?"

"Keep the heir-apparent from being assassinated," the general said.

Chas frowned. "That's Prince Ruan, isn't it?"

"The one and the same," her superior officer replied.

"Don't they call him the Wraith?"

"Aye, he is high up in the Order of Taibhse. Supposedly, he is one helluva warrior and if his documented kills are any indication, I can see where he's earned his nickname."

The frown on Chas' face deepened. "I am Protastnúach so I have never understood the Caitliceachs, Sir. The whole idea of a race of people governed by a ruling family is anathema to the way I was brought up. Anything that smacks of kingship and all that folderol just irks me," Chas remarked.

"It bothers me too, so I wasn't keen on the idea of us providing protection for one of King Declan Cosaint's brats."

"Then why are we?"

"Orders came directly from the Tribunal to us, Major. We didn't have any say in the matter. Despite our differences, the Caitliceachs are our allies."

"His people can't protect the heir-apparent?"

"Not as sufficiently as they would like. He's a handful, I hear."

"Aye, well, from what I've heard of Prince Ruan, he won't appreciate us providing protection for him. Isn't that what his surname means? Protection?"

"Aye, but protection of his people, not of himself," the general explained. "I'm told he tends to be rather careless of his own safety and his mother nudged the king into having their son placed under safeguard."

"Nevertheless, he might balk at me shadowing him."

General Morrison leaned forward and braced his elbows on his desk. "That's why he isn't to know who or what you are, Major."

Chas' eyebrows drew toward one another. "I'm not to tell him I'm an RG?"

"By all means, no, you aren't!" the general exclaimed. "The king's attaché was adamant about that."

"Then how in the blue blazes am I to protect him?"

"Stealth, my dear Major," the general said with a chuckle. "By using stealth!"

* * * * *

The prisoner slumped against the heavy chains weighing down his arms. It was hard for him to sign his name on the paper that had been thrust under his nose, but he would have done anything for a chance to have his life sentence put aside.

"The policy to grant clemency to prisoners capable of defeating one of our Riezell Guardians came from the governor himself. He thought it would be a good way to keep the RG on their toes if they knew assassins might be out there after their hides. You understand that you might die?" the warden inquired.

Shrugging as he let the quill drop from his fingers, the prisoner straightened as best he could. "You won't put me back in prison if I succeed will you?" he asked.

The warden snorted. "The chances of you taking out a Riezell Guardian are very unlikely but as long as you realize that going into the situation, that's all that matters."

"I've never been bested by a damned female and I'm not likely to start now," the prisoner boasted. He shook his wrists as the fetters were removed and contemplated strangling the guard who had squatted down to unlock the prisoner's ankle restraints. But the look on the warden's face and the scowling disapproval on the faces of the other five guards standing watch nearby was a very good deterrent for the prisoner not to act upon his natural proclivity.

"You'll be given a new set of clothing, identity papers and a weapon of your choice," the warden said. "Until you make contact with Major Neff, you will be required to wear the tracking device being applied now."

The prisoner glared down at the guard who had removed the shackles from his legs only to slip a tracking anklet in place before he got to his feet. The anklet was tight against his skin and he could feel a slight vibration from the transmitter.

"If you manage to take out Major Neff, the anklet will be removed, and you will be allowed to meld into the crowd and go your way," the warden reminded the prisoner.

"And not have you hunting me, right?"

"That's correct. You will be a free man," the warden agreed. "Until you commit your next crime and end up right back here."

"Won't happen," the prisoner protested.

"We'll see."

* * * * *

"The heir-apparent, huh?" Colonel Daniel Brock questioned as he scored the remainder of the thick steak on his trencher. "That should make an interesting assignment."

"I've learned a lot about Ruan Cosaint since this afternoon," Chas said. "I'm not sure interesting is the right word."

"He's a bad-ass," Daniel remarked. "Met him once."

Chas looked up from her trencher. "When was this?"

"Right after the war started. I was sent to Sciath to deliver a message from the Tribunal to King Declan." He stabbed a chunk of steak and popped it into his mouth, speaking around the obstruction. "I remember thinking it was the most beautiful palace I'd ever seen."

"Beautiful or not, I was looking forward to a little R & R," Chas pouted.

Daniel took a swallow of his Francach brandy. "When this assignment is over, I'll book a passage to that little *an Ghréig* island that you like so well. We can just lie around on the beach and soak up the old rays then take a dip in those beautiful turquoise waters. How's that?"

"It sounds heavenly," Chas admitted. "To just laze around with nothing to do in paradise…" She sighed.

Daniel took up his napkin and blotted his lips then neatly folded the linen and tucked it beneath the edge of his trencher. "Ready for dessert?" he inquired.

"I don't think I could eat another thing," she replied, repeating his action.

"Well, I'm still starving but it isn't for food," he told her quietly.

For the last four years, she and Daniel Brock had been lovers. It was an easy situation for the both of them since it involved little other than the satisfaction of physical needs. Neither had any desire for permanent bonds or Joining or making their relationship mutually exclusive. Daniel took his pleasures where he would, and she made sure her options were always open.

"I might have room for something salty," she said with a grin.

Daniel got up from the table, walked to her and held her chair as she rose. Taking her hand, he led her to the shadowy confines of his bachelor sleeping room, turning her to face him so he could slowly undo the buttons of her blouse.

"I have been waiting all day for this," he said in a smoky voice. His fingers were sure on the pearl buttons, his knuckles grazing her breasts as he worked his way down the bodice.

"Be gentle with me, Danny. I am starting to feel that Storian's love taps," she said as he pulled the tail of her blouse from her skirt.

"It'll be worse tomorrow and tomorrow night," he warned as he slid his hands along her rib cage and pulled her to him, flattening her lace-covered breasts against his chest. He bent his head to nuzzle her neck.

Chas had always enjoyed the foreplay Daniel instigated, though it was always the same each time. The man was very good at foreplay. He had an iron will, it seemed, and could go for an hour merely teasing and stroking her before feeling the need to stretch out atop her and take her in his slow, lazy way. Sometimes his restraint tried her nerves and she'd have much preferred for him to ravage her like a barbarian, but tonight she was glad for his self-control.

"You smell wonderful," he said, lapping at the tendon along the side of her neck as his hands smoothed up and down her back under the blouse.

"It's the gardenia perfume you brought back from *an Domhan* your last time out."

"I'll buy you a keg of it next time. I love the scent."

He eased her back from him and slipped the blouse from her shoulders, allowing it to fall to the floor behind her. Turning his right hand so the fingernails were against the hollow of her throat, he ran them down to the front closure of her bra and with practiced ease, flicked the hook apart with his index finger and thumb. As the garment separated, he hooked both hands in the straps and eased it from her body.

Chas had always been proud of her large breasts. They fit snuggly in Daniel's large hands and the prominence of her rosy nipples scraped along his palm as he gently massaged the ivory globes.

"You have the most beautiful breasts of any woman I know," Daniel said a moment before he lowered his mouth to the turgid points.

Their lovemaking was slow — almost choreographed — and while enjoyable, Chas could never call it spontaneous or exciting. There was never any deviation from one bout of sex to the next. She could almost count the exact steps that led to Daniel's oversized bed.

Unbutton the blouse, nibble the neck, remove the blouse.

Remove the bra, nibble the nipples then run the tongue over them.

Continue lathing the nipples, squeezing the breasts before sliding a hand down to the waistband of her skirt or slacks and cupping her sex through the fabric.

From there things heated up a bit, but they still went entirely too slow and too methodical to be anything other than pleasantly enjoyable. There was never any wild passion to claim either of them. There were no squeals of unbridled fulfillment or bellows of satisfied lust.

As he removed her skirt and panties, she threaded her fingers through his thick salt-and-pepper hair and held on as he went to his knees to worship at the juncture of her thighs.

Breathe lightly against the pubes and flick the tongue to the clitoris.

Part the lips with sure fingers and run the tongue along the folds, ending with a soft suckle at the core of her pleasure.

Insinuate a finger into her rectum, and pull her closer so his warm mouth could latch onto her sex like a giant leech.

That particular visualization never failed to bother Chas. She would squirm as the notion entered her head, and could have sworn she felt slimy *down there*. While his ministrations were highly pleasurable and always culminated in her being hot and ready to be impaled on his stiff cock, the routine of the lovemaking, the predictability of it, no longer brought the enjoyment it once did.

Lying beneath Daniel as he slipped into her, she stared up at the ceiling and tried to imagine being plundered by a brazen corsair from the barbaric coast of *an Tuirc*. She envisioned herself aboard that pirate's fast caramusal, its four sails snapping in the wind, eluding the blazing guns of the patrol boats as he carried her farther away from her home and deep along the wild shores of his. His hard body weighing hers down upon his bunk, his slick, hot cock buried deep in the honeyed folds of her cunt, he would ride her, ravaging her exquisitely until she would release a scream of sheer delight as their sweating bodies climaxed together. Thrilled by the howl of possessiveness that roared from his throat as he marked her his own, she would know true fulfillment.

"I love you, Chas."

Daniel's voice brought Chas back from the misty, foggy barbaric lands to the same old, same old trickle of pleasure that invaded her body as she came. It was a ho-hum release but it helped to soothe her aching body and as Daniel settled down beside her, his back to her, his snoring almost automatic as sleep claimed him, Chas lay awake and stared at the ceiling.

To fantasize of a bold pirate who could take her far beyond herself.

Chapter Two

Ruan Cosaint was scowling darkly as he stood in the open-air market at Gaillimh Bay. The sounds of the merchants hawking their wares had given him a brutal headache while the smell of animal feces from the pens caused hot bile to rise up in his gullet. He ignored the lovely woman standing beside him as she prattled on about this rug or that bolt of material, having stopped at numerous stalls to inspect the garish merchandise from time to time.

"Don't you think this velvet brings out the blue in our eyes, Ruan?"

"If you say so," he said through clenched teeth. The phrase had become a mantra to him over the course of the last three hours he had been forced to traipse alongside the latest simpering candidate his mother had foisted off on him.

"Just last week, I added several gowns in a variety of blue colors to my dowry, but none of them are this rich a hue," she continued, oblivious to his answer. "Don't you love the way the material shimmers beneath the sunlight?"

Ruan growled his answer and dug his fingernails into the palm of his hand. He'd like nothing better than to throw the bitch down, hoist up her skirts, fuck the hell out of her then get up and walk away. He had a feeling she would keep up a running commentary throughout the rape and never miss a beat. The thought made him grin savagely.

"I also have several silk scarves that would make a lovely sash for any gown made from this material. I will take eight yards, Citizen," she demanded of the merchant.

"Don't you think you've made enough purchases for one day?" Ruan snapped.

"Only a few more stops," she said and moved on, not bothering to see if he was following. She twirled the white lace parasol she carried to shade her from the hot Gaelachuan sun.

Rolling his eyes skyward, Ruan fell into step behind her and glared at the shapely bottom swinging from side to side in front of him. His hands were thrust into the pockets of his britches, his shoulders hunched with annoyance and his eyes narrowed. He was as miserable as he could ever remember being, and his only desire was to either hit or kill something, or ravage the nearest willing body. He wasn't particular which he did first.

Although of late, his conquests—entirely too numerous and all too predictable—had left him with a need he could not identify. It wasn't satiation, for all his partners managed to drain his cock. It was his soul that needed draining and not a one of the willing maids or horny ladies-in-waiting at his mother's court had been able to do that for many years. Not since he had been a randy fifteen year old had he known the kind of fulfillment he desired. If only he could find a woman who would reawaken the juices that flowed through his hard body...

It wasn't the scream cut-off in mid-vibrato that alerted Ruan to possible danger. The scream had been low enough to be ignored by most of the shoppers around him. It had been just loud enough to make the Gaelachuan prince turn and look to his right. What garnered his immediate attention was the flash of a blade in the morning light as it struck downward in the deep shadows of the alley beyond.

"I believe I like this corduroy much better for the settee. Don't you, Ruan?" Lady Siobhan Prentice-Hall inquired as she fingered the rich, nubby burgundy of the material. When no answer met her query, she turned to see the man she considered her soon-to-be-betrothed walking away, his back to her.

"Ruan?" she called out, standing on her tiptoes to try to see around the broad shoulders of the guards left behind to protect her. "Ruan, where are you going?"

Once more, the flash of deadly steel attracted Ruan's interest and the sound of scuffling in the alley made him increase his step. His hand went to the hilt of the razor sword strapped to his hip, and he closed his fingers around the grip.

From the corner of her eye, Chastain Neff saw a man hurrying toward them. From the Vid-Photo she'd downloaded that morning, she recognized him as being the heir-apparent to the Gaelachuan throne and moved back farther into the alley. The man hired to try to take her out was advancing, thick boning knife raised over his head.

"I'm going to gut you, bitch!" the man who had recently been released from the Riezell prison snarled. He slashed downward once more with the large knife.

"No. All you're going to do is go to hell," Chas said softly.

Though she had no weapon, Chas knew she didn't need one to protect herself against the threat of the prisoner advancing on her. Her hands were registered as lethal weapons with the Fleet Command and she knew her feet to be nearly as quick—and deadly—as her hands. There was no doubt of the outcome of the attack coming her way.

"I ain't going back," the prisoner snarled, and stabbed once more with the boning knife. He was hacking at the air, driving the blade downward with strokes meant to terrify his intended victim. "I've had enough prison life to last me."

"You've got that half-right. You have had enough life, that's for sure," Chas told him. Although she disapproved of Command's policy of giving a prisoner a chance to have his sentence put aside if he could take out a RG, she knew it wasn't ever going to happen. No criminal alive was as well trained as a Riezell Guardian. The outcome was never in doubt.

One moment Chas was pressed to the rough wooden wall of a building and the next, she was staring wide-eyed at the headless corpse tumbling toward her. So quick had been the blade that had lopped the attacker's head from his body, she had not seen it slice through flesh, tendon, cartilage and bone. No blood spurted from the deadly wound for the weapon that had taken the prisoner's head had seared the arteries and veins upon contact.

The swords wielded by members of the Order of Taibhse are razor-thin. The blade of that weapon is so thin and so sharp it cannot be seen by the naked eye. Upon contact with living matter, an electrical current is generated and the edge of the blade will cauterize nerve endings and blood vessels instantly. We're talking bloodless killing here, one of her instructors at the Academy had lectured.

As the body collapsed at her feet, Chas moved aside.

"Are you all right?"

It was a deep, husky voice that asked and it was strong, powerful hands that closed around her upper arms. The charge from that contact went all the way down her arm and spiraled into her belly, eliciting an unexpected gasp as he dragged her toward him. She felt as though she were drowning, being dragged down into a lightless, limitless maelstrom and she tried to jerk out of his grip only to be pulled up against a chest as solid as granite.

"Did he hurt you, lass?" that deep voice demanded, and when Chas did not answer, those powerful hands shook her lightly. "Listen to me—are you hurt?"

Chas looked up into dark blue eyes that seemed to be delving into her very soul. The closeness of the man's hard body, the uncanny electrical current passing from his palms to the nether regions of her body, an intoxicating smell of leather and cinnamon overpowered her and she sagged in his hands, unable to assimilate logically the sensations bombarding her.

Before she could protest, her would-be rescuer released his hold on her and swept her into his arms, holding her against him as though she were a child.

"Honestly, Your Grace!" The querulous inquiry was high-pitched and filled with annoyance. "Please do not run off like that. You know your mother…"

"Get the hell out of my way, Lincoln," Ruan snarled and swung around so that Chas' feet hit whoever had been speaking and knocked the speaker aside.

Chas had no choice but to put her arms around Prince Ruan's neck. His long-legged stride was churning up distance as he carried her along. All she could see was the underside of his lean jaw and was surprised to see a white anger line tight against his tanned flesh.

"Your Grace, really!" Lincoln protested. "Must you be so rough?"

"You ain't seen rough, yet, Lincoln," Ruan muttered.

Hurrying alongside the man he had been ordered to stay as close to as the Prince would allow, Lincoln ducked his head and tried to get a look at the woman in the Prince's arms. "Are you all right, milady?" he asked.

"I believe so," Chas replied.

Ruan carried her out into the bright sunlight and yelled at a merchant to vacate the upholstered bench upon which he had perched his enormous butt. The merchant struggled to his feet — helped by two of Ruan's personal guards — and stood fanning himself excitedly with a palm-frond fan.

Laid gently upon the thickly padded horsehair bench, Chas felt anew all the aches and pains she had developed from her last assignment. Unconsciously, she moaned as the strong arms were withdrawn from under her knees and shoulders.

"You are hurt," Ruan said, and before she could deny the statement, he was examining her arms.

"No, Your Grace. I'm just sore, that's all," she assured him.

He had hold of her hand and that strange tingling sensation was traveling up her arm and into her breasts, the peaks of which were straining against the fabric of her velvet gown.

"Why was he trying to kill you, lass?" Ruan asked, his sapphire-blue eyes locked on hers.

She stared up into a face she had long heard was the most handsome in the galaxy and added her own vote to that assessment. The man bent over her had the face of a god. A thick mane of midnight-black hair framed a swarthy complexion, the color of which set off a truly remarkable blue gaze.

"Enlil?" she asked and winced, wondering where the hell that had come from.

"Who?" Ruan queried.

Chas shook her head. "Black Gaelachuan," she whispered and could have kicked herself if she hadn't been lying flat on her back, her hand possessively held in his.

The right side of Ruan Cosaint's mouth lifted slightly. "Aye, that I am, lass. You are from Bhreatain?"

"Meiriceánach," she corrected, and watched his left eyebrow crook apparently with surprise.

"Meiriceánach? I like that answer better than Bhreatain," he quipped. "What are you doing at Gaillimh Bay?"

"I am to be Lord Hurlburt's new secretary. I stopped by the market to purchase my lunch and that is when that man…" She trailed off, turning her head away. "He said he was going to…"

Ruan tightened his hold on her hand and reached out to grip her chin and turn her face toward him. He wanted to groan when he saw the tears in her striking green eyes. "Try not to think about it, lass. Just put it behind you. You're safe now."

"Ruan! Whatever are you doing with that wench?"

Chas watched the handsome face hovering above her turn dark with anger. The finely chiseled lips hardened into a thin, uncompromising straight line and the warm blue eyes became as bright and brittle as shards of ice. When he turned to face the woman who had spoken, she could see a muscle working in his lean jaw.

"Have you finished your shopping, Maeve?"

Chas saw the woman stiffen and had to bite her lip to keep from laughing at the affronted expression on the dark-haired woman's pretty face.

"My name is Siobhan," she said, her chin going in the air.

"Whatever," Ruan said. "If you've finished, Lincoln will take you back to the keep."

Lady Siobhan Prentice-Hall's eyes widened. "You will not be taking me back to Sciath yourself?" she questioned in a disbelieving tone.

"No, I won't be," Ruan replied.

"Well, I never!" Siobhan stated and spun on her heel to flounce away.

Alistair Lincoln sighed deeply and hurried after the woman. "Stay right with him!" he told the guards. "Watch him every moment!"

Chas watched the Gaelachuan prince drop his head and shake it. His grip on her hand tightened almost to the point of being uncomfortable then he lifted his head and looked at the tallest of the four guards surrounding him. "Put a few yards distance between us, O'Malley," he ordered.

"Your Grace…" the man began, but his prince narrowed his eyes and the guard obeyed instantly, shooing the other men back.

"I think the lady is upset with you, milord," Chas said.

"She can go scratch her mad place," Ruan said with a snort. He helped her to sit up, frowning as she winced. "Are you sure you are all right? Should I fetch a dochtúir?"

She smiled. "I don't need a healer, but thank you for offering."

He moved back as she swung her legs from the bench, but kept possession of her hand as she stood because she wavered a little with the blood rushing to her head. He quickly put his arm around her shoulders.

The electrical current from that light embrace traveled all the way down her spine, fanned out like phantom fingers to delve through the crisp hairs at the apex of her thighs to touch her love-bud.

"Oh, my Goddess!" she heard herself gasp and her legs threatened to buckle beneath her.

"That's it!" he said, once more sweeping her into his brawny arms. "I'm taking you to a dochtúir!"

She could not seem to find her voice as he set off with her held protectively against him. She heard him speaking to the men flanking him in High Gaelachuan but only knew a smattering of the complicated language. She believed he had ordered one to run ahead and find a healer, telling him to make sure the place was clean.

All around them, people were moving out of the way, bowing to the prince as he passed. He nodded to a few who greeted him but kept glancing down at her, his dark blue gaze roaming over her as though he expected bloody stains to appear upon her person.

"This way, Your Grace! Here!"

He carried her beneath a wide awning and had to duck his head as he passed beneath a low doorway and into a cool, dark room that smelled pleasantly of roses.

"Lay her down here, Your Grace," someone said.

"Truly, Your Grace, I am…" she began but Ruan cut her off.

"Let him take a look at you." He slipped his arms from beneath her then reached out to gently cup her cheek. "I won't be far away."

The next person who entered her line of vision was an elderly man with a shock of wild white hair that haloed his wrinkled face like fluff from a dandelion stalk. He was smiling gently, and she recognized him as one of the healers from the Riezell Guardian HQ. She opened her mouth to greet him but he placed a finger to his lips and shook his head slightly.

"What are you doing here, Kaspar?" she hissed in a low voice.

"The general set it up," the Healer replied. "I am to do this."

It wasn't much of a cut but it stung just enough for Chas to draw in her breath and hand at the same time with every intention of hitting the elderly man for all she was worth. But her arm fell uselessly to the pillow and her eyes glazed as some potent drug took immediate effect.

"Don't worry, Major," Kaspar whispered. "It is only pairilis, one of the few Gaelachuan drugs they ever perfected. You'll sleep for about four hours then awake refreshed but in the safe arms of your target." The old man laughed. "And what a pair of arms to awake in, eh?"

"W...wha...?" was all Chas could manage before her world began to dim and shut down.

"Sweet dreams, beautiful Guardian," Kaspar said, patting her arm.

As darkness fell over Chas' eyes, she felt the healer's hands upon her clothing and would have protested had night not put out its leg to trip her.

Outside the healer's medical hut, Ruan shot up from the chair upon which he had been perched and rushed toward the healer as soon as he opened the door. "How is she?"

"Know you of a drug called pairilis, Your Grace?" Kaspar asked.

"Aye," Ruan snarled, his eyes burning like blue coal. "If you gave her that shit..."

"No, Your Grace, but apparently the man who stabbed her had coated his blade with it. No doubt it was meant to disable her so he could be about his perfidy."

The color drained from the Gaelachuan prince's face. "Stabbed? Where? I saw no blood!"

"Come," the healer coaxed and stepped back inside the medical hut. He led Ruan to the bed upon which Chas lay unconscious. "You could not see the blood for all the fabric surrounding her hips but he cut her here." He pulled the covers from his patient.

Ruan swallowed like an untried youth seeing his first naked woman. He barely noticed the shallow cut the healer showed him for his excited gaze was too busy crawling over the beauty that lay bare from the neck to hip, the blanket precariously covering the triangle between her legs.

"Lovely, isn't she?" the healer asked quietly.

"Magnificent," Ruan replied and felt sweat breaking out on his upper lip and under his arms. His palms itched to touch that flawless skin revealed to him. His manhood stirred, striving to raise its head to get a look as well. He had waited all his life for a woman who could cause such strong emotions in him, and this one was not only setting his juices to flowing but giving a tug to his heart, as well.

"Such a woman should be cosseted—do you not think so, Your Grace?" Kaspar inquired.

"Aye," Ruan whispered.

"Damn me if I would allow her to be out and about working for a man like Lord Hulbert. Why, the man is nothing but a lecherous libertine who would soon have this lovely maiden groveling in the street for a few coppers."

Ruan wanted nothing more than to reach out and touch the silky sheen of pale blonde hair that spread out over the pillow. He wanted to feel its soft texture between his fingers, to lift the strands to his face and experience the intoxicating scent he had only caught a fleeting whiff of when he had been carrying her.

"No real damage was done but it was a good thing you happened by else that miscreant would have brutalized her then, my guess, cut her throat to keep her from identifying him or else sold her to a brothel."

With passion-glazed eyes, Ruan looked over at the healer. The repercussion of what would have happened had he not come to her rescue did not bear thought.

"I am sure I can find her a much better position here at Gaillimh Bay, Your Grace. If you could see your way to giving her a few coppers to tide her over until then, I am sure she would be very appreciative."

Shaking his head, Ruan refused the offer. "She will be going with me," he managed to say.

"With you?" Kaspar asked.

"With me," Ruan stated firmly. He laid the backs of his fingers against her cheek and frowned when he felt warmth he thought too high.

"The pairilis is causing her a slight fever, but other than the cut on her hip, she is in very good health. She should be up and about in a day or two."

Nodding, Ruan stepped up to the bed and pulled the blanket over the sleeping beauty on the healer's cot. He tucked the coarse wool around her, flinching at the feel of it. Nothing, he thought, save silks and satins should touch this flawless flesh. Gently, he picked up his burden and held her high against his chest.

"Let my man know your fee, dochtúir. There will be a bonus for you. You have my gratitude for taking such good care of my lady."

Kaspar smiled and inclined his head. When the prince had left and his guard deposited a hefty sack of sterlings in the healer's hand, Kaspar chuckled aloud. "My lady, eh?" he repeated, tossing the sack of coins into the air and catching it. "Well, now. That bodes well for our little Riezell Guardian, it does!"

Chapter Three

Chas opened her eyes to find her bold corsair sitting astride a chair beside her bed, his arms braced along the chair's back. Her right hand was being held in both of his and his lips were placing the softest of kisses upon her fingertips. As he looked up at her through the falling sweep of a thick lock of his dark hair, his eyes shone with a light that took her breath away.

"I was beginning to worry," he said, and reached out to smooth the hair back from her forehead.

"What time is it?" she asked, for the room was dark with shadows.

"Nearly ten of the evening," he replied, and rested his palm on her head. "Your fever is gone."

"Thirsty," she said, and realized her voice was scratchy.

He was quick to release her hand and stand, swinging the chair aside. He took up a carafe and filled a goblet. "I have had them bring in iced water every half hour in anticipation of your awakening," he said, and stepped up to the bed. Gently, he slid his left hand under her neck and lifted her head, placing the rim of the golden goblet to her lips.

Chas drank greedily for her mouth felt encased in cotton. She closed her eyes as she swallowed the icy water. When she had taken her fill, she grunted and he removed the goblet, lowering her head once more to the pillow.

"Are you hungry?"

"No," she whispered, and drew in a long breath. The mattress beneath her gave her the impression that she was floating on a cloud, so soft was it. The sheet covering her was silk and the gown touching her body was of the softest muslin.

She frowned and opened her eyes. "Who dressed me?" she asked, looking up into his hooded eyes.

"A maid, although I swear to you I was this close..." He held up his hand with thumb and index finger only a fraction apart. "...to doing it myself, lass."

"For shame, Your Grace," she said, making herself blush on cue as she had been taught at the Academy.

"I am a man first, lass, and a prince second," he admitted.

"And a very inappropriate prince at that!"

The middle-aged woman who came striding into the room was beautiful, but her face was set in a disapproving frown. Two other women—equally strict in appearance—who were obviously her ladies-in-waiting accompanied her.

"You are well, young woman?" the older lady asked.

"I am, Your Majesty," Chas said and tried to rise, but neither mother nor son would allow it. The son stepped toward her only to have the mother push him aside. "Make yourself scarce, Ruan," she ordered.

"Mother, I..."

"Go!" his mother commanded. "This is woman's work and you will only be in the way!"

Grumbling to himself, the prince shoved his hands into the pockets of his britches and sauntered lazily from the room. His attitude was one that his mother was apparently accustomed to for she made no further demands on him but rather bade one of her ladies to shut the door behind him.

"And lock the damned thing," the queen snapped. "I would not put it past that poggleheaded son of mine to eavesdrop!"

Chas threw aside the covers and would have stood but the queen narrowed her eyes at her.

"And just where do you think you are going?" the queen asked.

"It is unseemly for me to be abed in the presence of..."

"Your employer?" the queen cut her off.

Brought back to why she was there, Chas settled back against the head of the bed.

"My son is a very brave man," the queen began as she took the seat Ruan had vacated. "But he is also a stubborn man." She lowered her voice and leaned forward. "Far too much like his father, I fear."

Chas smiled, but had no comment to make to that statement.

"I have been parading females before that boy for three years now and he has disdained every last one of them," the queen continued. "He says he will never marry but that is ridiculous and well he knows it. He is the heir-apparent and, as such, must marry and produce little Ruans to sit upon my knee. Do you not agree, Major Neff?"

"If that is what he wants, Your Majesty," she replied cautiously.

"Doesn't matter what the boy wants!" the queen disagreed. "He has obligations. He must marry and reproduce. That's all there is to it!"

"But he has yet to find a woman he would be comfortable with?" Chas questioned.

The queen flung out a negligent hand. "They have all been ninnies," she declared. "Knew them to be when I put them before him, but where was I to find the kind of woman he prefers? I certainly cannot be expected to traipse around the kingdom inspecting all the harlots that boy pumps, now can I?"

Chas did not need to practice the art of blushing for deep color came to her cheeks at such an unseemly remark by the queen.

"A strong woman, he tells me," the queen went on as though she had not seen Chas' embarrassment. "According to my son, he wants a woman who can hold her own against him in a horserace or on a chessboard. He desires one who isn't afraid of her own shadow and has no great desire to own every gown ever created. He certainly doesn't want one who will spend his money as though water through a sieve and neither does he want one who is so meek she can't ask for what she wants or needs. In other words, he wants a woman who will give as good as she gets, or so he challenged me. Where was I to find such a woman, eh?"

A shrug was all Chas could display, for she had glimpsed the merry twinkle in the Gaelachuan queen's eye and realized the woman was baiting her.

"And while I am guarding him, you want me to help you find such a paragon, Your Majesty?" Chas asked.

"Oh, I've found her already!" the queen stated. "Had a hell of a time doing it, too!"

"Then you want me to watch her," Chas suggested. "To make sure she is the right mate for him."

"Oh, she's the right mate, I've no doubt! I had the runes cast over a month ago and that is when we learned who she is. Twice more the runes were cast, but on the third casting? The third shocked even the mystic, for it told us this woman had been my son's mate many times over the millennia. Do you understand?"

Chas shook her head. "I know little about divination, Your Majesty, and I don't put any store in the old ways." She raised an eyebrow. "Does not the Caitliceachs' hierarchy teach such things are wrong?"

"As though we women would listen to a bunch of prattle from hateful old men who have never married nor are likely to!" the queen said, settling back in the chair. "We women hold to the old ways even while we smile and nod at the priests and pretend we accept their restrictions on our lives. What they don't know won't annoy us!"

Chas smiled. "And is this woman you have found for the prince a woman who won't buckle under to your priests?"

"Damned right, she won't!" the queen stated. "She's her own woman, she is!"

"And the mystics say she is the right one?"

"Lass, I am not a woman to leave things to chance. I believe in the old ways, but sometimes the mystics read the runes incorrectly. So I have had the woman investigated left to right, north to south, upside, downside and inside out. There is nothing I don't know about her and I—as well as my husband—have come to the conclusion that she will suit him admirably."

"So the runes were read correctly."

"You be the judge," the queen offered. "The first time the runes were thrown, two oak trees came up. That signifies what is. We knew we'd found the woman for him—strong like an oak just as he is. The second time the runes were cast, two mirrors came up."

"Doesn't that mean what was?"

"Aye, that it does. It means my son knew her in the past. According to the mystic, such castings are very rare where after two passes identical stones are thrown in the same positions."

"Then they should get along very well, don't you think?"

"One hopes so but…" The queen leaned forward, her face intent. "When the runes were cast the third time—and that's the charm or so they say—the mirrors came up again signifying what was to be. That casting astonished the mystic, let me tell you!"

Chas shook her head. "I don't understand."

"What do you see when you look into a mirror that is in front of another mirror, lass?"

The Riezell Guardian thought about it for a moment then nodded. "A multitude of reflections," Chas said. "To signify that there will be numerous reincarnations of them both and will always find one another."

"Precisely!" the queen said.

Chas held up her hands. "How do I fit into this, Your Majesty? I was told I was to guard him against a potential assassin. Is there really an assassin or am I here to help you procure this woman for your son?"

"Oh, the threat to Ruan is real enough, lass," the queen said, sobering. "There are those among the Order of Taibhse who would like to see my son in an early grave so they can be about their own wicked agenda."

"Which is what, Your Majesty?"

"Forming an alliance with the Storians to overthrow the Court of Cosaint and put a despot upon the throne instead."

"It wouldn't be the first time the Storians have tried something like that," Chas said.

"Well, it won't happen here and it certainly won't happen to Ruan! He is a prince, aye, but he is a warrior well-trained."

"I saw that today," Chas said quietly, remembering the headless corpse at the open-air market.

"When he slips into the wraith persona, Ruan is a man with whom to reckon and I have no fear for him. It is when he is being careless of his life that another score of gray hair shoots up from my scalp!"

"Every mother's worry," Chas said.

"Remind me of that when *you* have a passel of his brats tugging at your skirt hem, lass!"

Chas' mouth dropped open. She could only stare at the queen.

"Have I shocked you, lass?"

It took effort for Chas to clamp her mouth shut and even more effort to speak.

"You think I am this woman of whom the mystics speak?"

"I know you are. Your name was spelled out to us upon the fourth casting done at midnight under the dark of the moon. It was but a matter of finding the woman who possessed the name."

"Your Majesty, I am a commoner. How could you possibly expect your Tribunal or your son…"

"You were adopted at birth by a Meiriceánach family though you were born in *an Ghréig*," the queen said as she folded her arms over her chest.

"How do you know that?" Chas gasped, her eyes as wide as saucers.

"The Court of Cosaint has access to all the data contained in Tribunal records, lass. It was not hard to learn who your real parents were."

A deep chill went down Chas' spine. All her adult life, she had tried to discover her heritage but had been blocked by bureaucratic red tape at every turn. The laws that should have been changed centuries earlier had kept her from learning her true identity. She had long since given up trying to discover her roots.

"Well? Do you want to know?" Queen Annalyn asked.

"Who am I?" Chas whispered, afraid of what she'd learn.

"You are Gréagach. Your Gréagach name was Mylena Kolovos," the queen stated. "Your father was a prominent member of the Gréagach Tribunal. Lord Mykos Kolovos, I believe was his name. He and your mother, Katelina, were killed in a boating accident off Aegia while on holiday. The captain of the boat managed to save you though your twin brothers drowned with your parents."

"Captain Charlton Neff," Chas provided, seeing her long-dead adoptive father in her mind's eye.

"The captain's wife was infertile and they had long wanted a child. Rather than turn you over to Tribunal to be sent to a nunnery until you were of age, they left *an Ghréig* and immigrated to Meiriceán. Both were vehemently opposed to the Caitliceachs, the True Faith, so they saw no harm in stealing you away and letting your distant relatives think you had drowned with your parents."

"But I am Protastnúach," Chas protested. "Surely your Court will not…"

"Captain Neff was of the Protastnúach faith and brought you up with those beliefs, but you are of Eastern Caitliceachs heritage. You were baptized in our mutual Faith. Once baptized Caitliceachs, always a Caitliceachs, lass. As such, my Court has no objections to a Joining between you and my son. As a matter of fact, we were able to trace your maternal lineage back to Queen Medea, and that was enough to sway even the most virulent of my councilors."

Chas narrowed her eyes. "Gréagach royalty? You can't be serious," she managed to say.

"I am quite serious." The queen cocked her head to one side. "You are very lovely, so that will suit Ruan's desire for a pretty wife. The boy can't have a hag for the mother of his brats. You are shapely with a very fine bust, so that will soothe his baser needs and keep his hands otherwise occupied and off a sword hilt. You are well trained in combat and can hold your own against even a Storian primary assassin, so you won't be afraid of his quick temper when Ruan feels the urge to display it. That should fulfill my son's requirement to have a woman who can give as good as she takes."

"Your Majesty, I have…"

"An assignment that I believe will be both to your advantage as well as my son's," the queen asserted. "As a Riezell Guardian, you must carry out the assignment you were given. Am I correct?"

"Aye, but…"

"And the contract says the assignment must be finished to an end your employer stipulates."

Chas pursed her lips. There was no need for her to answer for obviously the queen and her councilors would have inspected the contract inside and out.

"I particularly like the motto of the Riezell Guardians—'To protect and serve with disregard to personal feelings or beliefs. To give my all, even should it be my life.'" The queen sighed. "That is so terribly romantic, don't you think?"

"And when he finds out what you are about?" Chas challenged. "Just how angry do you think he will be? With you? With me?"

"Oh, pooh!" the queen dismissed. "Let him bluster all he wants, but one bat of those pretty green eyes of yours and a hand placed in a strategic place should calm him down quickly enough."

The deep color returned to Chas' cheeks and she covered her face with her hands. "This can't be happening!"

"Do you find Ruan unattractive?" the queen demanded, her chin rising.

"No, of course not, but…"

"Do you find him offensive in manner?"

"Your Majesty, no, but…"

"Do you prefer Daniel Brock to Ruan Cosaint?"

Chas shuddered. "No, not at all, yet…"

"We have your psychological profile."

The paleness that washed over Chas' face made her head spin. "You what?" she asked through the slits of her fingers.

"I believe you made the statement to your analyst that you desired a man not unlike the corsairs of old." Queen Annalyn grimaced. "That hardly seems to suit the image I have of Daniel Brock."

"Your Majesty, you should not have…"

"Do you not," the queen said, coming to sit on the side of Chas' bed, "wish for a real man to warm you of a night, Chastain Neff?"

Chas could only gape at the older woman.

"Do you not want a man who will make your blood boil one moment, and then make it flow like hot molasses in the next as his fingers ply your flesh? Do you not desire a man who will take you soaring to the highest mountains then cradle you gently in his arms as he settles you back to earth?"

"Your Majesty," Chas protested, her voice a whine of complaint.

"I am told that when he laid hands to you in the marketplace, you were seen to shudder as though a lightning bolt had traveled the length of you. Is that correct?"

"While it is true I felt a charge from his touch, I…"

"Did you not call him Enlil?"

"Aye, but I don't have any idea…"

"Enlil," the queen said, "was the Lord High God of the Winds in ancient *an Iaráin*. His wife was Ninlil. That phantom woman you were in the distant past called out to her lover."

"That is only speculation," Chas denied.

"Had you heard the name before? Is it one you commonly use?"

Chas groaned with frustration. "No, Your Majesty. The name was new to me."

"No, it was love calling to love, Chastain. Ruan Cosaint is the reincarnation of an old, old love and he is the man for you, lass," the queen said, her statement brooking no argument. "And you are the woman for him! You were meant to be together! The mystic says so!"

"But when he finds out you hired me to…"

"Don't let him!" the queen snapped and rose from the bed. She smoothed the skirt of her gown. "Men don't need to know everything a woman does, lass. The sooner you learn *that* lesson, the better off you'll be!"

When Queen Annalyn left her, Chas went over the information regarding her heritage and realized she was crying. She had been trying for so long to find out who she had been, who her parents were, the reason Charlton Neff and his wife, Catherine, had adopted her, it was a relief to finally have answers. To learn she had been of noble blood? Unexpected and totally surprising. No wonder the Tribunal did not want her to know of her heritage.

As to the Gaelachuan queen's assertion that Chas and Ruan were fated to be mates? Well, she thought as she swiped at her tears, that remained to be seen.

Chapter Four

"You survived my mother's visit," he said as he stuck his head around the door.

Chas smiled. "It was touch and go but, aye, I managed to get through it."

He came into the room, leaving the door open, as he had no doubt been warned to do, and came to stand by her bed. All available chairs had been removed and Chas could tell he was annoyed.

"She tells me you will be here a few days," he said. "Is that at her direction or because you don't feel well enough to be up?"

"I believe her exact words were—'You will do as I say, lass, and I'll have no argument 'bout it!'"

"Aye," he said with a sigh. "That sounds like my mother. She is a formidable old biddy." He rested his hands on the footboard of the bed. "When I asked her what your name was, she ordered me to find out for myself."

"I am Chastain Neff, Your Grace," she introduced herself.

"Chastain," he said and the name on his tongue sounded sensual. "I am Ruan."

"Your Grace…" she began but he held up a hand.

"No, not Ruan Your Grace. Just Ruan," he corrected.

"I would not dare to…"

"My exact words are—'You will do as I say, lass, and I'll have no argument 'bout it!'"

Chas laughed for his tone and inflection mimicked his mother perfectly. Combined with the waggle of eyebrows and a forbidding glower lurking behind the sparkle in his blue eyes, his mimicry put her at ease.

"So," he said, leaning his elbows on the footboard and clasping his hands. "My mother and I have decided you will not be working for Lord Piss-On but…"

"Who?" Chas asked, her eyebrows rose.

"Pierceson Hurlburt," Ruan informed her. "He's nothing more than a cock with legs. You'd be compromised within half an hour of being in the same room with him."

"But I need a job," Chas protested. "I…"

"I need a personal secretary," the handsome prince interrupted.

She stared at him. "Don't you already have a personal secretary?"

He shrugged. "Alistair is more nag than secretary and besides, he hates the title. Too effeminate, he says. He'd much rather be training troops than attending me."

Chas looked down at her hands. "But you know nothing of me or my abilities, Your Grace." She looked up. "I might be a terrible secretary."

He cocked a brow. "Can you write?"

"Aye."

"Cipher?"

"Aye, Your Grace, but…"

"Then you're hired." He pushed back from the footboard. "You can start as soon as my mother decrees you able enough to leave that bed."

Chas watched Ruan walked to the door and she tucked her bottom lip between her teeth. Her sources had told her he was a brooding, no-nonsense man with a thick chip upon his broad shoulder. So far, she had not seen that side of him, but there was something in the purposeful way he walked that bespoke not only authority but also arrogant power. Ruan turned around at the door. "Any questions?"

She shook her head. "No, Your Grace, I don't think so."

"Good, then if the sergeant-major allows it, you can accompany me to Viridian tomorrow. I have business there. I'm sure she will see to having a portmanteau packed for you."

"The sergeant-major?" she questioned.

Ruan snorted. "My interfering mother who has decided you are to be the next wench she's going to throw at me. If royalty fails, look for a gently bred commoner whom she can train to be a noble."

With that said, he ambled from the room.

* * * * *

Ruan tossed and turned in his lonely bed, his thoughts on the beautiful woman two floors below his chamber. He kicked at the covers, pulled them over him, sat up and punched his pillow, dropped his head to it and then kicked the covers entirely from the bed. Next to be flung to the floor was the pillow, followed closely by another. Finally sitting up, the prince ran his hands through his hair and tugged viciously.

"Argh!" he snarled and swung his legs from the bed and sat there on the edge, glaring at the carpet.

The trouble was Chastain, he thought. Aye, that was who was causing his sleeplessness.

While it was true he had never seen a more beautiful woman, he knew this one had somehow gotten under his skin. That his mother had given her sanction of some sort bothered him, but then again, the old woman only had his best interests at heart.

Chastain.

Even the name filled his soul with vibrant images—blonde hair—long and silky, and curling to just above shapely hips that flared out at a perfect angle from a tiny waist and flat belly. Beautiful green eyes, the color of the early corn shoots in the late spring. Lush breasts that caused a man's eyes to go to them like an arrow to a bull's-eye. Long legs that curved sweetly to a nicely turned rump, slender arms, swanlike neck. And her face?

Ruan sucked in his breath as he raised his head and stared unseeingly at the wall before him.

Such a face she had, he thought. Smooth forehead framed by lustrous golden hair, a slight tilt to those glorious eyes, a pert upturned nose, lush lips that invited a man to taste their sweetness, a cute little chin graced with a seductive dimple.

Ruan shuddered and stood up. Padding barefoot to the window, he shoved the draperies aside and glared down into the moonlit courtyard. The fragrance of late roses filled the air and vied with the faint tang of salt that floated on midnight waves from the Northern Sea. If he listened closely, he could hear the roar of the ocean and…

Giggling?

He frowned and opened the window wider, poking his head out until the sound that had caught his attention made sense to him.

"Daval," he said, naming his youngest brother.

And Daval it was, running through the darkened courtyard behind one of the serving wenches. Both were as naked as the day they were born.

"You little bastard," Ruan chuckled and hunkered down so that his elbows were braced on the windowsill and he could spy upon his younger sibling.

The girl was much older than Daval and — as Ruan knew all too well — extremely educated when it came to sexual play. She was leading the young prince deeper into the garden, unmindful of any eyes that could be watching their frolicking and oblivious to the bright moon overhead that cast its light upon them like a beacon. Her naked rump jiggled in the moon glow and washed over her shapely body as though attempting to clothe her in its rays.

And Daval? The little son of a bitch was rollicking along the pathway with no care in the world. His wiggly was bouncing from side to side and — in imitation of their father — he patted his belly in anticipation of the feast he was no doubt contemplating.

Ruan couldn't help but chuckle as the young man rubbed his nearly hairless chest then reached down to grasp his cock to keep it from flopping so painfully.

Daval glanced back once at the keep then shrugged, picking up speed as he ran after the wench, still holding his shaft. The two were being uncommonly quiet so as not to rouse those within the keep, but now and again a giggle would erupt from the maze of shrubs through which the couple was running.

"I hope you get a briar up your toenail, you little fuck," Ruan whispered. "Or in your teeny, tiny prick!"

The couple stopped beside the fountain where bubbling water cascaded down from a tall statue of St. Padris. Stretching out along the fountain's wide rim, the wench lay there with one leg crooked at the knee, her arms held out for her young lover.

"Under the statue of a saint?" Ruan asked and whistled. "You'll go to hell for sure, Daval Cosaint!"

But what his young brother did next so shocked Ruan that his mouth sagged open, and he could not have torn his eyes from the scene under penalty of torture.

Daval had dropped to his knees beside the fountain and had buried his beardless face in the wench's lap, his actions leaving nothing to the imagination. The girl's hands were in the young man's hair, holding his head to the juncture of her thighs, and one of Daval's hands was squeezing the girl's breast as though testing a melon for ripeness.

"By the Goddess," Ruan whispered and realized the girl—what the hell was her name again?—was staring straight up at him, a knowing smile stretched across her practiced mouth.

As he watched, the girl put one hand to her free breast and circled the nipple with her index finger. She plucked at the stiff nubbin then put the finger to her mouth to wet it before returning it to her breast.

Ruan felt his groin tighten and wasn't even aware that he had put a hand to the thick bulge between his thighs.

Daval was showering kisses up and down the wench's thighs and up her belly. His lips locked onto one dark nipple and seemed to stay there an inordinately long time as the girl lowered her hand to her cunt and played with herself there.

Ruan groaned. Her eyes were on him, but her hand was between her legs, her hips arched upward as Daval kept on suckling her breasts — first one, then the other.

Watching the wench lowering and raising her hips, catching his breath as Daval reached down a hand to place his fingers where hers had been, Ruan began to breathe so quickly, so shallowly, he began to feel light-headed. The pressure of his own hand against his cock had increased and at some point, he had wrapped his fingers around the throbbing head.

He stared into the brazen hussy's eyes, yet he did not see the jaded, older-than-the-ages smirk that steamed from the wench's gaze. Instead, he saw Chastain's lovely green orbs looking back at him with hunger.

He increased the speed of his hand, tightening and relaxing only a little, tightening and relaxing even less as he pulled upon his shaft. The friction had brought sweat to his brow.

"Chastain," he whispered, feeling the itch beginning deep inside his belly and spreading downward through his cock.

The wench opened her mouth and ran her tongue over her lips, wetting them as Daval flung himself over her and rammed his young shaft to the hilt inside her. Even from the distance from which he watched them, Ruan could hear the grunt of satisfaction from the girl and the moan of pleasure from Daval.

Rocking the wench back and forth as he strove for his climax, Daval was unaware his oldest brother was watching him rutting like a stag in heat. Nor was he aware that with every stroke he took, Ruan took one in harmony.

Shifting his gaze from the wench — what the hell *was* her name? — Ruan stared at his little brother's ass. The muscles contracting and expanding as he pumped away at his midnight lover. He knew the exact moment Daval delivered his release for

Ruan's was close behind. So violent and so unsatisfying, it brought tears to the heir-apparent's eyes.

For over an hour Ruan sat slumped at the window. Masturbation was frowned on by the priests, and though he had done it far too many times as a youth, he had not indulged that wickedness for several years. A warrior had no need to take matters into his own hand when there were numerous wenches about with greedy hands and even greedier lips.

It was Chastain, he thought, as he finally pushed himself up and staggered to the bed. It was the thought of her luscious body that had driven him to such shamefulness and he knew—one way or another—he would have to satisfy the lust that roiled within him each time he thought of her.

Chapter Five

"He knows what you are about, Your Majesty," Chas warned as she was being dressed by the queen's ladies-in-waiting the next morning.

"Oh, he thinks he does, but when you slap him silly for attempting to seduce you this afternoon in Viridian, he will be beset with confusion," the queen replied.

"Slap him?" Chas gasped. "Milady, I could not…"

"Oh, hell, yes you can! The boy is accustomed to having any woman with whom he comes into contact jump into his bed the moment he grins at them. They throw themselves at him whether he appears interested or not. To my knowledge, Ruan has never been turned down. He's had more bed partners than his four brothers combined! Now a woman who makes him work for it will garner his interest quicker than one who simply splays herself down for his taking."

Chas winced at the image. "So I am to push him away when he tries to…"

"No," the queen drawled. "You are to slap him as hard as you can. Believe me when I tell you he will take that as a challenge and come after you with all his ammunition. It's time he did the hunting instead of having the bird dropped in his lap!"

Long after the queen and her ladies-in-waiting had left her room, Chas stood at the window and stared down into the opulent courtyard of Sciath Keep. Danny Brock had told her the palace was magnificent, but his description paled in comparison to the reality.

"A copper for your thoughts."

Chas turned at the sound of Ruan's voice and smiled demurely at him. "I was thinking how lovely your home is," she told him.

He came to stand beside her, looking past her. "My mother orders her gardens like she orders her children. One blade of grass, one twig or burgeoning shoot that does not conform to her sense of arrangement will be cut, or plucked or bent until it does."

"Are her children so easily bent?" she asked softly.

Ruan turned to her and reached out to drag the backs of his fingers down her cheek. "This one isn't," he answered and lowered his head toward her, but Chas stepped back, putting space between them.

"Have you been outside today, Your Grace?" she asked, going to the bed to take up the shawl that had been left for her use. "Will I need this?"

The heir-apparent shrugged. "Viridian is on the coast so it might be wise to take it," he answered. "My mother picked out your horse and the clothes you are to wear in Viridian."

Chas swirled the shawl around her shoulders and reached for her reticule. "I am ready, then, Your Grace."

He looked at her for a long moment, his eyes slightly narrowed, then walked to the door. "I'll meet you in the bailey," he said. "You do ride?"

"Aye, Your Grace, I do," she said. She wanted to ask why they would not be taking a shuttle, for Viridian was a good twenty miles from Sciath Keep, but he was already through the door, his boot heels ringing on the polished marble of the corridor.

Ruan shoved his hands into the pockets of his britches as he stomped down the hall. *So*, he thought, a muscle working in his jaw, *the chit was going to play hard to get*. Well, that was something new. But it certainly hadn't been in his plans for the day. Just staring at her had given him a rock-hard erection that needed easing and he had no intention of riding all the way to Viridian in that condition.

Lucia, the Spáinneach maid who at that moment was cleaning his quarters, had offered herself earlier. If she was still there, he knew relief was but a fumble away.

And the dusky, doe-eyed beauty was still in his quarters, her shapely rump in prominent view as she bent over his bed, rearranging the coverlet. She glanced around as he came into the room, kicking the door shut behind him.

Ruan's hands were already on the buttons of his fly, working through them with speed and purposefulness. Lucia smiled at him and turned her back, bracing her hands on the side of his bed as he stepped up to her, pushing her down over the edge of the bed with one hand as he continued to work his fly with the other.

Pushing the skirts of the servant's gown up her back, Ruan freed his cock from the restraints of his britches even as he nudged Lucia's feet farther apart with his booted feet.

With the Spáinneach beauty's rounded ass in the air, Ruan shoved his cock into her cunt with more force than he intended, for she cried out. He mumbled an apology—which surprised him since such behavior was not normal for him—then slid one hand up her back to grip her shoulder as he began thrusting into her.

Closing his eyes to the ebony hair of the woman rocking beneath him, Ruan replaced it with the pale gold of Chastain Neff's long braid. Instead the scent of harsh soap and furniture polish that clung to the servant, he imagined the delicate scent of gardenia that he had smelled on Chastain. Instead of the guttural grunts coming from the body under him, he replayed the soft sighs that had issued from Chastain's lips as she lay unconscious after he had brought her to Sciath.

Ramming himself into Lucia's willing body had always satisfied him, but at the moment, he was straining to come and having a problem doing so. She was tight enough still to give him pleasure and accommodating enough that he had nothing more to do than smile at her for her to drop to her knees before him. Well-trained in the arts of a whore, Lucia's lips were talented and her mouth was a wet, warm cavern that suckled better than any he'd ever known. Perhaps it was that muscle rather than the nether one he needed.

He pulled out of her and stepped back. "Suck me," he ordered.

Lucia didn't question his command but sank to her knees and turned around to face him. She reached for him and took him into her mouth. Wrapping her lips over the throbbing head of his cock, she looked up at him through her lashes as her experienced tongue lathed his straining flesh.

It was pale hair he wrapped the fingers of his hands into. He rocked his hips against questing lips that were not painted scarlet red but rather tinted a sweet shade of coral that needed no artifice to make them delectable. His hands moved through coarse strands of hair, but in his imagination that hair was silky soft.

The servant drew Ruan's cock down her throat until the tip of him could feel the slight protrusion of her uvula scraping along the frenulum. His breathing was harsh, quick, but the satiation he sought seemed just out of his reach. He groaned, needing something he wasn't getting and not understanding why.

Lucia reached between Ruan's spread legs and cupped his balls, working them gently. Tugging lightly, cupping then releasing, she slid her middle finger to the slight indention at the base of his cock and pressed upward.

Ruan had started to sweat, beads of perspiration standing out on his forehead and upper lip. He felt overheated, in need of a bath, but he kept at it, striving for a release he'd never had trouble having before now.

It wasn't until Lucia slipped her finger into his ass that he exploded in her mouth. But the satisfaction he normally felt was not there, and when he pulled away from her, he hung his head, drawing in shallow, unfulfilled breaths.

Lucia never seemed to mind not receiving her own satisfaction. She swallowed his cum and turned her head to wipe her lips on the shoulder of her gown. Remaining where she was, she looked up at the prince, awaiting his orders.

Ruan gazed into the servant's black eyes and knew a moment of shame that was so unlike him he flinched. He could not stuff himself back into his britches quickly enough, his fingers flying over the buttons. Turning his back on the kneeling girl, he hurried to the door and yanked it open with enough force to wrench his right wrist. Cursing at the sharp pain, he nearly ran down the corridor, walking so quickly he stumbled a few times.

Chas looked up to see the Gaelach prince striding toward her. His eyes were cold, his jaw set, and when he passed her without a greeting, her eyebrows shot up. She knew rage when she saw it, and the man who grabbed the pommel of his saddle and vaulted atop the prancing stallion's back was bristling with that raw emotion.

"Milady," the head groomsman said, offering Chas a hand up.

Frowning, for she would be required to ride sidesaddle—a position she neither enjoyed nor looked forward to—she accepted the groomsman's hand and put her foot in the stirrup, clumsily propelling herself up into the saddle and hooking her right leg between the pommels on either side of the seat and balancing herself, centering her weight through the right thigh.

"You don't like riding sidesaddle," Ruan snapped.

"I prefer not to," Chas replied.

"You want to ride like a man," the prince taunted, "but that's rather hard to do in a frilly skirt like that, eh?"

Chas lifted her chin. "I'll do well enough with the sidesaddle, Your Grace."

"If you fall your ass off, don't expect me to stop and pick you up," he told her and kicked his mount into motion.

Chas sat where she was for a moment, and then looked across to where a horse awaited a rider. She pointed to the stallion. "Is that horse prepared for someone?"

The groomsman frowned. "It is one of Prince Ruan's horses. We never know which one he will prefer to ride and…"

Before the groomsman completed his explanation, Chas was off her horse and striding purposefully toward the prince's roan stallion.

"Milady!" the head groomsman complained as he watched in disbelief while Chas reached up, grasped the pommel and pulled herself into the saddle. Without giving the groomsman another look, she clucked to the stallion and set it racing after its master, who had a fair-size lead.

Ruan glanced to the side as the thundering hooves overtook him. He blinked—recognizing his own beast—then looked up into the steady eyes of the woman sitting astride it, the skirts of her gown tucked up so a goodly portion of her shapely legs were showing. He arched an eyebrow at her but said nothing, merely kicking his mount lightly in the ribs to make it go faster.

But the woman riding beside him—leaning forward over her mount's neck—kept pace with him, their horses matching one another stride for stride as the miles disappeared behind them. By the time the signpost announcing Viridian came into view, the two riders were galloping along in tandem, neither looking at the other.

Chas could sense the anger roiling in Ruan Cosaint's brawny body. A white line streaked alongside his mouth and his eyes were narrowed. Although his hands were loose on the reins, she could see the coiled tension that had him sitting straight as an arrow in the saddle.

Slowing her pace as they entered the coastal village, Chas took a deep breath of the salt-sprayed air. Unlike Gaillimh Bay with its heavy scent of marine life, Viridian had a pleasant scent and the waters beyond were a lush turquoise blue. Beside her, the prince had reined his mount to a light canter and it was then she realized they had outdistanced his guards, leaving them far behind. Looking back, she saw the five-man escort bearing down on them, dust flying.

"Are you always so disdainful of your safety, Your Grace?" she asked, but received only an ugly snort for an answer.

Ruan led her to the inn where they would be staying the night. He halted his mount then flung a leg over the horse's head, sliding down with a gracefulness Chas could not help but admire. She dismounted before he had a chance to help her, and when she stood facing him — for he had come around his mount to assist her — she saw his lips twitch. Whether it was in amusement or annoyance she couldn't tell for his blue eyes were hooded as he spun around and headed to the inn.

The guard arrived as Chas reached the inn's door, frowning when she realized he was not going to hold the portal open for her. It had already closed behind his entry. She entered the establishment in time to hear the prince ordering two adjoining rooms.

He ignored her as she joined him at the innkeeper's desk. She could feel the stares of those sitting about the common room and heard a smattering of whispers that included the word doxy among them. Apparently, Ruan had heard the snide label as well, for he turned to survey the room with ill-disguised contempt.

"The lady accompanying me is of the royal house of Cosaint. Is there one among you who would like to repeat your insult aloud so I might deal with it?"

Shocked silence greeted the prince's challenge and eyes were cast down as faces turned red or white…depending upon the sex of the gossip. When no one spoke, Ruan Cosaint nodded, his eyes narrowed into thin slits of coldness.

"I thought not," he said and turned around to spear the innkeeper with a stony glower. "See to the lady's bath then prepare one for me. We wish to dine alone, so if you have guests who wish to use the dining room this eve, I suggest you discourage them."

"At your command, Your Grace," the innkeeper agreed, his head bobbing up and down as he twisted his hands before him.

Ruan spoke to the guards who had entered right behind them. "Contact Mayor Cronin and tell him we will meet with him at nine of the clock tomorrow. I expect a hearty breakfast be waiting when we rise. Is that clear?"

The Chief Guard clutched his fist and struck his chest over his heart. "At your command, Your Grace," he too, agreed.

"T-This way, milady," the innkeeper offered as he skirted the desk and held out a hand to show the way.

Chas glanced back as she followed the innkeeper up the stairs and saw Ruan entering what she knew must be the taproom. She frowned, for it was far too early in the day to partake of strong beverages. One sweep of her well-trained eyes around the room found no glaring threat to the target to whom she had been assigned and she relaxed somewhat, knowing his guards would bar entrance to the taproom and see to his safety while she washed off the road dust.

It was while she was lathering her long hair in the wide, deep copper bathtub that the door to her room crashed open and she gasped to find the prince standing in the opening, his white lawn shirt unbuttoned halfway down his chest. Standing beside him under the draped protection of his arm was a woman any reasonable person could see was nothing more than a common trollop.

"Chastain, meet Chastity," Ruan said, his words slurred. He grinned and lifted the bottle he had in his free hand to his lips and took a long pull.

"I doubt the name is fitting, milord," Chas replied. She locked eyes with the strumpet.

"Me name's Charity," the girl corrected.

"Help and assistance to those in need," Chas defined the name. "That fits, I imagine."

"I do what I can," the girl said with a giggle, and threw back her head as the prince's hand molded over her breast to fondle her.

Continuing to lather her hair, Chas ignored the duo in the doorway. The lush suds from the bubble bath hid her from the shoulders down, and unless Ruan came right up to the tub, he could see nothing more than her slender arms.

"How do you feel about a threesome, Chas?" the prince inquired with a leer.

"I prefer my men one-on-one, Your Grace," Chas replied. "Send the whore away and we'll discuss the matter."

"Look here!" Charity hissed. "Who you calling a whore?"

"Either take her to your room and hump her, Your Grace, or send her on her way. I don't share my body even for a Caitliceachs prince."

Ruan was well on his way to being rip-roaring drunk, but he wasn't drunk enough yet not to grasp the challenge in Chas' light tone. He cocked his head to one side and though the tub swam as though sitting under water, he screwed up one eye and studied the lovely woman reclining amidst the foamy bubbles. She was ignoring him and when she slid down into the tub to rinse her hair, he felt his cock go rigid with need.

"Go find my Chief Guard and tell him to pay you well for this afternoon, Chastity," Ruan said, sliding his arm from the strumpet's shoulders. He slapped her playfully—though a mite too hard—on her ample rear then left her standing in the doorway, her mouth a round "O" of surprise as he kicked the portal shut in her face.

Chas' head came up from beneath the water along with her shoulders and a goodly amount of creamy white bosom, the nipples barely hidden below the suds. "Her name is Charity," she said, not looking around at him as he staggered to the tub.

Ruan hunkered down beside the copper vessel and wrapped his hands over the curled rim. He lowered his chin to the back of his right hand and stared at her as Chas soaped a fleece rag and ran it down the length of her arm.

"You are beautiful," the prince whispered as he tried to see beneath the foamy bubbles.

"Thank you for the compliment, Your Grace," she said, casting him a quick look. She didn't like what she saw, for his eyes were red-rimmed with a sheen of sweat dotting his upper lip.

"I want to fuck you," he said.

"I don't like that kind of language," she informed him and when he snaked his hand out to grasp her wrist—belying the condition of his reflexes—she felt the strength in his grip and her heart thudded, for drunken men could be hard to control.

"Now, wench," he stressed, and tried to pull her toward him.

The slap was loud in the room and made even more so by the wetness slicking Chas' palm. There was enough power behind the hit to knock Ruan off center and he crashed backward to land partially on his ass and partially on the wrist he had wrenched earlier that day. He yelped, grabbing his arm as tears of pain flooded his eyes.

"No one manhandles me, Your Grace," Chas said between clenched teeth. "No one! Not even you!"

He stared at her, unable to speak as she rose from the water to stand over him. Dripping from head to toe, patches of foamy suds clinging to her lush form, she was an embodiment of the goddess rising from the sea. With her long golden hair curled around her shapely hips, her green eyes flashing, she was a sight to behold.

"I...I'm sorry," he heard himself say and the words surprised him, for apologies did not come naturally to Gaelachuan men, and especially not to members of the royal family.

She lifted one long, perfectly formed leg and stepped out of the tub, sloshing water on his legs. Standing over him, she locked her stormy gaze with his astonished one.

"If you want to make love to me, you ask and you ask in a gentlemanly fashion. I will not be spoken to like a common tramp, and I detest the word you used to describe the interaction with which you would like to engage my person. Never, *ever* use that word to me again. Is that clear?"

He could do no more than nod, for his attention was glued to the triangular patch of crisp golden curls at the juncture of her thighs. Tapered as though it were a silken arrow pointing to that part of her he desired the most, it beckoned him like a siren's call. He longed to reach out and touch it, but he feared she'd break his hand if he tried.

Though Chas was trembling from head to toe, she refused to allow him to see her condition. She walked elegantly past him, trailing soapsuds as she trod. Her bare feet slapped lightly against the wooden planking as she lifted her dressing gown from a peg and wrapped it around her, belting it about her slender waist.

Ruan managed to push himself up with the elbow of his left arm for he was cradling his right wrist in his left hand. He sat there with his knees raised and gawked at her.

"I want a man who will court me, not rape me," he heard her say and lifted his gaze to her beautiful face. She was standing there now with her arms at her sides, the lush, round globes of her breasts outlined against the pale green silk. The gown clung to her wet body and the prominence of her nipples made his mouth water. "I may not be of Gaelach royalty as you told the people in the common room but I have pride in myself, Your Grace. I know my own worth."

He ached to take her into his arms and hold her. He was shivering with the need of it, and the erection that had plagued him for most of the day was back in stony form. His palms itched to touch her. He wanted to kiss her until she swooned into his arms and then he wanted to...

"Perhaps you should leave now, Your Grace," she recommended. When he hesitated, she reiterated her suggestion.

It was difficult to get to his feet but he was able to do so with only a slight groan. His wrist was throbbing almost as much as his cock, but at least she wasn't looking at that stalwart soldier waving his bayonet at her. Her scrutiny was fused with his bewildered stare. Though his cheek stung and his tailbone ached from the hard landing he'd taken on it, he felt the pain of his embarrassment more than any other discomfort.

"I had too much to drink," he said and could have screamed as he staggered like an untried youth.

"Aye, Your Grace, that you did," she agreed as she walked to the door and opened it.

"Forgive me," he mumbled as he passed her on his way out.

"I already have, Your Grace. Have someone see to your hand," she said.

He turned once he gained the corridor and opened his mouth to say something else, but she shut the door in his face.

Ruan stood there and stared at the door as though it were an object he'd never encountered before. No one—not even his virago of a mother—had ever shut a door in his face. No woman had ever turned him down before. So completely beyond his normal experience with women, this episode felt as though he had fallen through a black hole and into a strange new universe.

He walked down the hall shaking his head.

Chapter Six

Chas was fully dressed when the light knock came at her door later that evening. It was time for supper and she was famished. Delightful smells had been wafting up to her from below stairs for the last few hours and her stomach was rumbling, her mouth watering at the succulent scents weaving their way through her nostrils.

It was the chief guard who stood at her door, preparing to knock again, when she opened it. The man's face was carefully blank but she fancied she saw a gleam in the pale gray depths.

"Prince Ruan sends his regards, milady, and bids you sup with him," the man said.

"Do I need my shawl?" she asked.

"Begging your leave, milady, but I don't believe you will. The dining room is quite warm, at the prince's request."

Chas carried on a light conversation with the chief guard whose name she found out was Patrick Murphy. He had been Prince Ruan's primary protector since the heir-apparent turned eight years of age.

"A handful, was he?" she inquired of the man who appeared to be at least a full score older than his charge.

"Still runs me a merry race, he does," Patrick admitted. "It was a relief when the queen decided to go before the Tribunal and hire you."

Chas stopped. Her eyes were wide as she stared at the chief guard. "You know what I am?"

Patrick nodded. "I have the queen's ear, I do, since it has been my duty to protect Prince Ruan. She went over your qualifications with me and asked if I thought you'd suit." He grinned. "In more ways than just job-related, I'd say."

Squinting, Chas asked him what that meant.

"The queen thinks you'd make a grand daughter-in-law. The mystic thinks so too, and Queen Annalyn puts great store in the throwing of the runes."

"And if I am not interested in being Prince Ruan's consort?" she asked, her jaw tight.

The chief guard actually laughed before coughing away his merriment. "That's your decision, milady," he finally said, and his tone left no doubt in Chas' mind that he thought she was pulling his leg. He opened the door to the dining room for her.

Mouthwatering smells enveloped Chas like a lover's embrace as she walked into the room. Prince Ruan was standing at the head of a long table sagging beneath dish after dish, the aromas of which made Chas giddy with hunger.

"My mother says these are all your favorites. How she finds out such things is beyond me but..." Ruan said, sweeping a hand over the steaming bowls. He stepped around to the right side of the table and pulled out a chair.

She went to him and took the seat he offered. As he pushed her chair up the table, she felt his fingers grazing the backs of her shoulders, and once more, that electric current passed through her body. She turned her head to watch him take his own seat.

"I dismissed the servants so we will have to serve ourselves," he said. "I hope the wine is to your taste."

Quietly—with no discussion of what had transpired between them earlier—they passed one another the bowls and platters of food. The conversation was light and pertained only to such mundane topics as the unseasonable coolness of late and the overabundance of crops that had not ripened sufficiently to allow the farmers to make money. When the last forkful of succulent beef had been consumed and dessert passed up by each of them, Ruan stood and held her chair for her.

"I am told the gardens here are quite lovely in the evening. Would you like to take a stroll?" he asked.

"I think I should fetch my shawl," she said, but he was shaking his head. He went to a side table, and took up a package and brought it back to her. "I took the liberty of procuring this for you."

Chas had no way of knowing the prince had spent the afternoon searching the markets of Viridian looking for something to give her as a peace offering. Neither did she know that such presents were never given by Ruan Cosaint, except to his mother or sisters. When she opened the tissue paper and discovered the lovely woolen shawl fashioned in an intricate Gaelachuan pattern of knots, her face brightened and she looked up at him.

"It is lovely!" she proclaimed.

"Not as lovely as the woman who will be wearing it," he said in a soft voice.

Chas draped the ivory shawl with its pale rose knot work around her shoulders then took the arm Ruan offered. She walked with him to the wide Francach doors and then out into the cool mist of the evening.

They did not speak as they walked through the sweet-scented garden. His free hand covered hers and she did not think he realized he was caressing her fingers. Overhead, the moon was full and heavy with a golden hue that softly lit the cobblestone pathway between the flowerbeds. When they reached the end of the cobblestones, they were standing at a wrought iron gate beyond which the waves of the Northern Sea crashed delicately against moonlit cliffs. She unhooked her arms from his and reached out to curl her fingers around the coolness of the wrought iron.

"I have never been this far north," she said.

He stood behind her, his body lightly touching hers. "I trained near here," he told her. "I've not been back since, but always thought I'd like to have a summer place in this county."

The heat from his body was intoxicating and she leaned back against him, closing her eyes as he put his hands to either side of hers, enclosing her so that she was pressed between his solid body and the wrought iron sea gate.

"Do you mean your training with the Order of Taibhse?" she asked.

"Aye. It was similar, I think, to your training."

Chas tensed. "My training?" she said.

He put his chin on her shoulder. "Think you I am not privy to the doings of my mother and her band of merry councilors?" he asked. He slid his hands over her arms and drew her closer to him. "I make it my business to know what that interfering old biddy is up to."

She tried to turn around but his hold tightened. "If you've known all along what I am…"

"I only found out this afternoon when I returned from the market," he said and she detected a note of coldness in his tone. "It took my spies that long to glean the information."

She wanted to face him, to see his eyes as he spoke. Even in the bright moonlight, she thought she could garner his feelings if she could but look into his face.

"So how much are you willing to do, little Riezell Guardian, to fulfill your contract to my mother and her pesky court of jesters?"

There was no mistaking the coldness now. His voice had turned hard and brittle, and there was rigidity to his embrace that suggested he had put some distance between them, though his body was still pressed close to hers.

"There have been attempts on your life and the queen thought…"

"She knows damned well I can look after myself!" he said, releasing her and stepping back.

When Chas turned, he was standing there with his hands shoved into the pockets of his britches—a defensive posture. He was not looking at her, but rather at the moonlight-laced surface of the sea.

"Is it that your mother thinks you need more protection or that it was a woman she chose to provide that protection?" Chas asked.

He turned his head and speared her with a hard look that sent a shiver down her spine. "My mother has been trying to foist this woman and that woman off on me since I gained my majority. The plethora of idjuts she's offered would fill a good-size mental institution. I told her I would choose my own wife, but does she listen?"

"And you are furious that she chose me to offer to you?" she said, hurt niggling at her heart.

"Oh, you'll suit me well enough," he said, turning away from her again. "With your training, you won't be a clinging vine twining around me to choke the very life from me."

"But you are still angry that..."

She got no farther for he snatched his left hand out of his pocket and reached out to grab her. He drew her to him so quickly, she had no time to react and when she found herself tight against him, the hardness of his erection made her knees weak.

"How far would you have gone in your charade, Chastain Neff?" he asked, putting his lips to her ear as he spoke.

The warmth of his breath sent a quickening of pleasure into her womb. He smelled of cinnamon and the heady wine they had consumed.

"I was drunk as a pissant as I wandered through that damned noisy market this afternoon. I could barely put one foot ahead of the other but I wanted to find that shawl for you so I could give it to you as a peace offering."

"I am grateful..."

"I felt bad, wench," he said through clenched teeth, "that I had acted like a randy youth and I wanted to apologize."

"It wasn't…"

"Imagine my shock to learn you had been hired to seduce me for my mother. I could have strangled you then!"

His hands went around her throat but Chas made no move to block him. Though her highly specialized training would have made it relatively easy to break his hold, she went limp against him, offering her neck as a sacrifice.

He looked down into her half-closed eyes — her slightly parted coral lips and lost himself. Swooping down, he captured her mouth with his and thrust his tongue past her lips to taste the sweetness.

Chas' arms went around his waist, pulling him to her as his hands slid up to her cheeks. He held her head steady, cocked slightly to the left as he claimed her mouth.

No eyes saw the prince and the Riezell Guardian slip to the night-misted grass that drew along the perimeter of the sea gate. No one saw them stretch out — he atop her. No one heard the soft gasps of pleasure as hands insinuated themselves beneath layers of skirt and inside the crisp lawn of a white shirt.

Ruan's fingers went unerringly to Chas' soft thigh and he caressed her, running his nails lightly along her flesh. Her fingers were entwined in the thick pelt of hair between his breastbones — her hands captured between their bodies.

"I knew the moment I laid eyes on you that you were the one," he said as he slid his lips down her chin and to the hollow of her throat. "The Goddess help me, but you are the one I have wanted and needed."

She pulled her hands from between them and encircled his waist, delighting in the feel of his weight lying upon her. His hand was between her thighs, the warmth of his palm pressed against the core of her through her panties as his fingertips probed at her anus through the fabric.

"Your touch electrifies me," she whispered and gently sank her teeth into the strong column of his throat.

"And yours me," he acknowledged.

Once more, he captured her mouth and as he did, his fingers slid under the leg band of her panties and into her.

Chas groaned beneath the imprisonment of his sweet mouth. His fingers delved lightly inside her — first one, then two. His thumb stroked sensually against her clitoris until she could do nothing more than wrap her legs around his hips, mutely beseeching him to thrust deeper.

Chas was no stranger to sex but everything this gorgeous man was doing to her senses was a new and delightful discovery. There was nothing bland about his possessive lovemaking. His fingers were knowledgeable and when they went deeper inside her, Chas felt as though she would explode into a million pieces. When he quickly withdrew those fingers, she shouted her protest.

"Easy, lass," Ruan said, his voice urgent. "I'll not leave you wanting."

Where Daniel Brock's limited imagination left off, Ruan Cosaint's was just revving up. His fingers closed around the leg band of Chas' panties and jerked, tearing the silk fabric as easily as though it were paper.

Here was her bold corsair! Chas thought as she felt Ruan fumbling with the closure of his britches. His hard tumescence had been pressing almost painfully against her right thigh, a slight dampness letting her know he was as primed as she.

He had pushed her skirts up above her waist and now the night air washed over her bare hips and thighs with a coolness that pebbled her flesh. The back of his hand was hot against her and when he moved it from between them, she sucked in her breath at the velvet smoothness of cock poking at her core.

"I want you," he said and took her mouth once more, his teeth nibbling at her bottom lip.

Chas arched her hips up to him. "Then take me!" she demanded.

Ruan's low chuckle was underlined with the heat of his hand positioning his staff at the entrance to her vagina. When he slipped that steely muscle inside her then pushed deep and hard and held it, she clawed at his back, rending the delicate lawn of his shirt.

His thrusts were as purposeful and authoritative as the man himself. That sensual probing left nothing wanting for his cock was rock-hard, sliding into her with sureness, with a command that had Chas panting with desire. He filled her to the brim and pressed his advantage deeper and deeper.

She clung to his shoulder, digging her nails into his back as he rode her. His pounding echoed in the night as he slapped his body against hers in a frenzy that left them both straining for that elusive climax each knew would be unlike anything either had experienced until now.

And when that climax came—his warm hand slipped inside her bodice to mold around her naked breast, and her legs wrapped so tightly around him his piston action could barely thrust—they exploded with a chorus of keening pleasure that was in harmony. Ruan's head was thrown back as he announced to the world his possession of this woman.

As the last tremor, the last squeezing of muscles, the last pulsation of sperm had subsided, Ruan lay collapsed atop her, spent and shaken to the very nucleus of himself.

Here, he thought as he rolled off her and gathered her into his arms, *was the woman he had been searching for all his life*. Here was the temptress who would make damned sure there would never be a need to stray. Here was the woman who could hold her own against his formidable temper.

Here was his Lady and there was no doubt in his mind.

Chapter Seven

Morning found the lovers lying side by side in Ruan's bed. Their fingers were entwined upon his bare chest, her head upon his shoulder, her leg thrown possessively over his.

"As much as I hate to admit my mother was right, this time she was," he said yawning, for there had been no sleep for either the night past.

"I questioned it myself, but there is no mistaking we were meant for one another," she admitted. "I believe I knew the moment you first touched me."

Neither heard the stealthy click of the lock for they were talking quietly, making plans for a life they were eager to share with one another. The soft snick of a booted foot against the carpet was lost upon the lovers.

The assassin was on them before Ruan could react. The prince's sword—that lethal weapon that could take the head off an opponent in a bloodless moment, was across the room and out of reach.

Chas' eyes widened as the shadow of the killer fell across the bed. She moved like a cat, throwing herself over Ruan as the assassin's blade struck downward, stabbing into her right shoulder instead of the prince's heart.

Ruan stared up into the eyes of his would-be killer and slid quickly out of the bed. As the man jerked his weapon from Chas' body, the prince was already in possession of his own blade and lunged forward, parrying the threat that thrust at him.

Struggling to push herself up, Chas groaned at the fierce pain enveloping her. The right side of her body was on fire and she was amazed that her blood was not spreading in a thick puddle beneath her. She could barely draw breath so knew her right lung had collapsed. She could hear the spark of blades clashing but could not seem to turn over. As the thunder of running feet broke through the agony engulfing her, she closed her eyes and sank into unconsciousness.

* * * * *

"She will not die, Your Grace," the mystic said, throwing the runes once more at the insistence of his prince. "You were meant to be together, fated as King of Gaelach and his Lady-Wife."

"Then why doesn't she wake?" Ruan demanded as he plowed a hand through his already tousled hair. He paused in his pacing to look at the mystic. "It has been over a week and she is no better!"

"She is healing, Ruan," his mother reminded him. "The dochtúirs have told you as much."

Ruan covered his face with his fingers. "I can't bear this!"

"She is resting quietly, lad," King Declan told his son. "There is no fever and no infection in the wound."

"Thanks be to the Goddess that the assassin used a Taibhsean sword," Queen Annalyn remarked. "At least the wound was cauterized and she lost no blood."

"And I am to be grateful that the bastard used a weapon of my Order against the woman I love?" Ruan barked.

The king and queen exchanged a look. It was the first mention of the word *love* their son had used. Though he had been at Chastain Neff's bedside from morning 'til night—even unrolling a pallet to place beside her bed and refusing to be cast from the room—he had not declared his affection for the unconscious woman.

"If the blade that struck her had been of ordinary steel, Ruan," his father said, "she could have bled to death."

Ruan slumped with his back against the wall. "I cannot bear the thought of losing her," he said.

"You won't, Your Grace," the mystic assured him. "On my honor as a prime mystic, I swear to you that your lady will be at your side for many decades to come."

Long into the night Ruan sat beside Chas' bed and held her pale hand within his. He stroked her long, delicate fingers and brought the tips to his mouth to kiss them softly. He spoke to her in the Old Tongue, crooning in a very pleasant voice, singing to her the legends of his ancestral home. His clothing was disheveled for he had slept in them for two nights now. Only once in the week since he had brought Chas back to Sciath had he allowed his mother to bully him to take a bath. Even he could smell his own ripeness, else he would not have given in to the demand. Now, he could smell the sourness of his sweat and though it annoyed and embarrassed him, he was loath to leave the room where his lady lay so quietly and still.

He stretched out his long legs parallel to the bed and with his elbow on the mattress, his hand holding Chas', he thought back to the man he had dispatched with such fierceness it frightened even him. He had been like one of the berserkers of old—slashing and thrusting with a steely purpose that carved limbs from his opponent in a frenzy of death-wielding that left body parts cluttering the floor.

Vaguely he remembered seeing the horror on the faces of Patrick Murphy and his fellow guards as Ruan carved Chas' attacker into nothing more than sections of singed meat. Repeatedly he had sliced at the body, cleaving head from torso, leg from trunk, arm from chest then scattering the pieces like confetti at a wedding. So furious, so enraged had his attack been, it had taken Patrick and two of his men to subdue their maddened prince, bringing him down to the floor like a stag to ground. Though he bellowed his rage, threatened bodily harm and eternal imprisonment, they had managed to bring him back to some degree of sanity.

Rushing to the bed, finding Chas comatose and laboring for breath, Ruan had thrown back his head and bellowed like his ancestors of old. He had not even felt the hilt of Patrick's sword crashing against his skull to render him unconscious.

Ruan had learned that Patrick had taken charge, sending for a dochtúir to treat Chas. It had been Patrick who had arranged the ship back to Sciath, taking a wild chance that the longer route would not be the death of the young woman. Patrick, it was, who had insisted the dochtúir administer a sleeping draught to the young prince to keep him out during the journey.

And it was Patrick, himself, who even now stood guard outside Chas' door to make sure no harm befell the woman his prince had claimed as his own.

As day broke over Sciath on the ninth day of Chastain Neff's convalescence, lightning flared in the distance and the ominous rumble of thunder shook the stone walls. A light mist of rain was already scratching at the windows, asking to be allowed in. It was the bright flash of a nearby lightning strike that woke Ruan.

He sat up in the chair, every muscle in his body aching from the cramped position in which he'd been reclining. He ran a hand over his whiskered chin and winced at his own body odor. He hated being unkempt—though he rather liked the scratchiness of the beard he'd never been allowed to grow. Turning his eyes to Chas, he saw that she was still sleeping and he sighed. Patting her hand, he drew in a long breath, exhaled slowly and then released her hand to stand. He put his hands to the small of his back and stretched backwards, feeling the muscles protest. He sighed again and walked to the window where lightning was now streaking across the heavens with increasing rapidity. Thunder boomed in answer to the loud crack of the lightning as he pushed aside the heavy drapes with the back of his hand.

The day was dreary and gray as befitted a wild storm—not untypical of Gaelach at this time of year. The fields—or so it was said—had forty shades of greenness because of these seasonal rains. Despite the fact that lethal storms roared along the coastline, the Gaelachuans loved their rain and reveled in the wild tempests that could turn so quickly to claim a life.

Reaching up to push the draperies back from the window so he could get a better view of the thunderstorm, Ruan cracked the window just enough to feel the delicious coolness of the rain against his face. He closed his eyes, breathing in the scent of spent ozone and the dusty smell of rain-washed fertile land.

He hung his head, the flash of the turbulent storm lighting him in relief from mussed dark hair to the soiled shirt he wore hanging loose from his britches. His bare feet were turning cold for he was standing in a small puddle of rainwater that was dripping from the windowsill, but he didn't care. There could be nothing colder than his heart as he strove not to think of losing Chastain.

She was meant to be his, he thought as rain fell on his hair and dripped from an errant lock that had fallen over his forehead. He braced his hands to either side of the window and barely acknowledged the moisture soaking him.

"In another life," the mystic had told him, "you were gods to your people. Where you went, your lady followed, even into the Abyss of Hell, Itself, she tracked you. A child—your child— grew in her belly and she wished for you to see its birth."

Old legends, Ruan thought as he opened his eyes and lifted his head. The mystic had spun images of legends so ancient they had become all but lost except in the mist-filled minds of the Ancients. He had regaled his prince with tales spun from strange fabric, from lands with Araibis names that rolled from the tongue like clattering pebbles down a mountainside.

"She will always be yours and you will always be hers. Your lives will always be intertwined and from one generation to the next, she will guard you as diligently as you will love her."

Ruan felt a hand upon his shoulder and his heart soared. There was no need for him to look around to know it was his lady's light touch that had asked for his attention. He reached his right hand across his chest to lay it atop hers and squeezed gently.

"How is your wrist, milord?" she asked, and he could hear the weakness in her sweet voice.

"It throbs a bit with this rain but otherwise it is fine," he replied, reveling in being able to speak to her again and knowing everything would be fine from then on. "My tailbone is sore, though."

He turned to her, his eyes traveling over her pale features, skipping past the pain in her pretty green eyes for he was the cause of that and it hurt him deeply. There were light splashes of color to her cheeks but that was good, he thought. No fever brightened her pretty flesh. He put the back of his fingers against her face.

"How do *you* feel, milady?" he asked quietly.

"Sore but well enough, milord," she replied, turning her face so she could kiss his hand.

Gently — and with infinite care — he put his arms around her and brought her to him. His heart was thundering in his chest to match the cadence of the turbulent storm outside.

"Had I lost you…" he began only to feel tears closing his throat.

"I am here, beloved," she replied. "Where I was meant to be."

He dipped his knees and swung her up into his arms to carry her to the bed. Putting a knee to the mattress, he lay her down gently atop the covers then stretched out beside her.

Outside the storm grew louder and rain lashed against the windows. The room had grown hot and stuffy so he sat up just long enough to peel the shirt over his head and toss it to the floor. He lay back down and for a long time he simply held her, feeling her fragile body pressed close to his. There was iron strength in this woman, but she was his to protect — to keep safe, warm and content. To rock their bantlings in her slender arms.

"Ruan?" Chas asked softly.

"Aye."

"I feel I am in need of a good fucking."

The prince lifted his head and stared down at his lady. He narrowed his eyes. "I thought you didn't like that word."

Chas shrugged. "I don't," she said, "but sometimes it's what a woman needs."

He looked at her for a long moment. "Are you well enough for such cavorting, milady?"

"I am." She ran her finger from his bare hairy chest down to his navel, circled the deep indention with a fingertip and then slipped her hand under the waistband of his britches to thread her fingers through the crisp, wiry curls above his shaft.

Ruan shuddered as her fingers wrapped around him.

"Fucking, eh?" he queried, and glanced down to where his soldier was moving from parade rest to attention.

"A good fucking is what I believe I said," Chas stressed. "In the manner of a corsair of old."

Ruan's left eyebrow shot up. "A corsair?"

"Aye," Chas answered with a sigh. "A bold and brazen corsair who has captured me and taken me aboard his ship. There to be ravished and ravaged and masterfully satiated."

"I'm not so sure ravishing and ravaging are such a good idea, wench," he said.

"Well, if you don't feel up to the challenge..."

He reared up and pushed her flat on her back, trapping her hand over his rising staff. "Be careful with your taunts, lass," he warned.

Chas pretended to shudder. "Oh, please, Captain!" she gasped. "I am but an untried maiden. I have never known a man. Please, I am saving myself for my betrothed, Lord Rufus."

"Rufus?" Ruan asked with a snort. "Some lover that fool would make."

Chas pushed weakly at the broad chest above her with one hand while the other closed around the prince's hard cock. "Please do not rape me, Captain. Please!"

Ruan's lips twitched. "Ah, but there is rape and then there is rape, wench," he said in a gruff voice. "Before all is said and done, I will have you begging for quarter!"

Reaching down to drag her hand from between their bodies, Ruan spread her arms wide, pinning them down to either side of her head. He swooped down and claimed her lips roughly, thrusting his tongue deep inside the sweet cavern of her mouth.

Chas wriggled beneath him, making sure her thigh rubbed against his rock-hard erection. When his lips slid from her to shower hot kisses down her throat, she turned her head away.

"Woe is me!" she cried. "Oh, woe is me! I am being violated!"

Ruan threw back his head and gave an eerie rendition of a villain's evil laugh before sliding his body down hers until he could press his mouth over the peak of one dusky nipple hidden behind the soft lawn of her nightgown. Sucking on the erect nubbin through the fabric, he gently closed his teeth around the protrusion.

Chas bucked beneath him, pressing her breast closer to his mouth. The sensation of wet fabric and the pressure of his teeth were sending shivers through her body. As his tongue flicked out to stab at the tender peak, she could not keep the groan of delight from escaping.

Ruan let go of her arms and sat up, straddling her. He put his hands to the bodice of her gown and ripped the fabric from neckline to waist, freeing her lush breasts.

"Oh!" Chas cried out and put her hands to his broad shoulders in an attempt to push him away. "Unhand me, you monster!"

Ruan moved off her just long enough to rend the gown all the way to the hem then jerked it out from beneath her.

Chas lay there with her eyes hot and filled with hunger as her lover tore the gown into strips. She put out her tongue to wet her lips, and as she did, she heard Ruan's low growl, for his gaze was locked on her mouth.

First, the right wrist was looped with a strip of torn gown. Stretching his lady's arm to the top of the bed, he tied the strip to the headboard.

"No, no!" Chas protested, weakly hitting him on his right biceps with her balled fist, but he captured her hand and before she could utter another denial had tied her left wrist to the headboard.

Feebly she kicked out at him as he made quick work of her ankles. She thrashed her head back and forth on the pillow, moaning and pretending to sob.

"Rufus, eh?" Ruan snarled as his hands went to the buttons of his fly.

"He will avenge me!" Chas pronounced.

"How, when the fop has no knowledge of which end of a blade to wield?" her ravager inquired with an evil smirk.

Peeling the britches from his hips, he stepped out of them, presenting the bold thrust of his erection to the wide eyes of his lady. "Now *this* is a sword, wench!" he bragged.

Slowly—very slowly—he put his knee on the bed and threw a leg over Chas' hips. He sat down gently—his cock stretched out along her lower belly and oozed a bead of love juice upon her flesh.

Chas shut her eyes and turned her head away. She struggled against the bonds holding her wrists, writhing sensually upon the tousled sheets.

Ruan leaned forward to put his hands on her breasts and began to knead them firmly. He ran his thumbs over the straining peaks then flicked the nails of his index fingers over the pebbled surfaces before lightly pinching the sensitive nubs, rolling them between his thumbs and fingers.

"No, please!" Chas begged.

"One more word out of you, wench, and I'll throw you to my men when I am finished with you," Ruan warned in a gruff voice. He sat up. "They want you as it is!"

Chas drew her lower lip between her teeth and shivered.

His hands spread over her rib cage and down until one hand—the heel just touching her pubic hair—was pressing firmly on her belly, one finger dipping into her navel. He smiled at Chas' moan and pressed a bit harder. As he did, he lowered his free hand to the spread V of her thighs and—turning his hand palm upward—slipped his index and middle fingers deep into her cunt. His thumb grazed her clitoris and when she cried out, he grinned mercilessly.

"I'll make you forget Lord Rufus No-nuts," he swore and moved his fingers in and out of her with a sure stroke.

"Lord who?" she asked with a giggle.

"Shush or I'll turn you over to my crew, wench!"

His fingers were easing in and out of her with a rhythm that had Chas squirming. She wriggled her hips, and her heels were digging into the mattress as she sought to elevate her lower body to the luscious torment he wrought.

"I'll tie you to the mast and let every man on board suckle your tits," he said and leaned down to capture a hard nipple between his lips, sucking the sensitive peak into his hot mouth as his stiff cock dragged along her thigh.

Chas was rapidly losing herself to the delicious pressure inside her cunt. His fingers were plying her as a master musician with his instrument, but she wanted something harder, something longer than those knowledgeable digits sliding in and out of her.

Ruan sensed his lady's need and pulled his fingers out of her. "You want me, wench?" he asked in a low, gruff snarl. "You want my stiff cock inside you?"

"Aye, milord!" Chas panted.

"Well, you'll have to wait," he snapped.

Chas started to protest, but her lover slid down in the bed, loomed over her and where his fingers had been ravaging, she felt his lips and tongue invading. She groaned as the hot moistness of that little muscle stabbed repeatedly at her clit.

"Ruan!" she cried.

He raised his head. "You dare to call another lover while I am fucking you, wench?"

"Nay," she said. "It is just that I..."

"Shut your mouth or I will gag you!" he cautioned. "A woman's mouth is good for only one thing and we'll get to that soon enough!"

A shiver of delight rippled down Chas' body, and it was all she could do not to make a sound as he continued to suckle her cunt and ply her vagina and ass with stone-hard fingers.

Ruan knew his lady was nearing a point where he could not control the sensations rippling through her. He snatched his fingers from her and stretched out atop her, settling his cock between her legs.

"I am going to fuck you, wench!" he chortled.

He was in her quickly, his throbbing shaft probing deep. His hands were on her hips, lifting her for his hard thrusts into her wetness. Fingers digging lightly into her rump, he brought her to him in lightning jabs that rocked her.

Chas felt the itch beginning deep inside her and arched her head back, giving herself up to the sensations between her legs. His cock was as hard as tempered steel and her warrior was wielding that delectable weapon with the expertise of a master.

As her climax shot over her in a rosy heat that made her release a soft scream of fulfillment, she felt him come. Long, hard and copious, the culmination of his lovemaking seemed to jerk inside her forever until he fell limp upon her, his face buried in the crook of her damp neck.

They lay there panting, trying to calm their heaving chests. The fingers of Ruan's right hand were on her left arm, gently stroking the underside from elbow to underarm in a lazy figure eight.

"Will you still turn me over to your crew, Captain Brazen?" she asked gently.

"Nay, wench," he denied. "No man will ride you save this corsair."

Chas closed her eyes and rested her chin on the back of his head, and sighed.

* * * * *

"What do you think of a springtime Joining?" he asked.

"They are nice. Do you know someone who will be Joined in the spring?" she countered.

"I thought perhaps you and me."

She pushed back from him a little and looked up into his tender eyes. "Well, if it is our Joining of which you speak, I would prefer summer," she admitted, "upon the Solstice."

He nodded. "Sounds like an auspicious time to me."

"There are, however, a few minor things that may prevent such a Joining," she said.

Ruan frowned. "And those are what, exactly?"

"No enjoying the honeymoon before the Joining," she said firmly.

The prince groaned but he nodded his reluctant agreement. "What else?"

"The groom has not asked the bride to be his mate. Don't you think he should?"

A slow smile dimpled Ruan Cosaint's handsome face and he released his lady. With manly grace, he went to one knee before her, took her hand in his, kissed it cavalierly and then placed the palm against his heart.

"Milady Chastain," he said, his eyes locking with hers. "Would you do me the honor of becoming my bride?"

"It would be my honor, Milord Ruan."

"Good then…"

Chas placed the palm of her free hand against his cheek. "There is one more condition, one of utmost importance at this precise moment."

The frown returned to the prince's rugged face. "That being what, milady?"

"You take a long, hot bath," she said, wrinkling her nose. "You stink!"

Ruan lowered her hand to the bulge in his britches. "Methinks I'd do better with a long, cold one, don't you?"

Chas grinned. "Perhaps, as long as you save the long, hot one for me!"

About the Author

Charlee is the author of over thirty books. Married 39 years to her high school sweetheart, Tom, she is the mother of two grown sons, Pete and Mike, and the proud grandmother of Preston Alexander and Victoria Ashley. She is the willing houseslave to five demanding felines who are holding her hostage in her home and only allowing her to leave in order to purchase food for them. A native of Sarasota, Florida, she grew up in Colquitt and Albany, Georgia and now lives in the Midwest.

Charlotte welcomes mail from readers. You can write to her c/o Ellora's Cave Publishing at 1056 Home Ave. Akron, Oh. 44310-3502.

Also by Charlotte Boyett-Compo

Why an electronic book?

We live in the Information Age—an exciting time in the history of human civilization in which technology rules supreme and continues to progress in leaps and bounds every minute of every hour of every day. For a multitude of reasons, more and more avid literary fans are opting to purchase e-books instead of paperbacks. The question to those not yet initiated to the world of electronic reading is simply: *why?*

1. *Price.* An electronic title at Ellora's Cave Publishing and Cerridwen Press runs anywhere from 40-75% less than the cover price of the <u>exact same title</u> in paperback format. Why? Cold mathematics. It is less expensive to publish an e-book than it is to publish a paperback, so the savings are passed along to the consumer.

2. *Space.* Running out of room to house your paperback books? That is one worry you will never have with electronic novels. For a low one-time cost, you can purchase a handheld computer designed specifically for e-reading purposes. Many e-readers are larger than the average handheld, giving you plenty of screen room. Better yet, hundreds of titles can be stored within your new library—a single microchip. (Please note that Ellora's Cave and Cerridwen Press does not endorse any specific brands. You can check our website at www.ellorascave.com or

www.cerridwenpress.com for customer recommendations we make available to new consumers.)

3. *Mobility.* Because your new library now consists of only a microchip, your entire cache of books can be taken with you wherever you go.

4. *Personal preferences are accounted for.* Are the words you are currently reading too small? Too large? Too...**ANNOYING**? Paperback books cannot be modified according to personal preferences, but e-books can.

5. *Instant gratification.* Is it the middle of the night and all the bookstores are closed? Are you tired of waiting days—sometimes weeks—for online and offline bookstores to ship the novels you bought? Ellora's Cave Publishing sells instantaneous downloads 24 hours a day, 7 days a week, 365 days a year. Our e-book delivery system is 100% automated, meaning your order is filled as soon as you pay for it.

Those are a few of the top reasons why electronic novels are displacing paperbacks for many an avid reader. As always, Ellora's Cave and Cerridwen Press welcomes your questions and comments. We invite you to email us at service@ellorascave.com, service@cerridwenpress.com or write to us directly at: 1056 Home Ave. Akron OH 44310-3502.

Make each day more *EXCITING* With our

Ellora's
Cavemen
Calendar

www.EllorasCave.com

THE
✟ ELLORA'S CAVE ✟
LIBRARY

Stay up to date with Ellora's Cave Titles in
Print with our Quarterly Catalog.

TO RECIEVE A CATALOG,
SEND AN EMAIL WITH YOUR NAME
AND MAILING ADDRESS TO:

CATALOG@ELLORASCAVE.COM
OR SEND A LETTER OR POSTCARD
WITH YOUR MAILING ADDRESS TO:

CATALOG REQUEST
C/O ELLORA'S CAVE PUBLISHING, INC.
1056 HOME AVENUE
AKRON, OHIO 44310-3502

Discover for yourself why readers can't get enough of the multiple award-winning publisher Ellora's Cave. Whether you prefer e-books or paperbacks, be sure to visit EC on the web at www.ellorascave.com for an erotic reading experience that will leave you breathless.

www.ellorascave.com